Conserve and Control

Otter Lieffe

This novel is entirely a work of fiction. The names, characters and incidents portrayed in it are the product of the author's imagination. Any resemblance to actual persons, living or dead, or events or localities is entirely coincidental.

Copyright © 2018 Otter Lieffe
www.otterlieffe.com

Cover design: Nataly Ozak and Mihailo Backovic
Editor: Liv Mammone

All rights reserved in all media. No part of this publication may be reproduced, stored in a retrieval system, or transmitted, in any form, or by any means, electronic, mechanical, photocopying, recording or otherwise, without the prior written permission of the author.

Conserve and Control was written in two very different places – the Mu Koh Chang Marine National Park and the ancient marshland—now covered by concrete and industrial beech forest—known as Brussels. It was accompanied by sex-changing parrotfish and nibbling cleaner wrasse, by polyandrous dunnocks singing proudly in the elder trees and peregrines hunting pigeons overhead.

This story is for them

Praise for Margins and Murmurations in the words of her fans

"As you can imagine being the only trans-woman in a facility is lonely and sometimes disheartening and so when LGBT books to prisoners sent me your book and I read the back cover, I was overjoyed to have a book with a character who I could relate to... It has helped bring some light to me in this place of darkness." Talia

"Amazing read! Compelling characters and stories, come to this if you've been longing to see yourself reflected in fiction and also if you're flagging on energy to resist the times. This book will both hold you close and fire you up." Felix

"It was beautiful to see myself reflected in a novel in a way that is extremely unusual for Trans women." Siobhan

"It's just so amazing. A very well written piece of speculative fiction/dystopia based so much on the world we live in that shivers will run down your spine. Sex workers, queers, trans people, disabled people as those forming the resistance, making the history - because their only choice is to fight or to be extinguished." Nellie

"Ahhh that moment when a self-published title blows you away! Otter Lieffe's novel Margins and Murmurations was fantastic. There's a hint of utopia as well: Before the State took control, this society had embraced and been shaped by all kinds of marginalized people. Glimpses of how wonderful that would be gave me hope." Monika, Lovely Bookshelf

"THIS IS SO FUCKING GOOD. Right from the beginning I knew it was going to be excellent - the writing is clear, the narrative gripping, the characters compelling." Liza

Acknowledgements

Solidarity is what brings a book like this into existence. Too often this supportive work goes unseen and although it's impossible for me to thank everyone here, I want you to know that I'm grateful every day to the uncountable new friends and partners in struggle that this process has brought into my life. I love you all.

Thank you, Melissa and so many others who supported the LGBT Books to Prisoners campaign to send copies of Margins and Murmurations to trans women incarcerated in US prisons. Thanks to the folks who have supported my Patreon or bought copies of Margins for themselves or their friends. This winter's writing would have been impossible without your support.

Thank you, James, and everyone at Active and AK Press, for printing and distributing my baby. Thank you, Jess for tours and gin-induced giggles. Thank you, everyone at Action for Trans Health and the other groups and spaces and beautiful humans that have organised events, podcasts and radio interviews. I am honoured to work with you.

Thank you, Nicole for keeping the website shiny and for being such a committed femme.

Thank you, Nataly and Mihailo, who not only sacrificed their restful Sunday to make the incredible front-cover but also fed me brunch while doing it.

Thank you, Natalie for being such a caring beta-reader, Felix for your lovingly detailed proof-reading and Liv for continuing to be the greatest editor I could have dreamed of. You all encourage and guide me to be the best writer I can be.

A special thanks to my darling Anja, who has housed and cared for me throughout this process and made sure I got my regular dose of walks and sky. This is all you, babe.

Writing from the Margins

Over the last year, the project of releasing Margins and Murmurations into the world has brought me closer to public recognition than any of the decades of political work that came before it.

I gave my first public book reading—on a theatre stage in Marseilles to a hundred and fifty sex workers and friends—and twenty more readings after that. In a squatted trailer park in Berlin I had my first musical collaboration with the non-binary duo, Body of Work. I gave my first radio interviews, in Germany and Australia. People I don't know come to talk to me at parties to get a copy signed. People I don't know have my book poking out of their sparkly handbags.

And it's odd because writing a book probably isn't the most important thing I've done. Don't get me wrong, I poured everything I have into Margins and I think it might even be important. But I've come to realize that a novel comes with a certain recognition that background, feminized, supportive labour never does. People whisper the word *author* with an awe that community organiser, cleaner, trauma supporter, squatter-gardener, therapist, or teacher just don't attract. Perhaps it's because novels are *art* and art is considered something very important by certain people with power. Virtually all successful authors are middle class for a reason.

Margins has connected me with literally thousands of people and for a person who lived her life in the shadows, working invisibly, it feels something like fame. It isn't, in any real sense, and it probably won't ever be. For one thing, I'm too precarious.

I scraped this whole project together with two years of seven-day weeks. I couldn't afford a proof-reader, so the first edition was full of embarrassing typos that I only caught when I worked myself to collapse recording an audiobook version. I had to crowdfund the editor's fees. I literally sat in a room on a mountain for a week teaching myself to typeset when I was supposed to be on holiday because that shit is expensive.

I carry copies in my luggage and distribute them one by one to sex shops and squats and community centres and activist meetings. Because trans women like me don't have publishers and poor people don't have the right contacts and, you know? I'm kind of amazed that this worked out at all. It wasn't supposed to. I don't belong to the class of people who are supposed to write novels. The class that has media friends and the right literary—or business—education and can afford to advertise themselves while taking a few years off work to write some nice stories.

But it *has* worked. Not in the sense of bringing me fame or riches, but that was never my goal. In fact, the one thought that has got me through the disappointments and obstacles is that this has never actually been about me.

Margins is about the starlings. Letting people know how fucking beautiful and heart-breakingly threatened they are in Europe.

It's about bringing nuance to conversations around sex work.

It's about having characters with oppressed intersections at the front of a story, just for once in this world.

It's about getting someone through their difficult week and keeping someone else up all night with excitement and bringing a third person back to activism after a period of burn-out.

It's been about connecting people through a crowdfunding project that printed and sent nearly a hundred copies to trans women incarcerated in US prisons.

My little book has crossed time zones and oceans with barely any resources except my stubbornness, a cheap laptop and the incredible support of the communities that came together around it.

A second edition printed by Active has funded a winter's writing and brought five hundred more copies into the world. The people supporting my Patreon have made a second book possible, and Action for Trans Health have given me two beautiful book tours. This is serious solidarity—which is rare in this world—and words can never adequately express how grateful I am.

The process through which Margins has travelled to some twenty countries on five continents has embodied the kind of grassroots community and networking, autonomy and solidarity that its story is all about.

That's how it happened.

It looks like people passing dog-eared copies to each other while discussing politics over coffee. It looks like learning all these new skills—social media, typesetting, publishing, printing, public reading, public speaking, recording, sound editing, interviewing—from scratch.

It looks like pushing through my fear, standing up in front of other people, and being seen.

Because of my own precarity, because I couldn't just click a button and instantly reach a million people, this project has literally brought new networks and new projects and new friendships into life.

My baby has achieved so much—so much more than anyone expected from her. And I couldn't be prouder.

Otter Lieffe

1. History

Prelude

The afternoon heat lay over the forest and stifled all sounds of life. At this hottest hour of the day even the insects had given up their throbbing hum and retreated under the tree bark to wait for evening to arrive.

The air-conditioned vehicles, immune to the heat, arrived as a noisy herd crashing through the undergrowth, their tyres tearing through soil that had taken millennia to form. Panicked animals fled along branches. The lucky few who could took flight away from the destruction. Nothing like this had happened here for such a long time, it took the forest inhabitants a while to remember. Some of them had lived this before.

By that evening, there was a hole in the forest; a gaping wound already surrounded by a chain-link fence and posted guards. At the centre of that wound lay a mountain of tree flesh, sustainability-certified, waiting to be turned into houses. Parts for a wind turbine were assembled, ready to be built. On the fence hung a development sign displaying artist impressions, in sickly pastel colours, of what was to come.

In a bold, dark green was written:

Eco-Homes: Living Sustainably Today for a Better Tomorrow.

Chapter one

And they ran. Through the flooded tunnel, through the darkness, bursting out into the sunlight with the sounds of horses and the cries of the injured echoing behind them. Some ran and some were carried as fast as they could go, out across the devastation and charred land that surrounded the City.

Out and out until, breathless, they paused to look back at the great walls that filled the horizon. They saw that the troopers had stopped their pursuit. As the last resistance members escaped, stumbling into the light, the troopers closed in behind them, forming a line and blockading the tunnel entrance with all the razor wire they could find.

With no way back, the resistance turned towards the forest; more than a hundred souls, stateless, homeless, but closer together than ever before. And they ran.

Teal realized she had been holding her breath and sighed loudly as she turned away from the projection, wiping her face with her sleeve.

Wow. Just wow.

She had seen it at least a hundred times. So often that in her mind the original resistance fighters—Ash, Pinar, Danny, Kit, and all the others—had merged forever with the actors who portrayed them. This documentary had been made to celebrate the seventieth anniversary of the Uprising and was already eight years old, but Teal had been fascinated with the resistance stories for as long as she could remember and could never get enough.

The language was quite difficult for her to understand; English had changed so much since second language speakers made it their own. The third person 's' and all those phrasal verbs. The pronunciation had moved on too and the difficult 'th' sounds had been replaced by 's' and 'z' and 't'. To Teal, it sounded archaic, almost nostalgic and she adored it.

She loved feeling like she was part of it all—resistance, struggle, uprisings—even for just a few minutes. With another sigh, she turned off the micro-projector and slipped it back into her pocket.

Back to t' present, she thought to herself. *Can't avoid work forever.*

She put up her long hair in a ponytail and, gripping the rope ladder with both hands, began to pull herself up into the forest canopy.

* * *

This is all so familiar.

Carl Kingson stepped off the transport onto the wooden platform and took in the award-winning station, the scents of pine forest and sea spray, and the light blue sky over a sparkling sea. He found it charming, of course, but also a little too much. Maybe he had been here too many times already and the wonder had worn off. Maybe it was just the jet lag. Either way, he would be glad to get away from all this natural beauty and take a well-earned nap. Maybe watch some porn.

Since starting his contracts with the Protection Service he had barely stayed still for more than a day or two and was deeply tired. At least he would be well taken care of, since he was keynote speaker at the conference that night.

I deserve nothing less. I mean, look at this place.

Waiting for an escort to arrive and take him to his suite, Carl sat down on a bench facing out over the sea.

Dignity Station was known across the Five Nations for its award-winning design and location. Its reputation was well-earned. Ahead of where Carl Kingson sat in an expensive suit fiddling with his phone, rocky cliffs dropped dramatically down to a pristine beach, water lapping gently at the shore. The stillness of the sea was broken only by the new reefs.

Built to protect the coast from increasingly violent winter storms, the reefs teemed with all manner of marine life. Carl knew, because he had designed them that way. It had taken two years of research and design and three years to genetically modify the corals themselves, but he had achieved what no-one could have expected—a coral reef in European waters well-adapted to the changing climate. And—most importantly to Carl—a booming tourist income.

And a new flat in London for t' genius that thought of it.

Behind him, enveloping the station, forest spread out for miles. The Union building emerged from the canopy. It was all reclaimed wood and cob walls and living roofs planted with roses and vegetable patches. Wheeling and calling above, flocks of starlings and ring-necked parakeets filled the sky.

Even the bench that Carl sat on was beautiful—a perfectly smooth cob design made of clay, sand and straw covered in tiny, holographic tiles that refracted the sunlight into every imaginable colour. He noticed vaguely that the bench had a plaque on it—to Kit and Nathalie, superstars of the resistance.

Esperans and their legends.

Carl returned to swiping his sauvite phone. After a ten-minute wait, during which he noticed nothing else except his overflowing inbox, a polite and well-dressed companion from the conference arrived on the platform and greeted him with a firm handshake.

Good. None of this four cheek-kiss business.

"Greetings, Mr. Kingson. So sorry for t' unavoidable delay. I trust your journey was pleasant."

"It was fine."

"I'm so glad to hear that, sir," said the companion, hiding the excitement he felt to be meeting one of his idols. "Our bicycles are parked just outside t' station if you would like to go directly to your hotel? It's only a small distance—but of course you know that—and I have a trailer attached to take your luggage, sir."

Carl sighed. "Still no cars in t' reserve, I guess."

"Only when necessary for long journeys, sir." The companion smiled broadly as he picked up Carl's suitcase. "'Protect and enjoy' and all that."

Carl grunted and followed the companion out of the station.

Sometimes I wish I never built this damn park.

Chapter two

"Hey, could you pass me up t' water bottle?"

"*My* water bottle."

"Just send it up, please. I'm dying here."

After a long trek through the jungle and an hour sitting in a canvas chair watching old movies, Teal had finally gotten herself up onto the observation platform suspended high in the forest canopy. She was soaked with sweat. The air was hot and humid in a way that only forests can be.

She'd had to wake up early that morning and had run back to camp twice to retrieve forgotten equipment. She was hot and grumpy, and her shift was just beginning. She would spend the next five hours on this uncomfortable wooden platform in the vain hopes of seeing something new, something that would keep her employed and, hopefully, protect this land from development.

Teal doubted she'd ever see anything more interesting than bugs up here. Her day was off to a terrible start. Shouting at her from ten metres below on the forest floor, her research partner Cyan was just making it worse.

"You left your spare bottle back at camp again, no?"

Teal was beginning to hate that I-told-you-so tone Cyan often had these days.

"Yes," she called back.

"Just like every other day this week?"

"Sure."

"You ever going to get your shit together?"

"Look, you win, okay? I'm a hot mess who take an hour in t'

bathroom and don't remember to bring water. All hail great Cyan, t' most organised human on t' planet. Always on their shit. Always perfect. Happy?"

Even from up in the canopy, Teal could see that they weren't. Without another word, Cyan tied the expensive water bottle—apparently indestructible, despite Teal's best efforts—to one of the ropes hanging down from the platform. Teal pulled it up, unscrewed the lid, and drank almost half of its contents in one go. Cyan silently hefted their heavy bag onto their back and turned towards camp.

"Thank you!" Teal shouted down hopefully.

Cyan turned back and growled, hands on their hips. "If you're finished scaring off every living thing in t' forest, I leave you to do some *actual* work for a change."

They stormed off and began the long walk to camp.

"Love you!"

Cyan resisted an urge to turn back.

"You should," they mumbled under their breath and kept walking.

***

"You are assigned for t' next two days to speaker E14, Carl Kingson," said the gentle robotic voice. "Proceed immediately to retrieve Mr. Kingson from room 412 and take him through Introduction. The conference start in two hours."

Aq closed the monitor screen on the desk next to his bed. It was nearly lunchtime and he was alone in the dorm room. His last shift had only finished eight hours before and he hadn't slept nearly enough.

He hated his job. Working security at the Union Building was barely survival money and the conference speakers treated him like their personal servant. Aq had learned quickly that anyone rich enough to be travelling between states was invariably privileged, spoiled and almost certainly an ego-maniac. Immediately after seeing his dark skin and slim, boyish body, they tended to see him as exotic and stupid in equal parts.

He took his time getting out of bed and made his way to the little bathroom he shared with ten other workers. The monitor had said to 'proceed immediately' but in truth he knew they always woke him up fifteen minutes before they needed to. He turned on the shower and the usual pathetic stream of super-recycled water dribbled down into the basin on the floor. He shivered as he got in—they hardly even heated the water these days—and knew he'd be seeing the water collecting beneath his feet again very soon.

All in t' name of t' environment.

The Union was a beacon of international environmental protection and Aq knew that, as such, its buildings were carefully monitored for water, electricity and other resource usage.

Naturally, the delegates in the Guest Suites several floors above the workers' quarters had all the shower water they could use and fresh drinking water—at twenty shell a litre—brought straight in from the southern springs. Aq hated them and he hated working for the Union, but he also knew he didn't have much choice in the matter. A job was a job, and he had a family to take care of.

When he had used up his allotted water, Aq stepped out of the shower and poured the basin water into the reclamation unit with his name on it. He dried himself off and took his security uniform from the cabinet where some other faceless worker had sun-cleaned it for him. According to the label, the light beige shirt was 'Organic, as Nature Intended'. It was scratchy, and it hung loose off Aq's slight shoulders. The pants and boots—'Vegan, for Sustainable Futures'—weren't much better.

Aq snacked on a seaweed stick as he took the twelve flights of stairs two at a time up to the Conference Level. He wouldn't have time to eat again until after the conference and knew he'd be hungry most of the day.

Shouldn't be like this, he thought.

But it was, and as far as Aq knew, it always would be.

* * *

The companion carried Carl's heavy suitcase up the six flights of stairs to room 412, opened the door and set it down inside. With a smile, he handed the key to the speaker. Carl looked at the ancient object with disdain. According to its tag, the key was 'simpler technology keeping traditions alive.'

Bikes, keys, sauvite phones that look like 21st century Nokias. This has all gone too far, he thought. Without a word of thanks to the companion, he stepped inside his suite and closed the door behind him.

The view of the forest and the coast was stunning. The outer wall of the room was all sauvite glass, curved and transparent, but he had seen this view before.

Hope I got time to rest before I have to impress t' crowds again.

He lay down on the massive bed—big enough for four people at least—and clapped his hands twice. The glass wall dimmed automatically until the room became dark enough to sleep.

Good. Something modern still exist in this place.

Chapter three

As usual, Cyan had too much to do and not enough time. The species richness reports from the previous week hadn't yet been entered into the camp's recorder and the new 'research assistants' as they called themselves—conservation tourists as they were known on camp—were arriving the next day.

The assistants brought very little meaningful to the project except a headache for Cyan, who had to 'manage' their 'assignments'. This mostly meant showing them around and making them feel useful. Babysitting the tourists was a part of the team's contract and Cyan knew, with painful clarity, that without that funding they'd all find themselves working in an eco-supermarket somewhere. Or the three members of the team who weren't from Espera, themself and Teal included, might find their visas revoked.

As they let themself in through the canvas door, Cyan saw that the small tent that served as both camp office and living room was a chaos of papers, soda cans and recording equipment. Months of research was organised—if that was even the word—horizontally across the desks and the tent floor. Almost by reflex they began tidying up the mess, arranging and filing away papers, putting the cameras carefully back into their boxes. They had done the same thing yesterday.

They ran their hands through their short, blond hair in frustration. Cyan knew that sharing an office and this tiny camp with their ex and two others was never going to be easy.

But when I spend my whole day tidying, I get no real work done at all.

The others weren't selfish, they knew, they all just lived differently. Teal claimed that she actually just couldn't *see* the mess she left behind in her wake. Cyan found that unlikely but knew that Teal did her best. They were very different, the two of them and it was hard sometimes to imagine that they'd ever managed to date for all those months.

But we did, and it was so incredibly hot.

Cyan's attention to detail combined with Teal's reckless abandon made them frustrating roommates, but awesome lovers.

Best sex of my life, thought Cyan.

They sighed and picked up another pile of papers.

* * *

Carl couldn't sleep.

Sometimes it happened that way. He was too tired and jetlagged from crossing three capital cities in two days even to jerk off. He was also too turned on to get the rest he needed. A mix of scenarios was passing through his mind, but he wasn't really hard; he couldn't really get into his fantasies the way he wanted to. He rolled over in bed and looked at the screen on the small cabinet.

Gotta get moving if I want to rest before t' conference.

With a resolute grunt, Carl stood up, unzipped his suitcase, and took out the box of projection slides. He found the holo-beamer just where he expected it to be and slipped in his favourite, a show just out of New Constantinople. Immediately, the room lit up and the beamer, adjusting automatically for size, projected four perfect men onto the bed.

The interactivity of the programme was still low—the company had promised to improve on that in their new releases—but it was good enough.

He climbed back onto the bed and nestled amongst the lithe, dark-skinned bodies, which were already kissing and penetrating one another around him. He was hard now and got to work.

* * *

It was late afternoon but if anything, high in the canopy, Teal thought it was becoming hotter and more humid than ever.

Not for the first time that week, she found herself wondering how she'd ended up here lying on a hard plank of wood in this sweaty jungle of eucalyptus and cherry trees and squawking parakeets. She was covered in bites and was stiff from sitting still for so long. She could barely move a muscle for fear of either disturbing the wildlife or—probably worse—incurring Cyan's wrath if she dropped any more equipment onto the forest floor.

It was only one time and t' camera didn't even break. They're always overreacting. And so what if I need longer in t' bathroom?

Although her hormones were finally kicking in and she had less and less facial hair, Teal needed to shave every day, twice if possible. And wearing concealer and foundation and make-up wasn't easy in the heat.

Especially if you spend all day in a damn tree.

That morning—like every other morning—she had fought with Cyan as they waited outside the little camp bathroom.

"How long can it take?" Cyan had shouted from outside the bathroom. "Would you hurry up already?"

Teal had emerged from the trailer with her hair tied up, her face a mix of foundation tones.

"Look, leave me alone, okay?" she had shouted back. "This stuff is complicated."

"Why do you even bother? No-one care what you look like. Who are you trying to impress?"

"Not you, that's for sure."

"You're being ridiculous."

"*Real? I'm* ridiculous? Look at you! Maybe if I came from your fancy family, I would walk around in crappy second-hand sweaters full of holes, but some of us have *dignity*."

"How dare you?!"

"Maybe if *you* had actually *been* homeless...you would...Has anyone called you trash even once in your life? You don't know anything!"

Cyan had opened their mouth to shout, but Teal had slammed the trailer door closed.

Remembering the fight, Teal felt her chest tighten, her shoulders lifting. She could think of a hundred other things she should have said.

Always fighting. Always hurting each other. Why do we do it?

She brought herself back to the present to find that a mosquito—or something that looked like a mosquito—had landed on her arm. Cyan would have known the genus and species straight off the top of their head, but for Teal, a bug was a bug. Staying almost still, she gave it a quick spray of citronella before it could bite her, and it flew away with an angry buzz.

She looked at the time on her sauvite phone: still another hour before it got dark and she was officially allowed back to camp for dinner. The humidity was still rising and off in the east she thought she might have heard thunder.

Cyan won't be pleased.

Teal hadn't recorded a single thing of interest today—just a fox passing by ten metres below her and a whole lot of bugs. Certainly nothing new; nothing that might help justify renewing their research contract and, more importantly, preserving this ecosystem. Certainly not the Red Shadow-Tail of local legend, a species so rare—if it existed at all anymore—that it hadn't been seen in the park for decades.

She knew that they only had a few more days left, and then they'd be in real trouble. From the platform, Teal could see the Conservation Perimeter fence that surrounded the park, giving it legal defence against any new development. Every day she saw guards coming and going at the control towers—all guys it seemed—armed to the teeth.

Eighteen-year-old boys in uniforms protecting t' forest. Is this real what Ash and Pinar fought for? Who they even protecting it from?

One way or the other, if her team didn't convince the board of the value of this particular stretch of forest, permission would be given to move the fence inwards by a kilometre and the land would be taken by developers for a new colony of expensive eco-homes for Union members.

Without us, this forest all gonna be villas. No more trees and no more animals. Money always always come first.

Teal looked up as the first drops of rain began to fall onto the platform.

"Fuck it," she grumbled as she reached for her bag and began to pack.

I'm just one person.

Chapter four

To get to the Guest Suites, Aq had to cross the Introduction Hall, built to showcase new holographic technology and to 'introduce' visitors to Esperan history. Aq passed it almost every day and had come to hate the holograms of rich white people narrating the official history of his country. He was usually a calm person—he had to be patient in his job—but on his first day he'd almost lost it.

"Don't listen to any of this!" he'd shouted at a group of delegates passing through the hall. "T' resistance fought *against* t' State. This *isn't* how it happened!"

He'd been severely reprimanded that time and had learned to keep quiet to avoid punishment and keep his job.

All lies, whatever they say. Already eight years since t' documentary came out. Already eight years since everyone who want to know, can know. But they like this story more than t' truth.

As quickly as he could, Aq crossed the hall. He could feel his anger rising as a holographic diorama popped up around him: a group of people of various skin tones—some in wheelchairs, some visibly gender non-conforming, all wearing ridiculously old-fashioned clothes—sat in a circle and signed to each other.

"—and here we see an example of a traditional resistance village," a voice announced.

Twenty-first-century English, Aq noticed. *Exaggerating t' 'eks' in example and swallowing t' final 'l' of traditional. No-one speak like that anymore.*

"It was in a village like this one, that Ash and Pinar founded the resistance that would one day bring diversity and ecology to the people of the State—"

Aq watched on with disgust as the 'resistance villagers'—still smiling big, wide smiles—began weaving baskets from a pile of reeds in the centre of the circle.

"—they taught us to embrace traditional technologies and to protect the earth, even before the plastic crisis of 2080—"

Bullshit. Everyone know it was t' plastic-killers that ended t' old technology.

In 2070, in response to overwhelming levels of plastic pollution, scientists in Espera began research on certain species of bacteria that had evolved to digest plastic particularly PETs. They developed an industrial spray of the bacteria and began a continent-wide spraying campaign on garbage dumps. The plastic levels were successfully reduced, but the bacteria adapted and quickly spread across the globe.

If t' plastic-killers hadn't taken over and start eating through everyone's sweaters and phones... if they didn't discover sauvite... none of this would exist. And I wouldn't have to suffer this awful display.

"Fuck all this shit."

He stormed across the hall walking right through the holographic village. A cleaner pushing an eco-buffer across the floor looked up and smiled at the outburst. Aq nodded back.

Well, he thought to himself. *At least someone understand.*

Finally, Aq arrived at the Guest Suites and made his way to room 412. Standing outside the door, he pushed the little call screen. After a few minutes a voice answered curtly: "Yes? What is it?"

"Hello, Mr. Kingson?" Aq said, as politely as he could. "I'm sorry to disturb you, but I'm here to accompany you to t' conference—" Aq paused. He still couldn't get used to having to say the next word, but it was part of his job and he'd already been told off for not saying it enough. "—*sir*."

"Wait out there, five minutes," said the voice emanating from the screen.

"Very good, sir." Aq leaned against the wall of the hallway and poked his shoe into the plush carpet. He was hungry already.

***

Teal's equipment bag was pulling on her shoulders. It was raining heavily as she pushed off from the platform and began to lower herself down through the dripping foliage.

As steadily as she could, she fed the rope through the number eight karabiner attached to her harness, careful to keep her wet hair well out of the way. She had paid dearly for all that sleek, chestnut hair and didn't intend to lose it here in this forest. Another gigantic bug landed on her arm, but her hands were busy with the rope. She could only watch as it stuck its long proboscis into her skin and drew blood.

Right now, dangling from a rope and being eaten alive by bugs, Teal wanted to be anywhere else but this jungle. But Cyan loved it here, and Teal loved Cyan. They both knew without a doubt that she'd follow them to the ends of the galaxy.

"Wait. What's that?" Teal spoke out loud before she could stop herself. She locked the rope in the karabiner and let herself dangle, trying not to make any more noise. She'd seen something up above her moving quickly through the canopy. It looked dark, fast-moving, and just the right size to be what they'd spent the past two months looking for.

This could be it, she thought, her heart pounding.

She reached behind her and carefully unclipped the holo-camera. In total silence, Teal took off the lens cap and pointed it up to where she'd seen the animal moving, her finger poised on the shutter button.

Looking through the viewer, she saw a mess of leaves glistening in the rain. There was no sign of the animal she'd seen—or thought she'd seen. It was already getting dark and she didn't have much time.

I could swear I saw—
There.
Just the slightest movement on a branch.

She could see its little chest moving, stillness betrayed by its need to breathe. It was young, she could already tell that much. Male or female, Teal had no idea. She had read it was almost impossible to tell. She could just make out its dark red fur, almost black against a soft cream belly.

So beautiful.

She lifted the camera and took a scan.

From here, she couldn't see much more than an outline, but back at the lab, the 3D projection collated from the scans would tell them everything they needed to know. Despite the fashion towards using the oldest possible technology, or new technology designed to look ancient, at the camp they had modern sauvite-based equipment at their disposal and this camera was all they'd need to prove presence in the park.

Teal was sweating with excitement. If this was really a Red Shadow-Tail, it would change everything. For Teal, for the team, and for this jungle that Cyan adored so much. She needed all the evidence she could get to prove the find and enough 3D scans to create a good image. Maybe even enough to animate it.

She pushed the scan button again, but this time nothing happened. A bright red light flashed on the camera and it let out a long, loud beep.

"Damn!" muttered Teal under her breath.

She looked back up above her but the branch the animal had been crouching on was empty.

Damn and shit.

Chapter five

Teal held the flashing camera in her hand and wanted to cry. She knew what the flashing red light signalled—it meant that in all her fuss leaving camp this morning, she'd brought the wrong battery. It meant that she had missed her opportunity to get the evidence she needed. It meant she would disappoint Cyan once again.

She let out a growl of frustration and looked around at the dark forest around her, knowing it was hopeless. The Shadow-Tail—if that's what it had been—was nowhere to be seen.

Maybe it was just a grey. Maybe it wasn't a red at all. Maybe I'm just a truly terrible researcher and should go work in a supermarket.

Not for the first time that day, Teal felt intensely angry with herself, with her own slowness and perpetual disorganisation. Leaving the camera hanging around her neck, she began to lower herself the last five metres down to the ground.

Why I am like this? How hard can it be to plan my day, to think one step ahead?

Teal's boots landed back down on the forest floor.

Still, I might have at least one good scan.

She cradled the camera like it was a new born baby and hurried back to camp to find out.

***

History

In theory, Introduction took twenty minutes. That's how much time was needed to cross the hall, stopping at all the indicated standing points marked by a green circle painted onto the floor and watching the holograms and narrations that appeared automatically around the person standing there.

Twenty minutes to cover the entire modern history of the land from 'T' Jewel of Europe' through 'T' Dark Days of t' State' and 'T' Founding of the Union' to 'T' Drive to Protect' and finally, shamelessly, 'Paradise.' It was twenty minutes that Aq had already suffered far too many times.

"And so," the old-fashioned voice read out. "Ash and Pinar reformed the State from within and ushered in the time of New Hope—"

Aq tutted. His great-grandfather had been resistance and was killed by the State. Despite his parents' insistence that they should 'leave t' past in t' past,' he had grown up hearing stories every weekend when his family would gather for dinner. And this official version of history—that Ash and Pinar and all the rest had been reformists who 'gently guided' the State to a new, better, kinder time—made him furious.

Co-optation of our story. Stealing our fuckin' history.

Fortunately, this time, Aq's delegate seemed as bored as he was and eager to move on. Carl Kingson stood impatiently at each point evidently unimpressed by the technology that could transform the hall floor into an aerial view of the northern continent or make a wall disappear into an apparently endless cherry forest.

Aq was used to the delegates living a life of privilege. If his designer suit and fashionable hair cut—buzzed on one side with a horizontal line wiggling towards the temple—was anything to go by, Kingson was no exception.

Always in a rush, always have something more important to do. Their time so much more important than mine. No problem to make me wait fifteen minutes in t' corridor while he jerk himself off.

Finally, after three standing points, Kingson began to look annoyed.

Here it come.

He turned to Aq and asked, "Do I actually need to go through all this? I really have better things to do."

"Not at all, sir," Aq replied, hiding his amusement. "T' conference hall is right this way."

"And now, I'm proud to present t' man who has been described as 'T' Architect of Paradise.' All t' way from London, our guest speaker, Mr. Carl Kingson."

There was loud applause. Carl stepped out onto the brightly-lit speaking platform and took the mic from the compere, who promptly disappeared off stage.

"Good afternoon. And thank you. I am honoured to be your guest here in Espera. It is indeed more beautiful each time I visit."

Carl stood before perhaps three hundred delegates from the Five Nations of the Union. As instructed, he was careful to use gender-neutral language. 'Ladies and Gentlemen' was considered irrelevant here he'd been told and, looking out over the diverse delegates, he could see why. Even back in London, the term had fallen out of use in the aftermath of the Gender Revolution.

Carl had daydreamed through most of his Cultural Sensitivity training, but today he was being as diplomatic as he could manage. He had a lot riding on the new contracts he hoped would be signed after this visit.

"As you all know, my focus has been on t' development of t' Conservation sector—" he carefully avoided the word 'industry' "— and my policy suggestions have been widely implemented in Espera with substantial success. I'm proud to see that t' *cerezo* forests are expanding once more, unhindered. T' beautiful new reefs that surround this complex are fully protected and t' air is cleaner than ever. International eco-tourism is booming and t' Esperan economy is more sustainable each year. Espera is, indeed, t' Jewel of t' Union."

There was more applause. Since the Kingson accords had been put into place over ten years ago, 'Jewel of t' Union' had become a slogan. Carl's policies had been implemented in other places as well but Espera was the headquarters of the Union and maintaining its reputation as a paradise was seen as a top priority.

"Before t' policies I designed, Espera was a different place," Carl continued. "A less protected place. A place where nature—in all her glory—was less well-cared for and less respected."

Some of the delegates, the Esperans especially, shifted uncomfortably in their seats.

"But that sad time is ancient history now. Due in part to t' hard work of t' Protection Service and t' research funded by this great institution we stand in today. I would like to begin this presentation with some scans of our great successes…"

Aq stood at the edge of the stage, just out of view, and yawned. He'd already stopped listening and was daydreaming about food.

* * *

"You won't believe what I found!" shouted Teal as she ran into the dining room holding a small metallic sphere.

Cyan looked unimpressed.

"Is it dinner? Because t' others ate half an hour ago and I'm starving. What took you so long?"

"I went to t' lab to process a scan and look—"

"Well, it better be good. I've been wait—"

"Just look!"

Teal couldn't contain her excitement any longer. She turned off the main lights, rested the holo-beamer sphere on a shelf and pushed a button. There was a soft beep and the room filled with coloured light. Cyan stepped forward towards the hologram several metres in either direction and began moving their hands through the air. The image rotated with them.

The team used the beamer, a form of Esperan technology, almost daily to collate and process scans. It had proven particularly useful for identifying shy and elusive species. Cyan noticed that this scan was very low quality: it was dark, and the resolution was low, as if it had been taken from only one or two scans in poor light.

"What am I looking at?" they asked. "It's very fuzzy."

"Look," said Teal, waving her hands in a top to bottom movement and shifting the image down half a metre. There was the branch, still so vivid in her memory, and—zooming in by separating her hands—the small, shy mammal she could now positively identify.

Cyan gasped and stepped closer.

"Real? Could it be?"

"Look at t' hair pattern, t' ear tufts, that red tail." Teal was grinning. "It's all exactly as t' reports have stated. It's so much smaller than t' Grey, and there's nothing else on record even remotely similar. It can only be a Red Shadow-Tail."

"Amazing," Cyan whispered in awe as they rotated the image again to get a better look. After a moment they said, "but t' scan is so dark. This obviously won't be enough for t' board. Where are t' other scans?"

"Well, I wanted to tell you about that—"

"Tell me later," said Cyan as they pulled Teal close and, without another word, kissed her full on the lips.

Chapter six

Teal was startled.

"I'll get t' others; you get t' champagne," Cyan continued, as if nothing had happened. "This calls for a celebration."

They ran out of the room to find Jade and Indi, their other partners on the project. Walking over to the fridge, Teal realised that she was smiling broadly, the sensation of Cyan's lips still on her own. She knew the kiss meant nothing. They were just friends; just research partners. They'd broken up for very good reasons.

It *had* felt good though. Familiar somehow, like an old skirt that still fitted perfectly.

But I'd rather they had checked first. It's not like Cy to forget consent.

Teal knew that the one scan she had managed to take wouldn't be enough. They would need more evidence to convince the board that there were Red Shadow-Tail in the forest, and that the forest was still protected under international law. That the new development should be stopped immediately.

They would need much more.

***

"Each one of us can make a difference here tonight. And together we protect this beautiful planet. Each one of you is powerful. You are amazing. Thank you for everything you do."

Mr. Kingson's speech was followed by a standing ovation. As he stepped off stage he was instantly surrounded by delegates and journalists. Dutifully doing his job, Aq kept the reporters at bay while the speaker paused briefly to discuss the plans he had presented with a few well-dressed white men who Aq recognised as Esperan industry leaders.

"Yes, that sound wonderful," the speaker was saying. "I have you booked in for an appointment... Yes, of course... I gonna be in town for t' next couple of days... A pleasure to meet you, too."

Aq had never seen anything like it.

This guy is a consultant, a businessman at best, but here he get treated like a rock star.

He pushed another reporter—as politely as he could—out of Mr. Kingson's way. Finally, they got through the crowd and headed back through the Introduction Hall. Aq was glad to see the holograms had been disabled to conserve power.

"They're pushy, no?" Mr. Kingson said, without turning his head. Aq was surprised: the delegates rarely spoke to him at all unless they needed something.

"Err...yes, a little I guess, sir."

"Is always like this. Everyone love paradise."

Aq wasn't quite sure what this meant, so he said nothing. The pair left the hall and turned the corner that lead into the Suite buildings.

"Speaking of which," Mr. Kingson continued. "After I get something to eat, I'm thinking of going to t' beach for some beers. That sand of yours look very good."

It's hardly my sand, Aq wanted to say. The few days he got off, he spent in the city visiting his family and helping take care of his siblings. He couldn't remember the last time he'd relaxed on a beach.

"Of course, sir," he said instead.

"Want to join me?" Mr. Kingson asked casually. Like it was the most normal thing in the world for a delegate to invite his security guard to the beach.

"I...erm," Aq began. "Thank you, sir, but I got another shift starting in two hours. There's a parliament gathering in t' Peace Buil—"

"Tomorrow then. Ah, here's my room." Mr. Kingson pulled out his archaic key and opened the door. "See you tomorrow... Aqua is it?" Aq's name was printed on the front of his shirt.

"Aq... short for Aquamarine, sir."

"Aquamarine!" the speaker laughed. "Well yes, I see why you shorten it! Funny, no? How everyone started naming their kids after colours? I was going to be called Scarlett when my parents expected a girl. They were disappointed when I came out with a dick and decided to call me Carl."

Aq was confused by this entire interaction.

Delegates never talk like this. Too informal. Too personal. What he want from me?

"Anyway, good night, Aq."

And before Aq could say another word, Carl Kingson stepped into his room and closed the door.

* * *

Teal's face ached from grinning. Jade was looking at the scan-projection of the Red Shadow-Tail for the third time. Indi had already drunk too much champagne and was passed out on the office sofa. Cyan had their hand on Teal's leg, and was talking fast, practically glowing with excitement.

"—I never thought we would actually find it," they were saying. "Honestly, I thought it had to be extinct. This mean more than all t' species richness and biodiversity reports in t' world—"

Teal just smiled. Cyan always talked a lot when they drank.

"—I mean those things are important, but ultimately, they just get reviewed by some obscure academic in a room somewhere and filed away for posterity. But *this—*" they gestured towards the magnified projection filling half the office "—this change *everything!* This is something t' campaign groups will get behind—even t' Union itself—no-one could resist this little guy. No-one could cut down his home. *You did it, babe, you really did it.*"

Cyan was actually shouting but Teal didn't mind. It was so rare for her to get into Cyan's good books those days, she was going to take all she could get.

Jade was fiddling with the beamer controls; brightening the projection, deepening the contrast to pick out the Shadow-Tail's fuzzy form better from the background. It was still dark and lacking in depth.

"That all I can do for now," he announced, stepping back from the projection. "It's time to collate t' other scans and see what we got. I hope we can animate it, maybe get enough for an internal scan. Where are t' other scans, Teal?"

"Ah," she said, fiddling with her fingers and looking down at the ground. "About that..."

Cyan was shouting again. Not in a good way.

"What you *mean* you took only *one scan?* That was t' first thing we learned about Esperan beamers! You *always* take at least three scans from different angles. You *always—*"

Teal had already explained about the battery; there really wasn't anything more to say.

"I don't know what to do with you sometimes!" Cyan stood up abruptly. "I don't know—"

Teal stared at a table leg.

"I'm going to bed!" Cyan stormed over to the door and called back without turning. "Good *night!*"

They slammed the tent flap down and stomped through the brush to their tent.

Jade and Teal sat in awkward silence for a few minutes. Indi was still curled up, snoring on the sofa. Finally, Jade reached over for the bottle.

"More champagne?"

Chapter seven

That night after his second shift was over, Aq returned to the stuffy dorm room where his ten roommates were already snoring loudly. The room smelt awful. He stripped down to his underwear and threw the uniform into the laundry chute.

He was exhausted but paused to check his personal info screen. Having grown up without a lot of money, he was careful and always made sure he had enough saved up to send some to his parents at the end of each week. He usually knew exactly how much he had in his account. But for some reason, each evening before bed, he checked the balance anyway just to see the reassuring numbers; just to feel like all of this was somehow worth it.

He touched the screen and opened the icon that related to his finances. He clicked 'Balance' and gasped involuntarily. One of his roommates grunted and rolled over in his sleep.

Aq's first thought was that he was imagining things—maybe he was really that tired—but the figures were right there in front of him. His account was one thousand shell richer than it should be. He clicked on the transactions for today and below his expenses for food and laundry and the daily salary—a barely liveable two hundred and fifty shell—there was a one thousand shell deposit made an hour ago.

He clicked it for more details, but it said only: 'TIP.'

A tip? From who?

In his ten years working at the Union, he had never received more than a few shell here and there. It certainly wasn't the elderly city woman he'd accompanied to parliament that morning; she'd looked at Aq like he had some infectious disease.

So it must be t' Londoner then from this afternoon—Kingson, was it? But why? And what he want for such a big tip? I knew there was something weird about how he talk to me.

Aq knew he was assigned to the guy again tomorrow.

I should ask him about it?

His head racing with questions, Aq climbed into his cold bed. Even tired as he was, it took a long time for him to find sleep.

* * *

Teal came to and rolled over in her bed with a sigh. She'd forgotten to set her alarm but she didn't need to this morning—the camp was already full of loud, excited voices.

Must be t' tourists, and what a noise they're making!

Over in the office tent, she heard Jade and Indi patiently explaining how to use some of the research equipment. They were being interrupted by a barrage of questions.

"Teal, I need you!" she heard Cyan calling, their voice full of stress. "Our *assistants* are here."

Teal grumbled to herself and got out of bed, her hair straggled over her face.

"Teal?" Cyan called again.

"Yes, yes." Teal slipped a shirt and pants over her underwear. "I be right there."

She grabbed her shaving kit and, moving fast to avoid the tourists, hurried over to the bathroom wagon. She took her hairbrush down from a shelf and looked at herself in the mirror. Her hair was a mess, her stubble a dark shadow.

This might take a while, she thought, and began brushing.

* * *

"I'm taking an extra shift up on t' platform," Teal announced when she emerged thirty minutes later from the bathroom and walked through the office—now the teaching room—to pick up a camera and the spare battery.

The new "assistants" were spread out in a semi-circle and Cyan was standing inside a holographic map of Europe, their hand hovering over the Union Building. They were mid-sentence and the interruption angered them.

"I need you here, Teal," they said, their voice carefully controlled. "We take a shift together this evening when t' *assistants* have their *assignments*." Cyan didn't mean to stress the words, but they found the entire thing so ridiculous they couldn't help it. They looked from Teal down to the eager faces of their new helpers.

These tourists are so excited to be here. They want so bad to help out. What a waste of time.

"I go over now for a while," announced Teal, "Just to see if, you know, our little friend come back again." She hefted the equipment bag onto her bag. "Don't worry, I have t' spare battery this time."

Cyan was speechless.

I got ten assistants to entertain, a mountain of research to write up, and a presentation to t' board due by tomorrow.

Indi had gone into the city for a meeting. Jade was nowhere to be seen.

I'm holding everything together just like I always do. I am tired of picking up your mess.

"You and you," Cyan said, pointing at two light-skinned Esperans whose names they had already forgotten. "Your first assignment gonna be assisting Ms. Moore here at t' observatory deck with an insect species count."

They paused while the team leader translated.

"Species guide books are over there and don't forget to collect lunch from t' kitchen on your way."

The assistants jumped up in excitement and, grabbing a pile of field guides, ran out to find the kitchen. Teal glared at Cyan for a full twenty seconds and stormed out of the tent.

* * *

Carl Kingson had a meeting with leaders from the Industry and Conservation Board in the Peace and Progress Building. Aq had been assigned to accompany him there and to the lunch hall afterwards. He was running a little late, rushing up the stairs eating a yat fruit as he went. He reached the corridor of the Guest Suites but stopped first at a terminal on the wall. Overcome by curiosity, he accessed his personal screen and opened his financial account.

His throat went dry and he swallowed hard. Another thousand had been deposited since last night.

Two thousand shell!

This was clearly much more than just a generous tip.

Aq realised his heart was beating hard. He was sweating. Of course he was excited—this was more money than he earned in a week. But he was also scared.

What this guy want from me?

He was determined to find out. He reached room 412 and knocked loudly on the door.

Chapter eight

An hour later, Aq sat awkwardly in a six-star restaurant while Mr. Kingson ate lunch. He still didn't know where the money had come from.

He'd had to wait a while for the speaker to get ready again and on the way to the restaurant Aq had tried to find a good moment to talk about the money but couldn't. He now sat in silence watching Mr. Kingson eat a meal which probably cost the same as a security guard's entire wage for a day. Spicy pasha seed soup and fried zag-fish from the reef on a bed of organic greens. All washed down with organic wine from the southern islands.

Aq knew these speakers and delegates ate well but he was still amazed at the decadence. And the waste. Kingson left half of his soup untouched, refused to eat the head of zag-fish—the best part in Aq's opinion—and ordered extra greens but never ate them. He talked almost without stopping.

"...and after lunch, I have yet *another* meeting. Red Rak, you know who he is, no? T' CEO of Rak industries—" he didn't wait for Aq to reply "—at this point in t' game, Red represent most of t' mining interests in Espera. Anyhow, I'm told he's super boring, but filthy rich with good business sense. He always—Aq, are you sure you're not gonna eat something? Some wine perhaps?"

Aq shook his head politely. He was far too proud to eat his delegate's fancy food. And besides, the only thing he wanted was to ask about the money. He was sure it was Mr. Kingson—*who else could it be?*—but he hadn't said a word, behaving like nothing had happened. Aq was burning with curiosity but wasn't sure how to get it into the conversation.

The speaker chattered on for the rest of the meal, and afterwards Aq accompanied him down to the station where they took a busy solar transport train towards the Rak Industries building.

The shuttle was completely transparent and the view as it raced along its rail over the tree tops and the Union bridge and into town was stunning. It was full of commuters and Union diplomats speaking at least ten different languages. Aq didn't take any of it in. He was tired and increasingly hungry.

"Beautiful, isn't it? In London this would all be commercials. Aq? You are listening to me?"

Aq re-joined the conversation. "Sorry, what, sir?"

"T' art." Kingson pointed upwards "It's t' best in t' Five Nations you know."

Aq looked up. He hadn't even noticed the holo-paintings on the ceiling. Constantly changing in every existing colour, fish morphed into people, people into poetry. He didn't care about art.

At home his father, who actively despised anything he considered middle class, would rant for hours about the wastefulness and elitism of the art industry. His mother, in turn, would accuse him of reverse classism. Aq just wasn't interested.

He watched as the mouth of a lizard holding an umbrella opened and released a string of words. It meant nothing to him. He sighed. His stomach growled loudly.

Maybe I shouldn't have turned down that meal after all.

"Here we are, sir," Aq announced as they entered the grand building of Rak Industries.

"Very good. Wait for me down here, no? I'm gonna be one hour."

Aq nodded and sat down on a bench. He was unsurprised to see that most of the foyer was covered in yet more holo-paintings. He tried not to look. Over near the foyer bar, he could hear a group speaking loudly in several languages.

Code-switching, he noticed.

Aq couldn't care less about art, but he *was* interested in languages. He spoke three by default—Arabic, the language of his parents, Esperan of course, and he had learned English at school. He wanted to learn more but had neither time nor money. He imagined in a parallel universe that he'd be a linguist and would sit around doing nothing but learning new languages.

I'd learn at least ten. Maybe twenty. Maybe all of them.

Whenever he could, he got books from the tiny staff library at the Union or searched what was left of the web. He was particularly interested in how languages changed over time.

Kingson, for example, he speak a lot like me, just his accent is different. English, for sure, is his first language. Somehow, when we all started speaking International English, it went back and influenced t' first-language speakers too.

Aq had always loved analysing the way people spoke. He would watch old twenty-first century films with his friend and by the end would have no idea who the characters were or what the plot had been about. The only things he paid attention to were the accents, the archaic grammar and pronunciation.

It was so much more complicated back then. All those phrasal verbs. And weird sounds.

His favourite old sound was the hidden or dark 'L'—the way many speakers would swallow the L in words like 'final' and 'table'.

Velarized alveolar lateral proximant, they called it. What an amazing name! No-one use that anymore. It's a shame really. I wish—

"Ahem."

Aq snapped out of his daydream and stood up.

"Sorry, sir. You finished early."

Mr. Kingson was grinning.

"T' meeting was a huge success. Aq, take me back to t' Union."

Aq led the way out of the building and into the street. When they arrived at the station, Kingson handed Aq a pile of coins to buy tickets.

"Sir, all public transport is free in Espera," Aq reminded him. "We didn't pay for t' journey here either."

Kingson hid his embarrassment with a cough.

"Of course, yes. In fact, that was one of *my* ideas I think."

"Okay sir," said Aq, looking at the coins in his hand.

I still didn't ask him about t' money.

Chapter nine

An hour later, alone and stretched out on his giant bed, Carl Kingson was still smiling. Just as he had expected, the meeting had gone well. Kingson had found Red Rak to be painfully boring, speaking in a low monotone that was hard to follow. He had noticed that many Esperans did that, and he assumed it was a language difference, but the process had gone well.

What they lack in conversational skills, these Esperans more than compensate for with greed and cunning.

As a good capitalist, these were two traits Kingson definitely appreciated. Over the last two decades, Rak had built a multi-million shell corporation mining for sauvite, the seemingly miraculous, clean-burning mineral that was used in almost every product in Espera; phones, computers, solar panels, biofuel generators and wind turbines.

By buying out a good portion of these 'green' industries, Rak Industries had made a name for itself as a protector of the environment. It was even an official sponsor of the Union's great park. During the meeting, Kingson had secured future contracts and greater collaboration with Rak Industries.

During a holographic presentation, he had learned that there had been unrest at the mines and an increasing number of incursions at the Perimeter. Using Rak's funds, the Protection Service would increase patrols at the fence and the mines. In turn, the Union would grant greater access for sponsorship at some of their international tourist sites.

It was a win-win and, of course, Kingson would be well

compensated for his work making the deal. He stretched again.

Enough business for today, I should treat myself to something nice. I'm celebrating, after all.

He woke up the tablet that connected him to the building's system and logged into the shopping section. He scrolled through several pages of ecological products, mostly Esperan but couldn't find what he was looking for. He looked through International.

Carl had always had a thing for expensive underwear and was sure that his cute security guard had never worn a pair of international designer silk boxers in his life. He ordered three of the most expensive ones available, guessing at Aq's size, clicked 'Gift', typed a small delivery note, and under destination entered: Aq Hass, Security Staff Quarters, Union Building 1. He had made a mental note of Aq's surname as soon as he'd received his allocation notice.

After all, you never know when that might come in handy.

Carl clicked 'Send' and lay back on the bed with a contented sigh. He reached for the beamer still containing the porn slide from the day before and clicked the switch to 'ON.'

* * *

If hell really exist, Teal thought, *it's being stuck in a tree counting bugs with rich people.*

She was furious at Cyan for putting this on her. She knew she was being punished for the mess with the camera yesterday. And for always being late. And just in general for being who she was as a person.

Teal didn't really know much about the insects here. She was a mammal specialist, a community ecologist. She'd even done a few marine biology placements. Anything to avoid entomology. And despite the enthusiasm of her two Esperan assistants, crammed together on the platform looking up everything they saw in the electronic field guides, she knew it was all busy work with no real goal.

One of the Esperans, who she read as a trans guy, although she couldn't be sure, looked up from the field guide and asked her a question. His English was much better than Teal had expected it to be, but whenever he got stuck for a word, his friend helped him with translation.

"Teal Moore," he began, using the Esperan formal way of naming people. Teal had thought of asking the volunteers to call her just Teal or Ms. Moore, but she found it endearing in a way and at least they couldn't misgender her that way. She had been called Mr. Moore more than enough times in this lifetime. "Will our research help t' forest?"

Teal replied, as diplomatically as she could, "Well, that's t' hope. You see t' fence over there?" The assistants looked up and nodded.

The massive fence that marked the edge of the park was only about thirty metres from the platform. A Protection Guard was patrolling, looking bored and uncomfortably hot in his uniform. Teal was beginning to know their schedule, their break times, everything. She saw them so often she almost felt like she knew them.

"That's t' Conservation Perimeter. There's a plan to bring it a kilometre that way—" she pointed to the east "—and open up all of this for development."

She paused while the young woman translated the word into Esperan.

"We hope t' biodiversity studies will be enough to prove how valuable this forest is and then t' perimeter won't be moved."

The assistants seemed happy with her answer and doubled their efforts to identify a dark brown moth they had caught in a sample jar. Teal knew she was overstating their importance. In her experience, biodiversity studies rarely protected land from development.

No-one really care about insects or plants. They don't care how many there are or how many gonna go extinct when t' bulldozers arrive.

As she often said, "Conservation is about money and money is about people."

And people only protect things they care about.

Back when such things still existed, it had been pandas and tigers and elephants and whales that had brought in the big bucks. The 'charismatic megafauna' as they were known in the conservation industry.

In Espera, lacking any large, attractive mammals, the Red Shadow-Tail, an animal so mysterious and full of stories—*and yes,* Teal thought back to what she'd seen yesterday, *so damn cute*—would have to do the job.

As Teal looked out over the forest, she flashed back to another forest platform near the equator—the project where she had met Cyan.

Chapter ten

In what had once been the Democratic Republic of Congo, Teal and Cyan had spent two years together in close quarters working in forest land protecting the last few remaining bonobos.

The intensity of the work—and their powerful mutual attraction—had brought them together, but from the very beginning their relationship was turbulent. They had skipped the honeymoon and gone straight to the fighting.

"Is it time to eat yet?"

"One more hour," replied Cyan, peering through binoculars. "I want to see if t' alpha gonna use her 'come over here' signal again. I feel like she keep changing it slightly and it might depend on who she's signing it too. If signs change depending on rank, that could be real interesting."

"Yes," said Teal impatiently. "But I think it's time to eat—"

"Shh! Look here she come again."

They had been lying on the platform for four hours in the rain, watching the troops passing below. Each day they were learning more about the form of sign language that the bonobos used to communicate their sexual desires. Cyan was enthralled and had taken pages and pages of notes since they arrived at the platform. Teal couldn't get comfortable. She kept moving around and finally sat up.

"Cy, she's fallen asleep. They're all asleep. Can we talk please?"

Cyan put down their binoculars and sat up too.

"Look, you should have brought more snacks with you. I told you—"

"It's not that. I'm worried."

"Okay."

"T' ranger said that there are rebel troops mobilising near t' edge of t' park."

"We're safe here," said Cyan putting their hand on Teal's knee. "They invested millions of dollars—and a small army—to protect this place."

"This whole region is so instable though."

"T' Congo has been unstable for a very long time, Teal…"

Teal rolled her eyes. She knew when she was about to get a lecture.

"Pretty much since t' early 1900's. When Belgian King Leopold brought slavery and half t' population—ten million people—were slaughtered."

Teal tutted. *Content warning.*

"And later under control of t' Belgian state, t' country continued to be gutted for resource extraction: diamonds, gold, even t' uranium that was dropped on Nagasaki and Hiroshima."

Yes, I know all of this.

"Then under a military dictatorship—backed by t' US of course—extraction expanded. By then it was mining for coltan, t' mineral that went into mobile phones and laptops across t' globe." Cyan took a deep breath. "Basically t' Congo being fucked over is nothing new."

Teal stared at them. She tried to control her voice, but she was shaking.

"I don't understand you sometimes."

Cyan looked confused.

"You *know* that my grandparents had to leave this place. It was *me*, not you that grew up fearing racism. T' Congo is part of *my* history. Why do you always tell me things I already know? Like you're t' expert on everything. Like you're t' only—"

"Shh, look! T' alpha's awake again."

"You know what? This isn't working. We should never have slept together. We should never hav—"

Teal stopped mid-sentence. A loud electronic beeping was coming from Cyan's bag.

T' sat phone. For emergencies only.

After hanging up, Cyan looked at the device in silence.

"Everything okay?" Teal asked, but she already knew the answer.

"We have to leave tonight."

"T' park?"

"Congo."

"But—"

"We always knew this could happen."

"What's gonna happen to t' bonobos?"

"We have to pack up camp right now. We have a flight back to Espera in eight hours."

Cyan unzipped their backpack and started stuffing their notes inside.

"But—"

"*Now*, Teal. We gotta go."

"Shit."

On their flight out of the country, they received word that the park—already the last protected island in a sea of destruction—was being invaded by various militias. The team got out just in time and the park was soon razed to the ground and gutted for mining. Without their forest, the bonobos were no more.

When they got back to Espera, Teal got a data-entry job in the city and didn't speak to Cyan for over a year. One day, out of the blue, they called her up and invited her to join a new team on a project in the *cerezo* forest. Teal was very uncertain, but the money they were being offered was good and her Espera visa was coming up for renewal. So she said yes. She still wasn't sure whether it had been the right decision.

Back in the moment, Teal continued to ignore her assistants busily taking scans of a mosquito.

I wish we could have done more for t' bonobos, but money and power always come first. While we were so focused on t' park, t' world was burning around us.

She sighed and moved to the edge of the platform looking out over the forest and the fence.

Nothing I can do about economics, but I'm sure gonna do what I can to save this forest. T' Union got a lot riding on its image as a defender of nature, a protector of t' planet. And if we can find substantial evidence of a Red Shadow-tail it's gonna change everything.

She was determined to find it, to get samples and a hundred scans if needs be, to prove its existence and to save the park.

I got to, she thought watching another guard patrolling the fence. *We're running out of time.*

Chapter eleven

"Package for Mr. Aq Hass!" announced Blue—one of Aq's roommates—picking up the package at the door and carrying it in. "Does our Aq have a new girlfriend?"

"I bet he does," said another room-mate. "Look at those skinny arms, if I was a girl I'd go for him!"

They laughed. Aq ignored them. They always made jokes like this. And, he noticed, they always assumed he was straight. Esperans were usually more flexible about such things and everyone in the dorms—the Union's security guards, cleaners and receptionists—were Esperans like him. But they were also all guys, and somehow when they were together in a group, they seemed to become a lot less smart. Besides, he had decided he probably *was* straight. He just didn't like people making assumptions.

"Let me see that," he said, taking the package.

He could see that it was sent from the Union Mall, which meant it couldn't be his parents. They always wrapped and sent his packages by hand. He turned the box over but there were no other clues. He noticed his hands were shaking a little.

This isn't right.

He took the box into the bathroom to open it privately. His roommates noticed and started wolf-whistling and hollering as he closed and locked the door behind him.

Aq tore open the box and unwrapped the contents. There were three pairs of brightly coloured underwear. He guessed they were made of some foreign fabric he had never felt before. He rubbed the material between his fingers. It felt amazing.

But why they're here? And who sent them?

Aq saw a small printed note attached to the inside of the box. It said only: 'You deserve some luxury, Boss.'

No name, no return address.

Gotta be that creepy delegate. I need to sort this out. This guy's obviously in love with me or something.

And what's with t' 'Boss' thing? Is he signing it Boss, or calling me his boss? This an English thing that I don't know about?

None of it made any sense. Aq noticed his hands were still shaking, but he wasn't nervous anymore, he was angry. He stuffed the package under his arm and left the bathroom and—ignoring his roommates completely—he stormed out of the dorm. Crossing the corridor to the stairwell, he paused to look at his watch. It was evening already. If he was stopped, he'd have no good reason in the world to be roaming the Guest Suites.

He started up the stairs: one way or the other he was going to get an explanation.

"What t' hell is this?"

Aq was shouting and waving the delivery package in the air. He knew he shouldn't be raising his voice—he shouldn't even be here, inside Mr. Kingson's room—but he was furious, and a little scared. He wasn't entirely in control of himself.

Kingson, for his part, looked calm, reclined on his massive bed, propped up with pillows, and sipping from a glass of Esperan rum.

"You don't like t' colour?" he asked disingenuously. "It's finest silk. Best on t' market."

Aq swallowed wrong and coughed hard. "Err no. Sir. T' colour is fine. It's just—well—why?"

"Consider it a tip, Boss."

That word again. What he mean by it?

Aq's English was good—it had to be in this job—but he just didn't understand. Surely, if anything, *Kingson* was *Aq's* boss.

"And t' money? That was you too, I guess?"

Carl Kingson smiled. "It was, Boss."

"Look," said Aq, swallowing hard. He looked towards the door for a way out. His head was spinning. "I'm not your Boss. I don't even know what that mean. And—" he subconsciously lifted his head, just a little "—and I don't need your money."

"But you do *want* it Boss, don't you?" asked Kingson, smoothly. "Because if you want it, it's all yours. And if you want me, Boss, I'm yours too."

"I—" Aq was speechless.

"Nothing sexual, Boss. Not if you don't want it like that. But if you want me to serve you, I can. I want to use what I have to make you happy, to make your life easier. You only deserve t' best in life, Boss. I see you work too hard."

Aq had had enough.

"This is disgusting!"

He spat the words and left the room. He tried to slam the door, but it closed softly behind him.

He stood in the corridor, breathing heavily, his chest tight. He reached up to wipe the sweat of his face but realised that in his right hand he was still holding the package of underwear.

I was supposed to leave it in t' room. I nearly threw it at him.

Aq realised then what had just happened. In a Guest Suite of his workplace, he had just shouted at a man rich and powerful enough to destroy his life if he wanted to. He swallowed hard and tried to calm his breathing.

And...and somewhere along t' way I stopped calling him sir.

* * *

"Look, you need to file t' samples away, like this. And don't leave t' camera on or t' battery gonna go flat."

They're so messy, Teal thought to herself. *How can they think they're helping t' project when I gotta watch them all t' time and make sure they don't break something?*

She noticed that they'd already drank the water they brought up with them. She gave it five minutes before they'd ask for her some of hers.

"Sorry, Teal Moore," said the youngest volunteer.

She looked about twenty and her eyes were a startling green that Teal found quite beautiful.

"That's—that's okay. Just try to keep things tidy up here and lower your voices a little. You never know when something interesting might pass by."

She hadn't told them about the Red Shadow-Tail and she didn't plan too. And yet she kept looking out at the canopy around them. She was sure of what she'd seen. Though the scan wasn't great, it had been enough to convince Jade—their resident sceptic. She just had to keep looking. It would come back. It had to.

For now, she needed to pee. She had attached the rope to her harness and begun lowering herself to the forest floor when the green-eyed Esperan woman gestured frantically at her from the platform. Her friend seemed to be taking scans of the entire forest, waving the camera and pushing the button repeatedly. Teal was already making her way up the ropes. Within a minute she was back on the platform, looking over to where the woman was silently pointing.

West. Towards t' perimeter fence.

Teal picked up the scope but at first she could only see the endless leaves of cherry trees and eucalyptus and a few finches perching on branches.

Nothing new, nothing worth making all this fuss about.

Then she saw it. Teal nearly shouted out but managed to contain herself. The Esperans were right—there *was* something out there. Something furry, she could see through the scope; something heading along the branches of the canopy towards the fence.

And behind it, that something carried a long, bushy, red tail. Trying to make as little noise as possible, Teal tried alerting the others over the radio. There was no answer. She turned back to the assistants.

"Can you get down t' ropes by yourselves?"

The Esperans nodded. Teal took the scan card out of the camera and handed it to the Esperan woman.

"I need you to run back to camp—just follow t' path same we came in—" she gestured towards the thin path that disappeared into the undergrowth "—and give this to Cyan. Yes, Cyan Tylor." Teal was already pushing off the platform, the camera—fitted with the spare scan-card—and the scope hanging around her neck.

"But Teal Moore..." whispered the Esperan woman. "Was it? Was it what I think it was?"

"Just go to camp as quick as you can and tell Cyan to come find me. This could be real big."

"And what you gonna do?"

"I'm gonna follow t' Shadow-Tail."

Chapter twelve

She was close. Teal tried to take another scan but even with the zoom, the Red Shadow-Tail was too high up, was moving too quickly through the canopy for her to capture it.

I gotta move faster.

The little mammal was almost at the fence. Teal ran, as quietly and quickly as she could. She stumbled over a root, twisting her ankle.

Shit.

She bent down to touch it. It was painful, but nothing too serious. She looked up again through the scope and her heart dropped. She watched as the Shadow-Tail leapt the several metres from one thin branch on her side of the perimeter to a branch on the other side.

It cleared the fence easily and Teal followed its course on the ground, arriving at the formidable barrier—ten metres high topped with razor wire.

Well, they call it Fortress Conservation for a reason.

She knew there was no way she could get over it. But there was no way she was giving up either. She looked for a way through, running along the fence while keeping her eyes on the spot where the Shadow-Tail had passed.

There.

Just the slightest opening cut into the wire, small enough to miss unless you were standing right up next to it. She had heard that despite all the security there had been break-ins to the park from time to time.

Someone cut this open and t' Protection Service must have missed it.

A tight squeeze, but I can make it.

She checked her watch—4 o'clock.

Time for t' guards to change over. Perfect. I got a chance.

Teal took a deep breath and then, expelling all the air from her body, she began to push herself through the hole.

She was almost on the other side when the sirens started.

2. Boundaries

Prelude

A woman stood in the middle of a supermarket aisle.

In one hand she held a tray with four perfectly ripe kiwis, organic but packaged in plastic. In the other hand were three more kiwis, unpackaged but polluted with pesticides.

She was somewhere else, outside of this store of impossible choices and compromises. She was in the street, shouting with all of the force in her lungs despite the tear gas. She was chained to a fence at a deportation centre. She was running a workshop and squatting a garden and painting a banner and supporting her friends and doing what she knew she must. She dropped the kiwis—packaged and unpackaged—onto the nearest shelf and headed for the door.

"Enough of this," she said to herself.

She had work to do.

Chapter thirteen

Teal tried to cover her ears to block out the deafening noise. She was through the fence. The wire had scratched her bare arms to bleeding. She couldn't go back to the other side—the Protection Service would be here in seconds. She was breaking no laws by *leaving* the park, but they had a reputation for shooting first and asking questions later. Besides, she knew there might not be another chance to get close to the Shadow-Tail and get more scans.

Glancing back at the fence one last time, she plunged into the darkening foliage.

***

"Cyan Tylor, Cyan Tylor!"

The assistants arrived at the camp, shouting, sweating and red from the run. Cyan emerged from the teaching room, surrounded by the other assistants.

"What is it? Is everything okay? Is Teal... *Teal Moore* okay?"

"Yes, yes! But..."

Teal's assistants started to talk quickly with the others in Esperan. The man waved his arms around, mimed something high up and made a running gesture. The woman was shouting in Esperan and looked like she was miming a long tail.

"We saw," the assistant tried again. "Err...it was..."

Cyan recognised the problem. *Emotional L2 interference.* They'd experienced the same thing themself many times when speaking a second language—their French was pretty good for example, but when they were scared, nervous or excited, it usually fell apart and they sounded like a beginner. Cyan wished Jade was here to translate, but he was out checking traps. The Esperan team leader finally stepped forward.

"They say they saw something in t' forest," he said slowly. "She think it was a...wait—"

He quickly asked her something in Esperan and she nodded her head. He seemed to ask her again and she replied with a definitive '*yes*'. Then the woman pulled the scan card out of her pocket, as if to prove what she was saying, and handed it to the leader.

"Well, I can't believe it's true." He looked at the card. "But she say they saw a Red Shadow-Tail. Do you know what that is?"

Cyan's eyes opened wide.

"Of course."

"They took scans—" he handed the card to Cyan "—and Teal Moore ran after it towards t'... what do you call it? T' Union's fence?"

"T' Conservation Perimeter," said Cyan, running their hand through their hair.

They were worried.

Teal know well enough to stay away. T' Service is all trigger-happy guys who didn't make it into t' police. They certainly don't need much provocation to start shooting.

But Cyan also knew how desperate Teal was to properly record a Red Shadow-Tail. They had given her a hard time over the battery. They unclipped the radio from their belt and dialled for Jade. He answered straight away.

"Jade here—"

"—Jade, I need you back at camp straight away. Take care of t' assistants. Teal's run off towards t' fence, they say she may have seen t' Red Shadow-Tail again."

The voice coming from the radio sounded concerned. "Yes, of

course. Is she okay?"

"I hope so," said Cyan. They turned off the radio and, without another word, ran to the path into the forest.

* * *

It was becoming darker with every step and Teal knew it was nearly evening. The trees here looked like second growth. It had all been logged at some point and it was increasingly difficult for her to keep moving forward through the thick undergrowth. Above the wailing siren, she heard a high squeaking sound above her. She had spent enough hours on the platform to know that that wasn't a grey or any kind of bug.

Gotta be t' Shadow-Tail.

Her determination renewed, she pushed on into the darkness.

* * *

Running as fast as they could along the forest trail, Cyan could already hear the sirens. They arrived at the platform and, just as they feared, there was no sign of Teal. They could see a trail of broken branches and snapped stems heading off away from the platform and towards the fence. They followed the trail, pushing through the forest floor bushes and vines when suddenly a crack rang out, loud even over the noise of the sirens.

Like a gun shot.

Cyan froze in panic, then looked down as something crunched under their foot. Beneath their boot, a water bottle lay in pieces, the thin sauvite split open and spilling its contents into the soil.

She must have dropped it.

"Not a gun," they said out loud with relief. "Not a gun."

But then there *were* guns, emerging from the bushes, four of them, and they were pointed directly at Cyan's chest.

Chapter fourteen

Aq put his rifle down on the canteen floor next to the others. He was eating cereal for dinner again. A few of his dorm-mates were at the table talking loudly about a sports game they'd seen at the weekend when he received a message to his faux-Nokia. He took it out of his pocket and read.

> 17.45 Unknown: Hi Boss, I hope You don't mind me writing to You here.

Aq choked on his cereal. Soy milk went up his nose and sprayed all over the table. He grabbed a tissue from the sticky dispenser. His colleagues paused their sports conversation.

"Everything okay, Aq?"

"Yeah, sure, all good."

Aq's wiped his mouth and cleaned milk off his phone. His fingers shook as he typed a reply.

> 17.50 Aq Hass: How did you get my number?

Just as he sent the message he remembered; every delegate was given their guard's private number in case of any problems or last-minute schedule changes. Shielding the sauvite screen from the others at the table, he replied again.

17.51 Aq Hass: Ah right. They gave it to you when you arrived.
17.52 Unknown: Yes, Boss. Is it okay for me to write to Your phone?

A pause.

17.52 Aq Hass: Sure.

Aq had noticed all the capital 'Y's in You and Your straight away. *A subordination thing?*

17.53. Unknown: Have You thought about my proposal from last night, Boss?

Aq's hand was shaking too much to reply. He put the phone back in his pocket. The others at the table had resumed their discussion and were practically shouting with excitement telling and retelling the game. Aq ignored them and continued eating. The only thing he cared less about than art was team sports.
What I'm gonna do? This is super weird.
He flashed back to the scene he had made a few hours before at the hotel room.
I shouldn't have shouted at him. I should have just said thanks for t' gift. Well, at least he don't seem angry with me.
Aq finished eating and stood up. His friends barely noticed him leave. He walked back to the dorm, biting his lip as he went. He had perimeter duty in a few hours and needed to shower. All the security guards had two all-night shifts a week in the control towers at the fence.
In theory, they were there to watch out for anyone trying to get into the park. But as nothing ever seemed to happen at the fence, he and the other guards usually spent the night playing cards or sleeping. Despite the boredom, he was grateful he didn't have to deal with any rich delegates looking down their noses at him.

He went into the bathroom and stripped. He pulled open the drawer with his name on it and took out his uniform. Shirt, trousers. But no underwear.

Shit, I'm still out.

Laundry service could only clean what he sent them and he'd been going without underwear for a week.

I'm not gonna have time to shop until next week.

Then Aq remembered the package. He wrapped a towel around his waist and went back out into the dorm. From under his bunk, he pulled out the box that Kingson had sent him. He looked up quickly to check that no-one was in the room.

I shouldn't. What if I need to give it back?

Aq took out one pair of boxers and went back to the bathroom, locking the door and checking the lock. His heart was beating hard again. He rubbed the material between his fingers again as he lay the boxers down on top of his uniform. They felt amazing.

I still hate him.

Aq got in, turned on the water and soaped up.

Or do I? I mean he's no worse than t' rest of them. He talk a lot for sure. But, he's okay really.

He knew Kingson was leaving for London the following day. He would have to move fast if he wanted to take him up on his offer.

Which is what, precisely? For me to take his money with nothing expected in return? To demand gifts and get them, just because this guy has too much?

Aq couldn't pretend to understand Kingson's motivations, but he had to admit, he was warming to the idea.

Aq stopped the water, dried his hands and took his phone out from his pocket. He looked again at the unfinished conversation and replied:

17.56 Aq Hass: I'm interested.

17.56 Unknown: Oh good, Boss. I really want to serve You.

Aq swallowed hard.
Here we go.

17.57 Aq Hass: But no sex, that clear? I only want your money.
17.57 Unknown: Of course, Boss. Anything You want. I give a great foot massage, but only if You want it. Or just money and gifts. I have a budget for this trip of 8,000 shell. All Yours if You want it, Boss.

Aq read the message three times. His head was spinning. Eight thousand shell was more than he'd ever had all at one time in his life. None of this seemed very real. To kill time while he thought, Aq entered Kingson's name and number into his address book.
I delete all t' messages when this is done.

18.00 Aq Hass: That's a lot of money.
18.00 Carl Kingson: Yes, Boss. I have cash, I thought maybe You wouldn't want too many transfers on Your account.
18.02 Aq Hass: Good thinking.
18.02 Carl Kingson: Boss, if I may. Would You like to call me, "sub"?
18.04 Aq Hass: Fine. Sub.
18.04 Carl Kingson: Thank you, Boss. I understand I've been allocated a new guard for t' morning. You are busy?
18.05 Aq Hass: Yeah, that's my roommate, Blue. I'm on duty at t' fence.
18.05 Carl Kingson: I see, Boss. You gonna have time to visit me, perhaps, before You go to work?

Aq knew that if he wanted to back out of this, he had to end it now.
But, what I got to lose? I might make some easy money. And besides, no-one need to know.

He made his decision.

18.07 Aq Hass: I be up in ten minutes, sub. Be ready for me.

The response was instant.

18.07 Carl Kingson: Yes, Boss. Thank you, Boss.

There wasn't time to finish his shower. Aq turned the water off and started getting dressed again. As he pulled on Kingson's gift he was, to his great surprise, rock hard.

* * *

"T' alarm has been triggered," said the Protection Service guard.
No shit, Cyan wanted to say.
The sirens were deafening and bright lights along the perimeter were flashing red. Cyan was looking down the barrel of the guard's rifle, so they held their tongue.
"You're with t' research team, no?"
Cyan was standing beneath the research platform with a camera and a bright green ID badge that said "Official Union Ecological Research" around their neck.
What else could I be?
They nodded politely.
"See anyone pass through here, into t' park?"
"No, nothing."
Cyan was happy to keep the guards distracted on this side of the fence for a while. If Teal really had gotten through, she'd need all the time possible to get away.
It's almost dark. How far out of t' park she gonna go? And how t' hell she gonna get back in?

"Could have been an animal, a pigeon perhaps, that set off t' alarms?" they asked innocently.

The guard looked at them as if they were very, very stupid.

"Just let us know if you see anyone dangerous."

He gathered his men and they headed back towards the control tower.

Cyan watched them leave.

Four young men with rifles and permission to use lethal force. Who in this world could be more dangerous?

* * *

Aq was back outside the door of room 412 of the Guest Suites. His stomach hurt. He knew this had to be a bad idea, dangerous even, but he was too curious, and yes, too *excited* to back out now. Maybe it wouldn't work out. Maybe it would end badly. But the delegate was leaving in two days anyway...

What I got to lose?

He knocked and heard Carl call in response.

"Open!"

Aq pushed the door and it swung open into the dark room. Unconsciously holding his breath, he stepped inside.

Chapter fifteen

The forest was almost completely dark and Teal was lost. She was pushing on through the foliage, but she could no longer hear the Shadow-Tail's soft sound above her. She'd lost all sense of direction. Was she still moving away from the fence or towards it? Sweat burned in her eyes.

She'd had no idea that crossing the fence would set off the alarm, but now there was no going back.

If t' guards catch me trying to get into t' park, I'm gonna be shot on sight. Official Union ID be damned.

She'd deal with that later. First, she had to get through this jungle. She was covered in sweat and felt dizzy.

I gotta find a way out.

* * *

Aq entered the room. He wore his uniform and carried his gun over his shoulder.

Carl Kingson—'sub' he supposed he should start calling him—was lying on the bed in his usual position, wearing only underwear and propped up against the headrest. But something about his expression was different. Aq couldn't quite put his finger on it.

On the bedside cabinet lay a wad of money. Aq could already see they were twenties.

Probably around a thousand shell.

An unopened bottle of Espera rum stood next to the money with two glasses. Aq stood still, trying to think how to start. He had spent the entire journey up the stairwell trying to imagine this scene, to think of what to say, what to ask for, to demand. He had already started doing it—'getting into role' he guessed it was called—this morning on the phone, but sending messages was completely different to actually speaking.

"Hi, Boss." It was almost a whisper.

Aq cleared his throat. "Hi...sub."

"Would you like to take some money, Boss?"

"Yeah. Erm...eighty shell."

"Of course, Boss."

Carl Kingson, business celebrity of the Five Nations and rich beyond Aq's imagining, counted out four twenties and presented them to him with both hands. Aq took the money and stared at it in what probably looked like disbelief. He put the money in his pocket. He was already hard again.

"Good, sub."

"Thank you, Boss. What else can I do to please you?"

"Pour me some rum," Aq said, in the most commanding tone he could manage.

I shouldn't drink a lot before my shift, he reminded himself, but he had a high tolerance for alcohol and he could see from the label that it was the really good stuff. *Just one glass gonna help take t' edge off, make all this seem a bit less weird.*

"Of course, Boss."

Kingson poured him a drink and presented it, again with both hands.

Aq sat on the bed and drank it down in one go.

"More, Boss?"

"More money."

"How much, Boss?"

"All of it. How much is there?"

"One thousand five hundred shell, Boss."

Emboldened by the rum already warming his chest, Aq said "Give it to me."

And he did. Aq stuffed it into his pocket and got up to leave. He thought of demanding a foot massage—he actually could really use one—but he didn't want to give him the wrong idea. Although he felt strangely turned on by all of this, Aq didn't want to have sex. He knew some of the others from the dorm slept with their clients—even beat them up—for cash sometimes, but he'd always said that was one boundary he wasn't going to cross. Aq took sex very seriously and it didn't feel right for him to commercialise it.

Besides I've already been paid way more than a simple fuck is worth.

He walked towards the door.

"What else can I do to please you, Boss?"

Aq turned back and looked around the room. His eyes fell on Kingson's suitcase. It lay open on the floor and was only semi-unpacked.

No going back now.

Aq knelt and started pulling things out. Inside he found some expensive-looking designer sunglasses and a shirt made of the same material as the underwear. He reckoned that he and Kingson were about the same size, so he took both and stood up.

"I'm taking these," he tried to say, but his throat was dry and the words didn't come out.

"Rum," he said finally. Kingson poured and presented him another shot. He drank it down in one gulp.

"I'm taking these," he repeated, decisively.

"Of course, Boss. Everything I have is yours."

Aq looked again at Kingson. He saw that same expression again and finally began to understand it. *Devotion.*

Aq felt light-headed. He looked over at the door. He'd already taken this much further than he planned to. He stood up, opened the door, and left without another word.

***

Like the difference between night and day, the forest ended. Teal stepped past the last line of foliage and she was out in the open. The sky was still light—she could see that the sun was only just setting on the horizon—and she felt completely exposed. She took an unconscious step back towards the forest and tried to take in what she saw.

Before her was a desert. There was no vegetation, no *cerezo* trees, nothing green or living of any kind. The air smelt bitter and she could see that the rocks and the ground were covered in a thin layer of pinkish dust. A wind was blowing. She had to brush her long hair out of her face. She could see twisters of dust spiralling up into the air.

What is this place?

Since arriving in Espera, she and Cyan had never left the park except to go to the city. They'd had no need to and the roads outside were notoriously badly maintained or just non-existent. She thought back to the camp's giant map of Espera geography. The whole area was coloured green, she remembered, indicating forest that stretched way beyond the Conservation Perimeter. But here there was no forest, there was nothing at all except rocks and dust.

Another twister blew by and Teal could see that it had picked up garbage, shopping bags, cans and paper, as well as that strange pink dust.

This place is dead, she thought. *Completely, tragically, dead.*

Chapter sixteen

Standing in the corridor once again, Aq looked at the shirt and sunglasses in his hand. He patted his pocket and felt the shell stuffed inside. He went quickly down the stairs towards his dorm, exhausted from the tension and increasingly nervous that somehow this would backfire on him. His shoulders ached and he felt nauseous. He had the sense of being on a tall building looking over the edge.

But he also felt good. Euphoric even.

I gotta talk to someone about this.

He paused in the stairwell and wrote a message to his friend, Moss Hiyat.

> 19.11 Aq Hass: Hey, mate. I got tower duty in a couple of hours. Want to meet up for a drink first?
> 19.13 Moss Hiyat: Staff bar in ten minutes?
> 19.13 Aq Hass: See you there.

Moss, who was Aq's best friend at the Union, worked on the main reception desk. He was the person Aq went to when he had family problems or needed to complain about work.

Aq knew that, like a lot of the guys, he also regularly supplemented his income by turning tricks, and sometimes dominating, for money. He was the perfect person to consult with. They sat at a table in the corner with their drinks as Aq explained the situation.

"Is it okay if I ask your advice about something—a client?"

"Sure. What kind of client?" Moss asked with a cheeky grin. He often liked sharing his sex work stories with Aq, even inviting him to join him on some jobs. Aq always refused. Not in a judgemental way. He just wasn't interested.

"He's an assignation," explained Aq. "A corporate big shot from London."

"Hot."

"Definitely not. Anyway, he sent me this message yesterday—"

He showed it to Moss, who read it over quickly and smiled.

"Calling me Boss and all that—" said Aq, feeling slightly embarrassed. "—It's a submission thing, no?"

"Yes, dear."

"Okay. I guessed so. T' thing is, I went to his room—"

"—Oh, this is where it get interesting!"

"No, relax. Never gonna happen, Moss."

"Nothing wrong with being a Danny, you know," said Moss, using the slang word for a male or nonbinary sex worker. The word came from a historical figure called Danny, a stripper and escort who had fought with the resistance. Sex workers who were women or nonbinary were often called a 'Kit', after another resistance fighter.

"No, sorry, of course not." Aq lightly touched his friend's hand. "I just don't want that job."

"Fair enough."

"Anyway, I go in, I demand money—fifteen hundred shell! And he gave it to me. And he already put two grand in my account without me asking. Also I... erm, I took some of his clothes? A nice shirt and that..." Aq was blushing. His friend was practically bouncing with excitement

"Cool! That's really good money, Aq! And he's definitely not after sex?"

"No. Well that's what he say. I mean I think he'd like to—"

"—Wouldn't we all?"

"Stop that. Anyway, he said sex is only gonna happen if I want it to happen. He just want to please me apparently. Can you imagine?"

"Very cool."

"But I don't understand what would make him want to do that. I mean, just handing me his money? Giving me his stuff? What do he get out of it?"

"You said he's famous or something."

"It's Carl Kingson," whispered Aq, although no-one was listening. Moss looked blank.

"He designed t' park and founded t' Protection Service. He's a huge Union celebrity. You know him, *everyone* know him."

Moss shook his head. "No clue."

Aq was always impressed by Moss's ability to know so much about the world but be so disconnected from it at the same time.

"But you know," Moss continued unfazed. "Big shot subs are all t' same. Too much power and control—they need to give it away. That's their fetish. Rich guys and top cops are t' worst. All they want in t' world is to give up control for an hour." Moss gave Aq a wink. "And that's why they pay Dannys and Kits to tie them up and kick their balls."

"Yeah, it could be that. But it seems like t' money's important in itself. I don't think he's paying for domination. More that t' money, spending it, giving up control of it, is t' fetish."

"Sound awesome to me."

"Yeah." Aq sipped his beer thoughtfully. "Maybe."

"You're not into it?"

"I am. I mean I got more than three thousand shell out of t' guy for doing nothing. What's not to like about that?"

"Hell, if you don't want him, give him to me!"

Aq chuckled. "I gotta go to t' Perimeter soon. Can I get you another beer?"

"Yep," replied Moss, already heading for the bar. "I think you can afford it."

BOUNDARIES

***

Cyan sat with Jade in the camp office trying to make a plan of action. Outside, Indi was back in the camp and was busy herding the assistants onto a bus back to the city. They were more excited than ever after the events at the fence and it took a long time to get rid of them. Finally, the bus pulled away onto the dirt track that led out to the main perimeter road. As they disappeared into the forest, Indi heard the tourists starting up a raucous song.

She opened the flap of the office tent and, almost bending double to fit her lanky frame through the gap, she squeezed in and joined the meeting. Cyan was talking frantically, waving their hands in the air.

"Hi Indi. Thank god we got rid of them at last. I was just saying, I left a radio and a flash light up on t' platform. In case, somehow, she come back tonight. And a spare harness below."

Indi pushed some papers off a chair and sat down. Cyan threw her a look but continued speaking.

"Anyway, after t' guards left, I found a gap in t' fence which I reckon she might have squeezed through but I guess they were watching me, so I headed back. Obviously, I called her phone about a hundred times and left messages, but it don't seem to connect."

"You think she would have crossed t' fence?" asked Jade, his arms crossed. "I hope she don't get caught—t' camp gonna be shut down for sure."

He was the oldest of the team, but Cyan often thought he acted like the youngest. They sighed.

"Your concern is touching, Jade, but yes, I think she left t' park. And that means there's no way back in."

"Maybe she could pass through t' fence again?" Indi suggested hopefully.

Jade shook his head. "T' guards will be paying more attention than normal. No way she can get back in."

"Oh, okay."

Indi looked down at the carpet and fiddled with her fingers. Cyan watched her out of the corner of their eye. Everyone knew how much Indi admired Teal. When she had first joined the team, Cyan had been a little jealous over the way she would follow her around, asking questions and subconsciously mirroring the way Teal spoke at the dinner table.

Teal had assured them that it was just respect; a cis woman in awe of the grace and strength of trans women, something quite common in Espera in those days. Cyan still wasn't convinced but it also wasn't the first time they'd been jealous either. They switched on the holo-beamer.

"Which just leaves t' main park entrance." A three-dimensional map of Espera filled the floor and they measured the distance to the gate. "About a twenty-kilometre hike through t' forest. And that's if she follow t' fence which wouldn't be real safe."

Indi coughed. "Sorry to bring this up—" she said softly, curling her hair with a finger. "But you know we gotta deliver our report to t' board tomorrow morning."

"Crap. I almost forgot." Cyan reached into their shirt pocket and took out the scan card the assistant had brought from the platform. "Can you two look at this, please, and see what we got? I hope it was worth it."

Chapter seventeen

Aq's phone was buzzing in his pocket as he arrived at the Perimeter for his shift. He looked at it quickly. As he guessed, it was a message from Kingson. Aq stuffed the phone back in his pocket without reading it. It had only been three hours since he had left the room. He was getting pushy and Aq hated pushy.

The Service jeep that had brought him along the perimeter road drove off and Aq climbed up the access ladder to the top of the control tower.

"Evening guys," he said cheerfully as he stepped into the room. Three guards sat around a table and seemed to be deeply engrossed in a game of cards. They barely acknowledged his arrival.

Aq spoke to them in English, as he usually did at work. He always found it odd that he lived in this language in Espera.

What's wrong with Esperan? Or even Arabic?

Although Arabic was embraced as part of the 'Great Esperan Diversity,' Aq knew perfectly well about the dirty looks he'd received for using it with his colleagues at work.

"Anything interesting tonight?"

The shift leader, a white Esperan who looked like he'd barely left high school, looked up from the card game.

"Something triggered t' alarms over by t' research camp this evening," he announced. "We checked it, but nothing. Only some white woman at t' observation deck. No-one unsafe."

Aq looked at the other guards. The leader was the only white person in the room. Aq was completely unsurprised that he equated whiteness with safety

Fuck that.

He had to spend the next twelve hours at the tower, so he kept his mouth shut.

"I can join in?" he asked gesturing towards the table.

"Sure," answered one of the other guards, giving Aq a weak smile. "We deal you in next round."

Aq sat down and settled in for the night.

Within an hour of arriving, he could feel his phone buzzing again. He took it out and looked. It was another message from Carl, a copy-paste of the first message.

22.21 Carl Kingson: Hi Boss. Thank You for earlier, it was amazing. But I want to give You more... I can?

Aq thought about telling him to leave him the hell alone. He'd only just seen this guy, and he already wanted more.

Just sending t' same message twice? That's too much.

But then Aq remembered their session. How much fun he'd had. And the pile of shell now hidden under his bed. He'd earned a tonne of money already—

If 'earn' is even t' word.

The card game was already getting boring and it was going to be a very long shift. Keeping his phone carefully shielded from the others as he typed, he wrote out a reply.

22.29 Aq Hass: Yep. I want to take more from you, sub. I'm at work but I got a sleep break at 12. I'm at Control Tower 16. If you can find a way to come pick Me up, we gonna drive somewhere and play. I got two hours.

As always, Kingson replied instantly.

22.29 Carl Kingson: I'm gonna be there, Boss. How much should I bring?

'One thousand,' typed Aq and then deleted it.

22.33 Aq Hass: Two thousand. And bring your tablet, I want to do some shopping too.

22.33 Carl Kingson: Thank You, Boss. I bring three thousand, just in case.

* * *

Outside the tent, Cyan selected Teal's number again and pressed call. Nothing.

Maybe Teal don't have signal out there, or she dropped her phone. Or something worse.

Cyan could feel themself becoming frantic.

How could this have happened? How could I have let this happen? I should never have given Teal such a hard time.

They looked at their hands grasping the phone and realised they were shaking.

I'm not going to get any sleep tonight.

They called again.

Inside, Jade and Indi were reviewing the scans brought back by the tourists earlier that day.

"Pretty good. Much better than t' other one at least." Jade switched off the beamer and got himself an organic beer from the cool box. "Want one?"

Indi shook her head. She would probably fall asleep after one bottle.

"I'm worried. About Teal I mean." She was curling her hair again.

"Her own fault," replied Jade sitting down and putting his boots up on a pile of papers on the desk. "What she was thinking?"

"Could you not?" asked Indi softly, pointing at the papers. "Some of those are important."

Jade grunted and put his feet back down.

"She gonna come back," he said and downed half the bottle. "Besides, we got work to do here. Data to collect. Samples to process. Science won't wait just because Teal decide to take a holiday."

Indi shrugged.

"Cy better get that extension tomorrow or we're screwed," Jade said.

"Cyan. You know they hate to be called Cy."

Jade rolled his eyes and finished his beer.

* * *

The car arrived at exactly midnight. Aq heard it pulling up outside the tower and was afraid Kingson would honk the horn to get his attention. He was relieved to hear the engine turn off and the night was silent again. Aq went into the break room where the other three guards were already sleeping and gently shook the shift leader awake.

"What t' fuck?" he said in Esperan and rolled over covering his face in the blanket.

"Sorry, but it's my turn to take a mandatory break."

Breaks *were* mandatory and Aq wanted to emphasise the point. From beneath the blanket, the Shift Leader grunted.

"I have a headache," lied Aq. "It okay if I go outside to take a walk? I'm gonna be back by one."

"Whatever, just let me sleep."

Before he could change his mind, Aq left the room, crossed the control room and went outside to the small balcony that surrounded the tower. He could see the car about two hundred metres along the perimeter road and, already excited, he started climbing down the ladder.

When he reached the car, Kingson was smiling at him from behind the wheel.

"Hi, Boss."

"Drive, sub. I'll tell you when to stop."

Kingson took off the handbrake and allowed the car to silently cruise down the hill he'd parked on. When they were sufficiently far from the control tower, Aq spoke again.

"Here is good. No-one ever use t' perimeter road at night."

On the dashboard, next to a pile of cash and a web-tablet, there was a Protected Area permit. He was curious to know how Kingson had managed to get permission to enter the park at such late notice, but he remembered that he wasn't here for chit-chat.

"Let's get down to it," he said, as much to himself as anything.

"I'm all yours, Boss."

He offered the tablet with both hands.

Aq took it and could see that it was already connected and opened to 'Shopping'. In less than a minute, Aq had found the perfume and scents section and clicked on one called 'Shadow's Attraction,' a kind that he'd tried one time at a Union shop and fallen in love with immediately. He had thought then that he'd never be able to afford a bottle so took an extra generous squirt from the tester. Billing Kingson's account, he ordered the biggest bottle available. It cost two hundred shell.

Despite his best attempts to maintain some kind of psychological distance from all this, Aq was beginning to really enjoy himself.

Damn t' risks, he thought to himself. *This is fun.*

Chapter eighteen

Teal's arms were still bleeding and her hair was stuck to the sweat on her face. The sun had set a while ago and for the first time since she had left the platform she was actually scared. She didn't know where she was and now that she'd lost the Red Shadow-Tail, she had no plan. She only knew it wouldn't be safe to go back to the fence for a while. If she could even find it.

She gritted her teeth against the dry wind and continued dragging her tired body through the desert. It was all she could do to stop herself from crying. To keep herself from exhaustion, she began to analyse the darkening land around her.

She could tell that this wasn't a natural desert. She had worked in several deserts: the kind that had been there for a long time, intact ecosystems full of animals and plants adapted to a perpetual lack of water, and the human-induced kind, desolate and all but lifeless. This was definitely the second.

But how? Why? And why we never heard about this?

She had many questions, but she also knew she had to get back to camp. The temperature was dropping fast with no forest or clouds to retain the heat and this wind and dust were terrible. She didn't want to sleep out here. She'd seen the sun set to her right and knew that she was moving south. She decided to follow the perimeter fence south and east around the park until she arrived at the park entrance.

Not too close though, I never need to hear those sirens again.

She kept going for what must have been two hours, eventually navigating by the stars when the sky was too dark to see where the sun had set.

Thank goodness for Jade and his star-gazing evenings. It would be easy for me to get real lost out here. T' horizon's flat and there's nothing at all—

Until suddenly there was something. Stumbling through the dark, she saw vague forms all around her. In the starlight, she started to pick them out from the land. They seemed to be buildings, houses, a settlement of some sort. Distracted by the shadows, Teal forgot to watch where she was going and bumped hard into what looked for all the world like a kitchen sink elevated on wooden slats. The quiet of the night was broken abruptly by plates and cups falling and smashing on the ground. Teal heard voices all around her. Even not understanding the words, she knew that the voices were scared. Scared and angry.

Chapter nineteen

Teal was surrounded by people all shouting at her at once in the darkness. She couldn't understand a word. She couldn't really see the people and was barely able to discern them as shadows against the dark. She had no way to know if they had weapons.

Someone shouted: "And who's she? Which lettie did she come from?"

Another looked at her and asked, "You ain't savvy?"

She stood as still as she could with the palms of her hands presented forward in the dark. The shouting continued unabated. More shadows arrived.

"Sorry," she was repeating softly. "Does anyone speak English?"

Nothing. More shouting. She knew just enough Esperan to ask the same thing in Esperan. Still nothing. Desperate, she repeated the phrase in French, then in Swahili. Just more shouting. One of the group ran off into the settlement and soon came back accompanied. A voice that sounded like it belonged to an older woman rose above the noise.

"Who are you and why you don't speak Polari?"

"Thank god you speak English!" said Teal, almost crying with relief.

"No flies, you don't screech Polari?"

Teal looked blank.

"So you're from t' other side?"

"Yes! Yes!"

What is this language they're speaking? Who are these people?

As she always did when she was nervous, Teal started speaking very,

very fast.

"Yes, I'm from t' other side. I guess. I mean for me, this is t' other side. Anyway, I'm so sorry to disturb you all, I don't mean any harm. I don't even know where I am, to be honest. It's just that I came through t' Conservation Perimeter—t' big fence, you know? I was following a Red Shadow-Tail actually, I'm from a Union research team and—"

The woman put up her hands. "Stop, stop. Slow down, *please*," she said.

Teal stopped gabbling. She apologised again.

"You're from t' park?"

"Yes. I came through t' fence."

"Why?" asked the woman, in a tone that suggested it was a very strange thing to do.

Someone next to the old woman asked, "Who's t' palone, why is she at our lettie? Is she a National charper, are there dowry others on t' way?"

"Nish t' chat...and nanti that," the old woman replied, then turned back to Teal. "Why you came?" she repeated.

"I was following a Red Shadow-Tail," said Teal slowly.

"A Red Shadow-Tail. *A Red Squirrel!*"

The crowd around Teal gasped and started talking to each other again. The woman silenced them by raising her hands.

"You are sure?" she said to Teal.

"Yes, I have proof."

Teal suddenly wondered if she should be having this conversation at all.

"Then please, come into our home and have some tea. We have much to discuss."

Teal gasped as she stepped through the tent doors. The inside was stunning. The massive central pole holding up the structure was intricately carved and decorated, the designs and images seeming to move in the flickering candlelight. The ground inside was covered in a thin mat that looked like it might be hand-woven. Following her host, Teal took off her dusty shoes in the doorway, relishing the cool mat under her tired feet.

"Please, sit."

The old woman gestured towards a long, thin table, perhaps only half a metre off the ground. She put her walking stick down first and lowered herself. Teal sat cross-legged and shuffled her legs under the table.

"There that's better. My name is Azure."

"Teal."

"Teal...a beautiful name."

"Thank you. I guess there really weren't so many choices now that—"

"It's a beautiful name."

"Thank you."

"Your pronouns?"

Teal was a little taken back by Azure's directness. In Espera, trans, agender and non-binary people were very much a respected part of society, but politeness generally dictated that people tried to guess the pronouns that each other used. There was a whole diplomatic dance of trying to avoid gendering new people at all until someone dropped a clue.

"She, her," she responded.

"Me too."

Wow, that's much less complicated.

Teal smiled. Azure abruptly turned her head back towards the entrance and shouted very loudly.

"Rouge! Order lau a bevoir, duckie. T' bona stuff!"

She turned and smiled at Teal. "We gonna have tea first and dinner should be served soon. You join us, no?"

"I..."

Teal noticed that Azure had a very intense way of making eye contact. She had an air of confidence and an expectation of being followed.

I wouldn't want to get on t' wrong side of her.

"Yes. Thank you."

"Good. You came a long way, you gotta be hungry."

"I am actually."

When I last ate? It feel like days ago.

A young person arrived carrying a tray with a simple teapot and cups and a plate of blackberry cookies.

"Thanks duckie," said Azure. "Pavare t' others to order munjarry when its ready. She is hungry. And so is your mother!"

"Pardon me for asking," Teal's voice was quiet, polite. "But what is this language you're speaking? I've been in Espera for five years and I never heard it before.

"Polari."

"Polari...?"

"Polari. Now drink your tea."

Teal sipped quietly at her drink and looked around at the candlelit communal space. It was mostly reclaimed wood and tarps, but it had clearly been arranged with real love and attention.

It's beautiful here. I love it.

The food began to arrive.

"So, you're a park researcher?" Azure asked Teal.

Her mouth full, Teal couldn't reply. She nodded instead.

"I see."

The tent became busy. Teal counted twelve people—ten adults, two children—gathered around the table sitting cross-legged, eating and talking very, very loudly.

Who eat this late? she wondered. *And so much noise!*

Even Teal, who enjoyed the chaos of big family dinners, was overwhelmed. She was also confused by the strange language they were speaking.

Some words are definitely English, and some of it is kind of familiar. But what could it be, and why only here? What is this place?

Teal was determined to find out, but Azure seemed more interested in asking questions than answering them.

"So you're paid by t' Union?"

Already asking about money—she's so direct! I guess I did turn up unexpectedly at their doorstep in t' middle of t' night. But still...

"Erm, yes. T' team is funded by t' Union and a private board of conservation industry representatives."

"Conservation industry representatives," Azure repeated and passed Teal more flatbreads. "Here, eat some more."

Teal was already overfull, but she took the breads dutifully.

"Thank y—"

"And you say you saw a Red...*Shadow-Tail* as you call it. We believed them to be extinct in Espera."

"Yes."

"Tell us more."

"I mean, I guess you know t' main sto—"

"Please, tell us."

Teal noticed that the room had quietened down and everyone was looking at her, waiting.

Well at least this is one story I know well.

She put the bread back down, sipped some water and began.

Chapter twenty

Well, as you know, t' Red Shadow-Tail used to be super common across Europe."

People around the table nodded.

"Then in t' 1870s, Greys were introduced from t' US to t' UK to look beautiful on fancy estates. Unfortunately, t' imported Greys had some immunity to a virus they carried, but Reds didn't. They also outcompeted t' Reds for food and did better in destroyed habitats."

This part of t' story everyone know.

"Within a few decades t' Reds were almost gone in t' UK. And t' same thing happened in t' north of Italy."

Everyone had stopped eating now to hear the story. Even the children were quiet.

"But everywhere else, t' Reds were doing okay because Greys hadn't arrived. Then, in 2025, Greys finally made it to Brussels. In fact, it was only a single pair that got across t' channel. Some believe they were brought as cute pets for diplomats, others think they hitched a ride in a truck or a train. Anyway, they brought t' squirrel parapoxvirus with them and, as Shadow-Tails do, they bred and spread super fast. T' virus can kill nearly a hundred percent of infected Reds in five days—and it was a total disaster. Populations crashed and in less than twenty years there were already local extinctions."

Teal looked around her at the silent villagers.

This is kind of a crappy story in t' end. I'm sure Jade could present it with cold statistics in that distant way of his. But actually, it's sad.

"And in Espera, t' Red Shadow-Tail was last seen in t' 2040s," she concluded looking down at the table. "And then it was gone."

"Until now," said Azure. "According to your research."

"Yes! Right! I didn't see t' scans yet but I'm sure—"

"I believe you."

Wow, if only t' board were so easily convinced.

"You're not t' first to see one near here."

"Oh..."

Azure nodded.

"And..."

I answered your questions, please tell me something.

"...and where is 'here,' can I ask? What is this village, and this desert? I live five years near here and no-one ever told me about this place."

Azure stood abruptly.

"Tomorrow I answer all your questions."

"Tomorrow...?"

"You're gonna stay over of course. T' park's too far tonight."

"Oh..."

Teal had been so overwhelmed by the events of the day, she hadn't even thought about where she was sleeping tonight.

"Thank you. I would lov—"

"My daughter, Rouge, will show you to your room. Good night, Teal."

As abruptly as she seemed to do everything, Azure went to bed.

Chapter twenty-one

Cyan was on the solar transport from Union to downtown. The train was travelling fast on its elevated rails across the bridge and over the city buildings. They looked out of the transparent wall and saw the early morning light reflecting over the harbour.

Espera City is so beautiful sometimes.

But they couldn't enjoy it; they were worried about Teal. They still had no news from her and, although Jade and Indi were back at camp with strict instructions to call if they heard anything, Cyan was anxious.

I gotta pull myself together.

They checked their phone. Only an hour and a half until they needed to give the team's report. They were unprepared, but they hoped the research the team had produced would be sufficient to impress the board and at least get them an extension on their contract.

Cyan, Indi and Jade had stayed up late deciding whether or not they should present the Red Shadow-Tail to the board but they hadn't been able to make a final decision. Without a good plan for making the information public, it might not be the best thing for the park.

"Last thing t' forest need is even more tourists," Indi had said. Cyan agreed with her.

Distracted and tired, they looked at the train map above the door for the tenth time. Six more stops before the financial district.

Super weird, they thought. *That conservation meetings happen among t' skyscrapers and boardrooms rather than in t' diplomatic meeting rooms of t' Union.*

But the board always met there. The restaurants were better, apparently. Cyan shuffled through their papers and tried to prepare something resembling a professional report.

Aq was texting on his phone as he got onto the solar train and sat down. Kingson was leaving for London in an hour and had messaged to say goodbye and to let Aq know that he'd left a package for him at the new private mailbox he'd opened under his name. He already knew it was the rest of his eight thousand shell—Kingson's entire budget for the trip. It was all the money in the world to Aq, thirty-two day's wages to be precise. For doing not much of anything. Not even sex.

In a way, he felt relieved that this bizarre game was over. The gifts he'd bought himself last night would be arriving over the next few days to his mailbox; hundreds of shell worth of clothes, new boots, expensive perfume. But he kept imagining getting more.

Like an addict, he thought vaguely, scrolling through his phone. *Where I'm gonna get my fix? Anyway, I need to stop thinking about all of that.*

He put away his phone. Just like every week, he was heading to Oak Grove to visit his family. He'd be able to give them more money this week though, quite a bit more.

He yawned and gazed around at the other passengers on the transport. Next to him sat a very pale person—their skin tone was the same as Kingson's, Aq noticed, but their hair was darker. And very short. They wore an ID around their neck that said 'Official Union Ecological Research'. He wondered if they were from the team near the tower. He'd slept barely two hundred metres from the camp the night before.

He was curious.

The gentle voice of the train conductor announced the next station in three languages. Cyan looked up from their papers and checked the map yet again.

Four stations, I can't forget to get off.

They noticed the person next to them was looking at their badge. He—Cyan guessed he—had the same lopsided haircut most of the Protection Service guards had. Maybe it was a soldier thing.

He's cute, they noticed vaguely. *Skinny, but defined. Definitely a guard of some kind. Actually, he's still looking at me. Look away now. Stop staring.*

They thought of moving to another seat or standing up and waiting by the doors, but before they could, he spoke.

"I saw your badge," he said in perfect English. "Are you researching in t' park?"

"I am," Cyan replied politely, but carefully.

"Are you on t' forest team over by t' perimeter?"

"I am."

"I was over that way last night. I'm a guard with t' Service."

Cyan smiled politely.

"It's beautiful over there. T' forest and that. How is t' research? You find anything interesting?"

He's not creepy, he's sweet, Cyan decided.

They looked over through the window. They had just gone through another station. Three more to go.

"Actually yes. Something very interesting. A Red Shadow-Tail."

They were shocked by their own admission.

Why I'm telling him that? Shut up Cyan!

Teal was missing, their whole project was riding on a major meeting and suddenly Cyan was discussing the Red Shadow-Tail with a total stranger. A park guard nothing less.

Well, they figured, *this guy just gonna think I'm delusional.*

The guard paused a moment, possibly trying to understand their pronunciation of the word.

"A Red Shadow-Tail? Like a red squirrel?" he said, using the old name for the animal.

Cyan nodded and the guard blew air out of his mouth in a way that Cyan guessed could either mean surprise, amazement, or disbelief.

"Precisely."

"I saw one too once, from t' tower. No-one believed me, but I swear I saw it. It made a sound high up in the trees like *'chitterchitterchitter'*. It was very cute."

Cyan smiled at his impression. They were about to ask him a question, when they realised that their train was already about to leave their stop.

"Sorry, I have to go!" They jumped through the closing doors just in time.

Chapter twenty-two

Thirty minutes later, Aq got out as the train pulled up at Oak Grove station. The platform itself was a world away from the award-winning station at Dignity or any of the modern stations down-town. Every available space was covered in posters for fast-food or recruitment to the Protection Service. About half the lights were turned off—'Reducing Our Footprint for a Better Tomorrow,' according to another poster—and the benches were covered in spikes to prevent people sleeping on them.

Or sitting on them, apparently, thought Aq. *Why even bother having benches?*

He left the dreary little station and headed out into his old neighbourhood. Aq loved Oak Grove, in the way that someone can love old sneakers despite the fact that they just don't fit any more and they let the rain in. Oak Grove certainly wasn't his home anymore, but neither was the Union with all its rich, white delegates. As each year went by, Aq was less and less sure he belonged anywhere.

He walked around a pile of recycling that had spilled onto the pavement. Separating recycling was mandatory in Espera but in Oak Grove weeks could go buy before anything got collected. Aq kicked a can out of his way and it rolled off the very high curb.

No matter how many recyclers go on strike, t' Union always manage to have clean streets. And frikkin' flowers everywhere. Always enough money for t' Union to look pretty.

He arrived at his family's home and walked up the little driveway. He passed the proudly maintained juniper bushes and pristine paving slabs that his father swept every morning without fail.

Aq could smell his mother's cooking before he even knocked on the door.

*＊＊

Cyan walked from Central Station to the building where the meeting would be held. Their entire walk was filled with flowers. The platform was planted with aromatic herbs and hanging baskets. The pavement was lined with thornless roses, carefully trimmed to allow enough room for everyone to pass. They stood in front of the building, filled with awe.

It was grand Esperan architecture. Five stories of cob, recycled wood, and sauvite glass. Just below the steps, which led to an equally grand entrance, was a monument surrounded by a permaculture garden of olive trees. Cyan ran their hand over a vine that had created a thick carpet around the tree trunks.

They planted sweet potato for ground cover. Real smart.

The garden was in full bloom and was one of Cyan's favourite places to pause when they were in town. They stepped in front of the statue.

Hand-carved from Esperan stone, a giant Ash and Pinar stood together on a pile of rocks, holding hands calling out to an invisible crowd. Their hands were mid-sign. Cyan read the plaque.

'From one of t' most iconic scenes in t' Exodus, here we see t' great Ash and Pinar a few hours before they led t' resistance to a battle against t' corrupt and violent State and its policies of destroying diversity.

They are signing in USL—Universal Sign Language, formerly Resistance Sign. It is t' word for 'home.'

Today, Ash and Pinar have become synonymous with protecting the environment, just as their friends Kit and Danny have become synonymous with empowered sex work. We honour them and all t' resistance today with this statue.

May we all be as strong as they were. Espera City Council, 2110.'

Cyan looked over the garden and saw a solar tram trundling quietly by.

How things have changed since those days. T' resistance, T' queer purges, T' Exodus. Things are so much calmer now and yes, in many ways, better. Except maybe these god-awful meetings.

Cyan touched the statue in reverence, climbed the steps and entered the building.

***

Aq was already tired of his family. He loved them dearly but his father seemed more difficult each year. His three younger brothers were causing a riot in the tiny flat where, with Aq's sister and mother, they all lived together crammed into three rooms. At least lunch was sure to be amazing. He always missed his mother's cooking.

They code-switched effortlessly between Arabic, Esperan and the occasional English. All except Aq's youngest brothers, who had declared they wanted to be 't' best Esperans,' and would never speak any language other than Esperan again. Over tea and cookies, the conversation quickly turned to money.

"Never been this high, I swear to you Aquamarine, they make it harder and harder to stay here."

Aq sighed. He hated that name, but knew his father would never get used to calling him Aq.

"I know Papa—"

"And in frikkin' Union they got all their fancy turbines and solar panels and I don't know what, but we're stuck here with Espera Power threatening to cut us off from their unreliable electricity if we don't pay last month's bill. But how can we? How can—"

Aq's three little brothers came running through the dining room-kitchen and knocked over a chair with a loud crash. Squealing, they rushed away again. Aq's father continued as if nothing had happened.

"Also, your sister's starting high school next month and she need a new uniform—"

"And new shoes," said Aq's mother, turning from her cooking to point at her daughter's feet with a wooden spoon. "She's been wearing those old things for a year and a half."

"It's fine, Mom. Don't make such a fuss," said Aq's sister. A fiery eleven-year-old, Mauve shared Aq's thick black hair and blue eyes.

"If someone say something I take them out. I could you know."

She clenched her fists to emphasise her point.

Aq's mother rolled her eyes. "Yes dear."

"Well actually, Mom, Papa, I want to talk to you about money."

This is it, thought Aq. *T' first time that Kingson's money gonna mean something in t' real world.*

"I brought a little bit more this week. I took some extra shifts at t' Perimeter."

"How much more?" asked Aq's father, suspiciously.

"Blue!" admonished Aq's mother. "What your father mean to say, is thank you Aquamarine, that's very sweet of you."

"I'll just put it in t' pot." Aq pointed at the small tin of money on the kitchen counter.

"Thank you, dear."

"No problem. And also—" Aq hadn't really thought this through. If he was going to be bringing more money home, he'd have to find a better back story. "—My commander said that if I kept working as hard as I have been, I might be, erm... up for promotion?"

He didn't mean it to come out as a question.

"A promotion!" exclaimed Aq's father. "Well about time! You're gonna be a delegate soon, my boy. Why should it be only white people become diplomats and politicians? They're supposed to represent

Espera, but Espera isn't rich *or* white. Plenty of families like us, came here to escape war. I don't know wh—"

Aq's mother brought over a tray of cookies.

"That's great news, dear. Here, have another cookie and tell us all about it. Lunch is nearly ready."

Chapter twenty-three

Cyan was always impressed by the decadence of the conference hotel. Everything that could be was made of dark, polished wood, and thick carpets covered every floor. The reception that served both the hotel and the six-star restaurant—named 'T' Shadow-Tail's Table' no less—was decorated with polished bronze lamps, a bronze bell, even a bronze-embossed visitor's book. Somehow it all reminded Cyan of colonial hunting lodges back in Africa.

The receptionist, a polite south Asian person with their hair in a bun, directed Cyan to the elevator. They stepped inside—more thick carpet and polished rails—and pushed PH for 'Penthouse and Meeting Rooms'. Everything in the building was written in English and Esperan, the most prestigious of the national languages.

The elevator delivered them to the top floor and they made their way over to room three, which was the meeting room. They checked their phone

Good, right on time.

Holding the research files tightly to their chest, Cyan lingered near the glass wall of the meeting room until they were beckoned in by the committee director. They took a chair and waited for the rest of the committee members to arrive.

"Thank you all for coming!" The director's voice was loud and penetrating. Cyan guessed his suit must have cost more than their team's entire budget for the year. "I hope you won't suffer too much with the hotel's cuisine!"

There was polite laughter from the board. Cyan looked around the room. Everyone in the room was white, probably Esperan, and wearing a fancy suit.

These people probably always eat well. But T' Shadow-Tail's Table? Even I've heard of this place.

"As you know," continued the director, "Our group is committed to delivering t' finest cutting-edge research in service of our planet. Today we gonna hear presentations from members of three of our research groups doing valuable work in t' Western Forest, t' Union reefs and t' city's parks. Money, like so many things in life, is a sadly limited resource and, as you have read in our pre-meeting update last week, we only gonna have finances to renew two of these projects into next season. But I'm sure our researchers gonna be real happy to put on a show and convince us of their worth!"

It wasn't really a joke, but the board laughed anyway.

"First up is Cyan Tylor, who say her team in t' forest have something *very* interesting to show us all. Cyan Tylor, if you would?"

"Yes, thank you Director," Cyan paused. "But, it's *they*, not she."

"Oh yes, yes of course." The director coughed. "They, of course, they."

It wasn't the first time that Cyan had been misgendered by officials, but it was considered a serious social faux-pas since the Gender Acts. Espera prided itself not only as the 'Jewel of t' Union' but the 'Queerest of t' Nations.' Misgendering a non-binary person in the workplace was taken very seriously in law. In reality though, people were just as uneducated and made as many assumptions as anywhere else. Cyan had stated their pronouns the first time they and the director had met.

He really has no excuse. As if I wasn't nervous enough already.

"My name's Cyan Tylor," they said quietly. "I erm, well for t' last three months, my team and I—" they tried hard not to think about Teal, wherever she was "—have been researching the Western *cerezo* forest to establish its biodiversity and resource value, particularly with regards to Union proposals for reducing t' area protected by t' park's perimeter."

They paused and tried to steady their voice.

God, I hate public speaking. Jade should be doing this. He'd wow them with all his numbers.

"T' research that I gonna now present to you is living proof of t' value of this forest to t' Protected Area. As such I hope that you come to appreciate its great value to all life on this planet."

I'm saying 'value' too much. But that's what these people know, that's what they care about. Value, worth, profitability.

Their hands shaking, Cyan opened their files. They linked up a series of graphs and lists from their phone to the main screen and began the presentation.

It was soon clear that the board were not going to be easily impressed. Even after seeing all the species richness charts, the comparative diversity studies, everything they had on the *cerezo* forest, the eight people sat around the table looked bored to death.

Cyan knew there would be a lot of money being offered by Eco-Homes. They'd heard that the company might be bought out by Rak Industries sometime soon.

Adverts on every solar train platform. They're even sponsoring our lunch. They could buy t' whole park if they wanted. What chance do we have really?

The wooden clock on the wall said that Cyan had only five minutes left. Five minutes that would make or break their project. They swallowed hard and took the scan card from their pocket containing all the scans of the Red Shadow-Tail, collated and cleaned up by Jade in the early hours of this morning. They still couldn't guess what the impact might be if people knew that the Red Shadow-Tail was real and living just an hour from the city.

Fuck it. What's t' worse that gonna happen? Better a home full of tourists than no home at all.

"There is one thing more that I'd like to show you today."

They put the scan card into the room's beamer sphere and

switched it on. The lights automatically dimmed and the projection filled the space over the table. The board members gasped in surprise. Even the director looked impressed.

They love t' theatre of it all.

"Here, in t' *cerezo* forest—" Cyan was speaking as dramatically as they could "—threatened with losing his only home—"

They paused, looked around, making eye contact with the powerful board members.

"I present to you t' Red Shadow-Tail."

Chapter twenty-four

"Mom, I can't, really. I'm gonna die if I eat one more mouthful."

"Nonsense dear. You're too skinny. Have another pie."

Aq's father sniggered.

"What's that, Blue? Would you like another pie too? Oh good, look there's one more left."

It was Aq's turn to laugh. His sister had eaten so much, she looked like she might pass out. His brothers had run off before the second round of pies had appeared out of the oven.

Aq leaned back in his chair and rubbed his belly. He was blissfully happy.

No matter how poor we get, Mom always gonna find a way to make our stomachs hurt.

He looked over at his father and smiled. He was already asleep at the table with his head in his hands.

***

Brunch with the board was everything Cyan expected it to be: tiny piles of gourmet food on gigantic plates and terrible conversation. The restaurant was decorated pretentiously in black and white. Even the food was monochrome. Cyan had the impression they were in some old science fiction movie.

Next they're gonna have a big old robot come serve us our drinks.

But the scans of the Red Shadow-Tail seemed to have had the desired effect. During the meal, under the pretext of asking Cyan more about the project, the director swapped seats so he could sit next to them. While the other board members were busy eating, he leaned close enough that they could smell his heavy cologne and whispered:

"Your find was real interesting to me, Cyan, real interesting indeed. Between you and me, you got your grant."

Cyan was elated and could barely stop themself from squealing with excitement.

"Thank you, director! That's wonderful news!"

The director gave them a well-polished smile, turned abruptly and began a conversation with one of the other well-dressed researchers.

Wow. An extension gonna mean everything to t' project. And to t' forest!

Cyan poked thoughtfully at their expensively colourless food.

Now we just gotta find Teal and we gonna be back on track.

* * *

Aq waved goodbye to his family and began walking the kilometre and a half back through the neighbourhood to the nearest transport station. Oak Grove looked worse each time he visited and today there were more people begging in the streets and pushing shopping carts than he could ever remember seeing before. Sweating from the morning heat, he arrived at the station and showed his transport card to the guard.

Just as he was getting onto a train headed back to Union, Aq's phone buzzed in his pocket. He took it out and was surprised to see it was a message from Kingson. As far as Aq knew he was supposed to be back in London already. Intrigued, he opened the message.

14.03 Carl Kingson: Hi Boss. Good news! Been invited to give another policy presentation next weekend and t' Union has extended my visa an extra seven days. I wasn't ready for London weather anyway. I've rented a place in t'forest—more discrete than t' Guest Suites—so we can meet there. Just if You want to Boss. Do let me know. Your boy.

Aq looked out over the decaying, forgotten neighbourhood covered in carefully separated recycling blowing around in the wind.
No question.

14.06 Aq Hass: Good boy. Let's make a plan.

And before he could change his mind, Aq clicked send.

"I'm very happy to see you, Boss."
"As you should be, sub."
It had almost become their formal greeting, already a cliché, but Aq liked it, although the truth had become somewhat more complicated. When he had arrived at the last stop on the train line and the flashy Union vehicle had been there right on time to pick him up, Aq had realised, without a doubt, that he was also happy to see Kingson.
"I'm going to use you hard today, boy."
Since when is this vocabulary so natural to me?
"Thank you, Boss. I hope you like t' new place. You can use me here whenever you have time, Boss."
He pulled into the driveway of his 'new place'. Aq already knew it was the house of his dreams, although it was more luxurious than even his dreams could have conjured up. It was a massive property with bay windows in the British style overlooking the palm trees lining the driveway and beyond it lay the *cerezo* forest.

Beautiful, Aq realised despite himself. *Decadent and beautiful and perfect.*

"I like it, boy."

"Let me show you around, Boss."

The inside was even more grand, the living room all decked out in dark wood and chandeliers. The spiral staircase led to no less than four attic bedrooms with a stunning view over the trees. From here, Aq saw there was a massive pool in the back patio. When he thought of his family's tiny flat in the city he found himself disgusted by all this wealth and space. He was, he realised, also strangely aroused.

"Fuck!" he said, despite himself.

"I'm so glad you like it, Boss," said Carl, already pouring Aq a drink. "It's rented for t' next month for you. And Boss, one day, when you're ready..."

"Yes?"

"I'd like to buy it for you, Boss."

I'm dreaming.

***

Teal woke with a start.

Where am I?

Then she remembered: the village. She looked around her. The guest tent was cosy, her bed warm and soft. Despite being overstimulated and overfull from dinner she had fallen asleep immediately.

I was real tired, I guess.

She rolled over and looked at her phone. Still no signal.

Shit, how did I sleep fourteen hours?

Teal rubbed her eyes.

God...Cyan will be frantic worrying about me. I should find out how to get back from here. Wherever here is.

She stood, and her head almost touched the ceiling of the small tent. She stretched a little, bending down to touch her toes. But she felt dizzy. Nauseous even.

Strange, she thought.

Then everything went black and Teal was gone.

3. Deepening

Prelude

The family stood beside their hut in traditional hunting gear. They were wearing heavy headpieces covered in leaves and holding spears.

The tourists had only just arrived and the photo shoot had already begun. With their cameras clicking, they stood close to their bio-fuel jeep—for safety, just in case—while the family, wearing clothes that not even their grandparents had used for hunting, growled and shook their spears.

The mother looked past the tourists, to the savannah beyond their jeep and out to the distant fence. Ten metres high, barbed and electrified in places, she knew that the only way for her family to stay on this side of it, on this land where she and everyone she knew had been born, was to continue with this insulting theatre. To live in their bug-infested home and to hunt with spears. Was it still worth it? She couldn't make that decision for her people. Not yet.

A brave tourist came close to her, pointing, laughing and speaking with his friends in a language she couldn't understand. She tightened her hand around the spear and thought about the damage she could inflict. A simple jab to the throat and he would be dead. It would be quick.

If they want a vicious hunter, I'll give them one.

Chapter twenty-five

What t' fuck?

Teal was no longer in the guest tent in the village. She was... well, somewhere else. A city. Concrete, buildings and filthy air.

Pollution, she realised.

There were vehicles everywhere, and they were incredibly loud.

What t'—how did I—what t' fuck?

She stood in a square. The sky was bright, the air cool.

Springtime maybe?

But Teal had never experienced anything like this. Less than a minute before she had been somewhere else, just waking up.

I'm dreaming. This is a dream.

Teal had been lucid dreaming her whole life and she knew about dream signs—the things that happened only in dreams and not in waking life. For her it had always been her hands. When she was dreaming, she would have six fingers or seven. They would move and blur. When that happened, she knew she was dreaming and could initiate a lucid dream or wake herself up.

She looked down at her hands and counted her fingers. Five on each hand, clear, just where they should be.

I'm not dreaming then. This is real. But how? And where—

A loud bang rang out and the quiet square was suddenly flooded with people. Protesters. Banners. A samba band. People all around her were talking in excitedly and smiling. Their speech was strange and unfamiliar in a way she couldn't pinpoint for a moment, until she registered the 'th' pronunciation among the garbled sounds.

Twentieth-first century English, she realised, recognising the outdated way of speaking from movies and documentaries. *Am I? Did I somehow—?*

The crowd around her took up a chant.

"We won't be silent! We want our say! The femme riots start here, today!"

This is impossible.

Teal looked around her and took in the details. The long dresses and baggy jeans, the practical boots and glittering heels. The banners declaring "Masculinity *isn't* neutral" and "More Fats, More Femmes" and "Fems en colère" and "Femme is working class."

She saw lines of carefully prepared Molotov cocktails in gin bottles. Somewhere in the distance she thought she could hear what she guessed where old police sirens—so much more aggressive than the gentle song of Esperan police vehicles.

This is real. 2017. My god—

And then, just as suddenly, Teal was back in a small tent in a desert on the wrong side of the fence. She fell to her knees and threw up.

Chapter twenty-six

"Ms. Teal, are you okay?"

Teal was still kneeling trying to process what had just happened.

I'm in shock, she realised distantly. *And I puked.*

She looked down at the vomit already soaking into the hand-woven carpet. She looked up at the other person in the room, Azure's daughter Rouge, who she had met yesterday.

"I...oh my God, I'm so sorry. I don't know why I—"

"No problem, Ms. Teal. Maybe you're not accustomed to our food. I gonna bring something to clean it."

Rouge turned and shouted at the top of her voice: "Mother! Our visitor is moby! She faked a mess on t' shagpile!"

"Take her to t' communal tent!" Azure shouted back. "I make us some tea."

Teal looked at her hands. She was shaking and felt far away from her body.

Dissociation, she realised.

She stood up and allowed herself to be led to the communal tent where she had eaten last night. She felt very, very unsteady and thought she might be sick again.

What's happening to me?

"And then I was back here. Back in t' guest tent. And I...I threw up. I'm real sorry." Teal put her hands around the cup of tea for comfort.

Azure was silent for a while. She looked at Teal, her eyes intense, her face giving nothing away.

I should say something? She's pissed with me?

Then Azure did something unexpected; she reached out and took Teal's hand between hers. It was the first physical contact they had shared.

"I knew you were coming," she said, her voice controlled. "This has happened before. This is how it start for you."

Teal had no idea what her words meant or why they affected her so strongly but as Azure lifted her hand and touched Teal's cheek gently, she realised she was crying.

"I knew you were coming, dear. Ash told us."

"Ash?"

"This is a resistance village."

The way her morning was going, Teal was feeling pretty unshockable, but still she couldn't help but let out a gasp.

"Resistance. Wow..."

Teal stared at the table for a moment.

"But... didn't... haven't? Wait, what?"

"Didn't t' resistance join t' Esperan state and become part of t' new eco-paradise?"

"I..."

"That's what they've always told you, isn't it?

"Well..."

"We've been out here for a very long time." Azure's voice was calm. In fact, she seemed to get calmer the more confused and overwhelmed Teal felt. "We've been here since my grandmother and her friends fled t' State. Since before t' Esperan state expanded and took over t' City."

"Your grandmother?"

"Yes." Azure smiled. "You heard of her of course. Kit was her name."

Teal spilt tea all over her shirt.

Kit...Kit from t' uprising? Kit from t' Exodus? Could it be?

"Kit?"

Azure smiled. "Yes."

Teal was stunned into silence. After a moment she tried to speak.

"I'm sure you've heard of my grandfather too. Danny. He was with her in t' exodus."

Teal couldn't speak.

She stood up and ran to the door. But it was too late, she fell to her knees and threw up again.

"Kit and Danny were your grandparents," Teal said very slowly after she had cleaned herself up a second time and come back to the table. Azure had poured her another cup of tea.

"Yes."

"OK. Wow. But wait, wasn't Kit...? I mean, how did they?"

Azure seemed to read her thoughts. "She's famous for being lesbian, but she wasn't. Bisexual erasure is still around, it seems."

"—Oh...yes, of course, but actually I was going to say *trans*. I mean how could they—"

"That's a very personal question to ask about a person's grandparents," said Azure. She wasn't angry, but her voice was firm. "These are not abstract people to me, dear. Heroes to be worshipped in your museums and documentaries. My grandparents were there for me all through my childhood. I loved them intensely."

"God. I'm so sorry, I didn't mean..."

"—And before you ask, no, they never joined t' state, Esperan or otherwise. There's a lot of convenient mythmaking about my family."

"Sorry..."

"We've been out here for sixty years, you know? T' resistance live on."

"I had no idea."

Azure nodded slowly. "I know. But here we are."

Chapter twenty-seven

Aq sat back in a comfortable chair on the balcony of Kingson's villa and looked out over the forest. It was afternoon and the tourists were beginning to head off in their bio-buses, leaving only the sounds of blackbirds and wrens behind them. The afternoon was warm, with a light breeze cooling the humid air.

He checked the time on his phone, more a compulsion that anything—he'd checked it just five minutes ago and knew he had an hour and a half before he'd need to get the train over to Union for his evening shift. He didn't really want to go to work.

He took a sip of the rum he had been served. He could smell lunch already being cooked in the kitchen downstairs.

This is much more interesting.

"Your dinner, Boss. I hope that it's good enough. I tried to make it just how you ordered me to."

Carl laid the food on the balcony table for Aq. Fried fish with Tyalas salad, roasted peppers and a bottle of wine. Aq wouldn't say it of course, but it looked delicious.

"I'm gonna leave you to enjoy your meal, Boss. Unless there's anything else I can do for you?"

"My uniform gonna need pressing"

"Of course, Boss. I should have thought of it myself."

"Just do it, sub."

"Yes, Boss."

Carl Kingson scuttled off to press Aq's uniform. Aq poured himself a generous glass of wine and started eating.

This is how it should be, he caught himself thinking. *But is it? Isn't it a bit much? Yesterday he offered to buy me an* entire house. *Maybe this is going too fast.*

Aq took a mouthful of delicious pepper and sighed.

After he had finished his meal—which was even better than it looked—Aq found himself in two minds. He was full of food, a little tipsy from the wine. After the exhausting time with his family the day before, he was feeling a bit lazy. If he didn't go to work, he wouldn't get paid—for all its human rights declarations, the Protection Service didn't give sick pay. Aq made his decision.

After all, as Moss say: if your job treat you like shit, calling in sick is an act of resistance.

"Sub, get up here!" he shouted. Carl appeared in less than a minute. "Bring me five hundred shell—" Aq's daily salary was just two hundred and fifty "—and I wanna watch you put them in my wallet."

"Of course, Boss."

"And bring me my phone. I'm gonna call in sick."

Carl tried to conceal a smile and ran downstairs to fulfil his wishes.

* * *

"Time to return you to t' park," said Azure in her usual abrupt manner. "Your friends gonna be worried about you."

Teal still sat holding her empty cup. She was trying to process the things that she'd learned, but she felt shocked, and disconnected.

'T' resistance live on,' Azure had said.

How many more villages are there? Why we were never told about this?

"I have so many questions," she said distantly, following Azure outside.

"On t' way. It is a very long walk. Especially with my knees."

Teal noticed that Azure always walked with a stick. She looked tired.

"You don't have to come with," she said carefully. "With a map, I could probably find my way. If it's painful for you to walk, I mean. Or if you'd rather rest."

"I'm chronically ill, young Teal. Pain and insomnia are just a part of life at this point."

Teal didn't know how to respond. Sometimes she felt the privilege of her good health very strongly. She looked up to the eastern horizon and could just make out a dark line that marked the forest, the park. Everything between there and where she stood was pink, dusty desert.

I didn't even ask about t' dust yet. What happened out here?

Azure was speaking to her daughter.

Teal realised that she was slowly beginning to understand the bizarre slang they used. Polari seemed to have enough English mixed in to guess some meaning from context. Azure seemed to be saying that she'd be back in a few hours and to prepare some food for their walk. Rouge ran off and came back a few minutes later and put a backpack of food on the ground. Azure hugged her, she nodded politely to Teal and left.

"Teal," said Azure, looking east.

"Yes..."

"T' day is getting hot already. Let's go."

"Yes, thank you."

Azure walked away at a brisk pace out into the desert without turning back. Teal realised that she wasn't going to wait and, picking up the backpack, she ran after her.

Chapter twenty-eight

"It wasn't always like this," said Azure cryptically, as they crossed a dry arroyo with nothing but pink dust at the bottom.

"T' desert you mean?" Teal was out of breath. "What caused it?"

"Industry. Forestry. Civilisation. Progress. This is what that look like."

"I guess so," said Teal. In truth, she wasn't sure how she felt about those things. She had certainly seen civilisation destroy a lot of things in her work, not least in the Congo, but, like Cyan, she also had a general faith that things were getting better. That things were bad, sure, but they used to be even worse.

They walked over a hill. The scenery spread before them was just the same: more rocks, more pink dust, no forest at all.

"And t' dust?" she asked. She had noticed that the dust was a light pink colour, but the ground and the rocks seemed to be either beige or grey. *So probably not erosion.*

"It's sauvite dust. From t' mines."

"Sauvite?" said Teal, surprised. "'T' Miracle Mineral?'"

Across the Five Nations, sauvite had become known by this catchphrase. Although Espera prided itself on 'Traditional Technology' as a legacy of the resistance, sauvite was everywhere now. The unique properties of sauvite had been discovered at the end of the twenty-first century, just as plastic had become all but redundant.

It burned clean, producing only water and oxygen and had become widely used as a domestic fuel. It was selectively conductive and was used in almost all household gadgets, phones, computers and car parts. It was tough and lightweight, and the solar panel and wind turbine industry had exploded because of it. Teal had heard they'd even starting to powder it and use it to fertilise the biofuel plantations. It certainly seemed miraculous.

"Yes, that's what they call it. It's mined over in t' west. My daughter, Rouge, go there each morning, she work there, in t' mines."

I guess it gotta come from somewhere. I never thought about it.

"And, is it good work? Is she happy?"

"I think you can imagine," said Azure flatly, closing the conversation in her unique way.

It end so suddenly, Teal thought as they got closer to the park. *Forest, fence, then nothing, just dust. Thank god for that fence.*

"We lived there before, you know," Azure said suddenly, breaking twenty minutes of silence. "In what you call t' park."

"Real?" Teal had never heard of resistance living in the park before. But then, she'd been told the resistance had disappeared when the state had been reformed and there was nothing left to resist. She realised that a great many things that she'd heard about Espera might not be true after all.

"I'm not surprised that you didn't hear about it."

Teal waited for her to continue.

"We were there until 2080, in fact. I grew up in t' park. Near t' other side, far from here. My family lived there for many years near t' river after t' Exodus."

Teal looked at the desolate landscape around them.

"Why did you leave?"

"We didn't choose to."

"What do you mean?"

Teal caught a look in Azure's eye. Something between sadness and rage. "Well, they kept us for a while. For as long as we played t' role they wanted. You've been to t' Ash and Pinar museum, I assume?"

Teal nodded. The forest museum based around the cabin that Ash and Pinar built was one of her favourite places to visit as a child. She loved using the well and harvesting the rose petals. She loved learning about the old ways.

"So then you already know how Espera love to fetishize t' resistance at t' same time as co-opting it."

"I guess so," replied Teal thoughtfully. "I hadn't thought about it like that bef—"

"We watched them as they built t' fence around us. Of course, they used cheap immigrant labour. Every year a few more kilometres. Eventually we had to get a visa just to stay on our own land."

"I'm sorry. I see that fence every day. I mean, I know Big Conservation has a history of fences and exclusion, but I had no idea that happened here."

"It did."

They fell quiet as they picked their way across a particularly difficult arroyo. On the other side, Azure continued.

"They kept us for a few years after t' fence was finished. I worked as a forest guides for tourists, who, by the way, are t' stupidest people on t' planet."

Teal couldn't help but smile as she thought of the research tourists back at the camp.

"Tourists came every day to our village. Everyone wanted t' authentic resistance experience. Until we didn't want our photos taken anymore. Until we criticised Espera and t' mining industry. Then they removed us real fast."

"Enforced primitivism..." said Teal, thoughtfully.

"What's that?"

"That's what it's called in t' industry."

"What do it mean?"

"Well, it started in t' 1970s, I guess. For a while it was part of an official programme of some of t' largest conservation organisations to keep people out of highly protected National Parks."

"That sound familiar."

"Exactly. Or at least t' idea was to keep *indigenous* people out. Tourists and researchers and park managers had access. Indigenous people could only stay on what was often their own ancestral land, if they lived in a 'traditional manner'. Similar to what you were describing. They could hunt with spears, for example, but not guns. They could live in huts, but not houses."

"To fit t' stereotypes of their backwardness," said Azure with bitterness in her voice. "And be good for a photo shoot."

Teal nodded.

"Of course t' resistance isn't indigenous to this land in t' same way," Azure continued. "But we sure as hell protect it. Without us, t' forest wouldn't be here at all."

"Which is pretty much universal. All this idea of untouched, virgin wilderness is a myth. Nearly always, t' biodiversity that t' parks set out to protect is a direct result of t' people who have been living on it and protecting it for tens of thousands of years," said Teal.

"Yes. Big surprise, it wasn't t' rich white tourists, game hunters, researchers and park managers."

They fell silent again, Azure faultlessly navigating the way through the desert. Teal was suddenly very aware that she was probably on the wrong side of this from Azure's perspective. It wasn't the first time she'd thought about her role in conservation.

But all industries have their shadow side. And there are probably worse things I could do for a living.

But t' resistance villages. This land destroyed by mining. Talk about a cover up.

As they walked, Teal's head was occupied with processing all the things that she had heard and felt in the last twenty-four hours. Azure had taken the news of Teal's 'episode,' as she was thinking of it, very calmly. And she still hadn't explained what she meant when she had said 'This is how it start for you."

What do that even mean? How is this a start? Start of what? I never want to feel like that again.

Still, for a moment, hiking through the mesmerising landscape, Teal allowed herself to dive back into that sensation. The look of the sky and the sound of the voices. The police sirens and the music.

Whatever that was, it was kind of amazing. It was real like I was there. Like I travelled somehow. Could such a thing be possible? Could t' legends about Ash be true—?

"We're nearly there," announced Azure, interrupting Teal's thoughts. "That's t' gate about a kilometre ahead."

"Ah right, I see it!"

"I'm gonna leave you here. Once you get to t' gate, you'll get your phone service back and can call your friends. They block it beyond t' fence on purpose so we can't use it. Same as t' water and electricity."

"Espera know that you're out here?" asked Teal, surprised.

Azure tutted.

"Of course, dear. Here, take this." The older woman gave Teal a piece of paper. "This is a map back to t' village. You'll need it when you come visit."

"Thank you, I mean I would lov—"

"We see you there in two days."

Azure turned and walked away, leaving Teal standing holding the map, utterly confused.

Chapter twenty-nine

"Oh my god, I was so worried about you!"

Cyan ran from the car, kicking up a cloud of dust behind them. They grabbed Teal and hugged her so hard that Teal found it hard to breathe.

"Are you okay? Where were you? We were so worried!"

"I'm fine, I'm... *fine... need... oxygen!*"

Cyan released her but held her close as if scared she would disappear again.

"You went through t' fence didn't you? You're such a fucking idiot!"

"Good to see you too, darling," laughed Teal. "Let's get in t' car and—ooh is that Indi and Jade I see?"

Indi opened her door and came running to hug her too. Jade waved from the car.

"Okay, okay enough with t' hugging already, you trying to kill me?" Teal laughed. "I'm glad you all managed to miss me so much in less than twenty-four hours."

"We were so worried!" said Indi.

"Yes, Cyan mentioned that already. Let's get back to camp, shall we?" She looked down at her dust-covered clothes. "I really could use a shower." Indi looked at her impatiently. "Yes, yes," Teal laughed. "And then I tell you everything. I got a hell of a story for you."

As Cyan drove them on the main highway that connected to the park's Perimeter road, their phone started buzzing.

"See who that is, would you, hon?" they asked Teal pleasantly, already regretting calling her a 'fucking idiot'.

Teal took the phone out of Cyan's pocket and opened the message.

"It's from t' board director, he says that—oh my god! They renewed t' contract!" She flung her arms around Cyan's neck, even though they were driving and planted a big kiss on their cheek. "You're a frikking genius."

Teal turned around to look at Jade and Indi who were grinning in the back seat.

"What do you say? Let's stop off in t' city on t' way home? I think we got some celebrating to do!"

The bar they chose was quiet and an Esperan couple were playing an instrument that Teal had never seen before, some kind of cross between a piano and a violin that needed two people to play. Although they really couldn't afford it—not even with the new contract—they ordered good Esperan wine. Local and organic like pretty much everything in every bar in Espera.

The four of them took a table in a corner where they could talk without being disturbed. Teal didn't sit down. She stood awkwardly curling her hair.

"Cyan, did you bring t' thing I asked you for?"

Cyan looked blank for a moment and then remembered. They reached into their backpack and passed her a small make-up bag which Teal knew had her shaving gear in.

"Thanks, babe."

Teal went to the bathroom to shave.

Sometimes they get it right.

By the time she emerged, the others were already on their second glass of wine.

"So...?" asked Indi impatiently, her eyes bright with curiosity.

"So, yes..." began Teal. "I went through t' fence."

"And?"

"And as I'm sure you noticed I tripped an alarm somehow. There was a gap, just a small one that I guess t' guards never noticed. I squeezed through and—" she interrupted her flow of words with a sip of wine "—and I got away from them, t' guards, but I also lost t' Shadow-Tail. It was a red, I'm sure of it now. God, I was so scared though when t' alarm went off. I ran for hours—"

"Yes, t' scans certainly look optimistic," said Jade distantly. "With t' new budget extension we have a good chance of success."

"Erm, yes. Anyway, I was terrified. And cut myself on t' fence I guess. I lost t' Shadow-Tail along t' way and I got lost myself—"

"I showed t' scans to t' board," interrupted Cyan. "I wasn't sure if it was a good idea but that's what got us t' extension."

"Okay…" Teal wasn't sure she was being listened to.

There's more to life than t' project and budget extensions.

Indi spoke in her quiet voice.

"Are you okay, Teal? It sounds like a very scary experience."

"It was." Teal curled her hair with one finger. Cyan noticed that Indi was doing the same thing. They immediately put their arm around Teal's shoulder.

"Of course she's fine, aren't you Teal?"

Teal knew it was a sign of possession, but Cyan's arm felt good around her, so she didn't say anything.

"I am. Some weird things happened while I was on t' other side. I met some people—"

"What people?" asked Jade suddenly, even aggressively.

"I…" Teal wasn't sure she was ready to share her stories yet. Jade was a patriotic Esperan and she doubted that he'd take too kindly to learning that the resistance was alive and well—and profoundly anti-Esperan. She would make that decision later. "Just some people who live beyond t' fence. They let me stay t' night."

Cyan knew they weren't getting the whole story and pulled Teal a little closer.

"That's okay, when you want to tell us, you can tell us. Another glass of wine?"

Teal smiled and nodded. *Yes, sometimes they get it just right.*

Chapter thirty

Aq made the decision as he was walking through the bedroom on the way to take a shower. The bed looked like pure luxury compared to his bunk in the dorm room—it must have been big enough for at least three or four people. He touched one of the pillows.

Stuffed with feathers or something.

It was probably the softest thing he'd ever felt in his life. Kingson was in the bathroom tidying his toiletries—most of which he'd been bought in the last week—as Aq walked in.

"I'm taking a shower," he announced. "And I'm staying t' night."

Aq knew he wouldn't be missed at the dorm—he was supposed to be at the control tower anyway. He had taken another shift in the morning, promising that he'd be well enough by then, but that still gave him eleven hours.

He realised that it was a big decision for him to stay. Apart from a few flings here and there back when he was younger, he had almost never slept the night with someone who wasn't either in his family or in the dorm. It took trust, he realised, but Kingson had given him no reason not to trust him.

And besides, he got a lot more at stake than I do. What gonna happen?

Nothing Aq had was worth stealing, and the things of value he had—not least the two-hundred-shell perfume and the stacks of money lying around the house—Kingson had either bought him or given him.

He could be an axe-murderer, Aq supposed, but he knew he could take the delicate diplomat any day in a fight.

Kingson's face lit up.

"Real, Boss?"

He was clearly pleased, but Aq tried to ignore it. He was here for his *own* pleasure. That was the role and he liked it just fine.

"While I shower, prepare t' bed for me and bring me another glass of rum. You gonna rub my feet and when I fall asleep, you're gonna go downstairs and sleep on t' couch."

"Yes, Boss. That sound wonderful."

Apart from their initial handshake—*what, three days ago only?*—they had never actually made physical contact. Aq was being careful not to let this lead in a direction he didn't want it to. He was in control, so he was supposed to get whatever he wanted.

"Get to it then, sub."

* * *

Cyan was nearly asleep at the table.

Jade had checked out of the conversation and was reading a report on lichens.

Typical Jade, Teal thought as she finished her drink. *He like books and budget sheets so much more than stories or people.*

Cyan was trying to get information about Teal's adventure.

"So who were these people you met? Did they feed you? Were they Esperans?"

Teal slurred a little. "It's kind of a long story."

Jade looked up from his papers.

"Of course they were Esperans, all that land is part of Espera."

"Well..." Teal began. "That's not t' whole story."

"Wait, is wasn't one of t' villages?" Jade carefully put his report away in a folder.

"You know about those?"

"Everyone know. There was a report on Esperan TV about it recently. Squatters who didn't want to work anymore so went off to live off-grid. They made a real mess of t' land, apparently—it's like a desert out there now. Espera try to take care of them, but they're anarchists from what I heard and refuse our help."

Teal felt her cheeks flushing.

"That is *not* what's happening out there at all!"

Jade rolled his eyes.

"Yes, please tell me about my own country. I'm sure you know more."

"Have you ever *been* out there?!"

"Have I broken Esperan law and gone through t' fence you mean? No, not so much."

"Jade, you're being an ass," said Cyan, who was awake again. They spoke much more loudly than they meant to, and the table fell silent for a moment. Cyan and Teal glared across the table at Jade, who glared back with his arms crossed. Indi finished the last of her orange juice and stood.

"Okay, I think we've all drunk enough for this evening," she said softly. "Shall I take us home? It's good to have you back, Teal, we missed you."

***

Carl was working on his tired feet, and Aq couldn't remember when he had felt such luxury.

He's good. Maybe he studied somewhere.

Aq had nothing to compare it to. People like him didn't get foot rubs.

That isn't how t' world work. Until now.

Suddenly here was this person, rich and practically a celebrity in a country that worshipped Big Conservation, rubbing oil into Aq's feet and smiling like it was the greatest day of his life.

Aq finished his rum and lay his head down on the pillow. His eyes were already heavy and just as he was dropping off to sleep, a thought popped into his mind.

How quickly we adapt.

Maybe he even mumbled it out loud. And then he was asleep.

Chapter thirty-one

"Right, let's get going!"

Everyone was surprised to hear Teal's voice so early in the morning. Cyan, who had only just out of bed themself, emerged from their tent and was amazed to see Teal already dressed, shaved and brushed, with a camera and a scope slung around her neck.

"Breakfast is on t' table," Teal announced. "I'll meet you all at t' platform!"

Cyan was too confused and, they were beginning to realise, too hungover to say anything. They managed a nod and a half-hearted smile and Teal was already off down the path into the forest.

What t' hell happened to her out there? they wondered and reached for the coffee.

***

"Boss... Boss?"

Aq rolled over and grunted. His head hurt.

"Boss? I'm sorry to wake you, but your shift start in an hour."

Aq grunted again. The bed was too soft and Aq didn't want to leave it. He hated mornings. He needed caffeine.

"Would you like me to call in sick for you, Boss?"

Aq sat up and rubbed his eyes, trying to rouse himself. He could just imagine Carl Kingson, famous London businessman, calling in sick for him to his squad leader. He'd never explain that one.

"No. Bring me breakfast."

"It's all laid out for you on the balcony, Boss. Your uniform is cleaned and pressed, and your new boots arrived this morning. I polished them for you, Boss. The train leave for Dignity at ten thirty-four, unless you would like me to drive you."

T' new boots are already enough, I'm gonna look pretty suspicious if I arrive for work in a Union vehicle.

Aq's head was pounding from the rum—he was processing information slowly.

"No I'll take t' train. Run me a bath."

"Already running it for you, Boss."

"Then go—" Aq had no idea what else to do with him. It was too early to be in role, too early to make someone else's decisions for him. "Go clean something."

Kingson looked a little crestfallen, but obediently went off to find something to clean. Aq looked around him at the giant bed, the light coming in through the French windows.

Still better than waking up in t' dorm, he thought and got up for breakfast.

* * *

"Beautiful, no?"

"It always is."

Teal and Cyan were up on the platform. They were setting up motion sensors around the forest linked up to a computer back at camp in case the Red Shadow-Tail came back when they weren't here to scan it.

The first light was breaking through the thick forest canopy and the air was abuzz with life.

"I don't think I really appreciated it before, you know?" said Teal, watching a blackbird flit between branches. "How lucky we are to be here, to be in a position to maybe do something useful for this place."

"Well, I hope we can," replied Cyan, fixing one of the motion sensors to a branch and running the wire down. "And if t' Red Shadow-Tail *is* real-"

"Oh, it's real. You saw t' scans."

"I did. But you know, there are a lot of weird things in this forest—"

Teal made her decision

"It *was* a Red Shadow-Tail. T' *resistance* certainly had no doubt about it."

"T' resistance...? Wait, what?"

"I want to tell you more about what happened to me out there." She looked over to the fence. "But I need you to listen."

"Of course."

"I'm serious. You might not like everything I have to say."

Cyan gave her a confused look.

"Okay, Teal. I'm sure I'm ready for it, whatever it is."

"T' villages that Jade was talking about, they're resistance. And they've been out there for a very long time."

Cyan opened their mouth to say something but stopped themself.

"They lived in t' park before. And I had t' impression that they come back sometimes too."

"Real?!" Cyan blurted out.

Teal nodded.

"*Into* t' Protected Area? But no-one's allowed into t' park, they'd be shot on sight."

"No-one except us. And t' eco-home developers. And t' tourists and t'—"

"Yes, okay. But, wow, I mean, how do we not know about this?"

"Some things are kept secret for a reason."

While Cyan thought about what to say next, a guard came down from the tower, pissed against a tree in full view, and went back up.

"Cyan?"

"Mm?"

"Are we doing t' right thing? Here, I mean. Is this how t' forest get protected? With fences and soldiers and guns and laws?"

"I think so. I mean, you heard what Jade said. It's all desert out there."

"It is. But I don't know if that's related to t' park. Azure told me that—"

"Who?"

Teal laughed. "Relax, not everyone in t' world is your competition you know."

Cyan smiled despite themself.

"Anyway, Azure said it was sauvite mines that caused t' devastation out there. Not t' villages."

"Okay."

"And I don't know. Doesn't it sound a bit familiar?"

"What do you mean?"

"Like last century when basically four big conservations organisations owned twelve per-cent of t' world's land—"

"—to protect it."

"Sure. But they also evicted indigenous people from half of it in t' name of conservation. T' very people who had created biodiversity for tens of thousands of years were driven away and into poverty and became poachers to survive—"

"I know, I know," said Cyan as patiently as they could. "I was in t' Congo too, you know? I'm not saying it's okay, but we didn't make t' rules."

"We're not nearly rich enough to make rules," Teal joked to break the tension. Cyan smiled.

"Tell me about it! One day when you be queen of t' world you can sort all this stuff out, okay?"

Teal stretched.

"I wouldn't mind trying it out for a day. Or I could join t' resistance."

"I..." Cyan gave her a look. "I'm going to pretend I didn't hear that. We are all set up? Shall we get back to camp?"

"I'm gonna stay a while if you don't mind. I have some thinking to do."

"Okay hon," said Cyan softly, moving to the edge of the platform and taking the rope. "See you back at camp?"

"Yes."

"Don't cross t' fence this time."

Teal smiled. "I won't cross t' fence this time."

After Cyan was gone, Teal sat for a while, replaying their conversation in her head.

I hope I did t' right thing telling them. They're so hot and cold. After all these years I still never really know how they're gonna respond.

Watching the cherry leaves moving in the breeze around her and hearing the echoing calls of green woodpeckers, Teal began to feel calm. Even the gentle buzz of insects was making her feel relaxed.

I love this place, she realised. *I'm so lucky to be here.*

Deepening

Chapter thirty-two

Aq had been gone for an hour and Carl was already lonely. He imagined that Aq must be at that very moment meeting his 'assignation' for the day and working hard accompanying them around the Union building, meeting their needs. Maybe taking them through that terrible Introduction Hall.

Carl didn't have anything official to do until the evening when he'd be discussing a new policy proposal for the security of the Conservation Perimeter.

He had already put Aq's laundry in the machine, washed the dishes from this morning, and cleaned the bathroom, kitchen and bedroom. He thought of taking a swim in the pool, but his heart wasn't in it. What he really wanted to do was have Aq there all day to make his decisions for him. He wanted to submit to his Boss and let him control his every move so he wouldn't have to. He stood now in the massive living room under a glittering chandelier, lost.

Usually when he was feeling like this, he bought something. Somehow spending money gave him the feeling that he'd achieved something with his day. But what could he buy? Certainly he didn't need anything. He had a whole other house waiting for him back in London. Maybe Aq need something nice to make his day at work easier. Carl knew he couldn't send flowers or anything so obvious, he didn't want to cause him trouble with his work-mates.

What then? I want to make my Boss happy, I want to serve him, but I don't know what to buy.

Carl sighed and collapsed into the sofa.

***

Aq was suffering. His assignation for the day was some corporate type working with Rak Industries—a muscled guy in an expensive suit—who needed accompanying the entire day. Apparently, he couldn't even find the bathroom by himself.

"Ready!" announced the assignation as he emerged from the bathroom shaking his perfectly manicured hands. Drops of water landed on Aq's new boots. "These eco-blowers never really work, have you noticed that?"

Aq gave a non-committal nod and led the way to the Business Chambers.

"This meeting gonna be a big deal," continued the businessman, talking more to himself than anyone else. "We're on quite a roll with mergers and acquisitions this month…"

Aq nodded again.

"I mean, Espera might be full of gays and refugees, but they certainly know business and there's enough sauvite out there to keep t' Five Nations in phones and solar panels."

Aq didn't nod this time.

He even hear himself speaking? Gays and refugees? This is Espera—He could get his visa revoke for talking like that.

They arrived at the chamber and, without a word, the assignation handed Aq his jacket and closed the door in his face.

An hour later he was still standing in the corridor, waiting for the businessman to emerge and, almost certainly, start gloating about how well it had all gone. As far as Aq could tell, these meetings always seemed to go well.

Aq stared at a broken light fixture in the corridor.

Why is it, that t' people with t' most power, t' most money, t' most respect and influence are t' ones who decide who live and die? Who can immigrate or not? Who can stay on their land or have it blown apart for mining? And why they always such damn assholes? What about money make them that way?

Carl is one of those assholes, he reminded himself.

Although he was practically worshipped for his work 'protecting the environment', he made a tonne of money for himself doing it. A lot of money that Aq was now helping himself to. He looked down at his new boots.

Is this actually any better?

Aq's assignation emerged, smiling, from the chamber.

"Take me to t' restaurant!" he all but shouted. "T' acquisition was a great success and it's time to celebrate!"

Absently, Aq wondered if he'd get bought some champagne to celebrate too.

But no, he reminded himself, *that's t' other evil corporate guy in my life.*

He lowered his head and led the way to the elevator.

Later, as Aq made his way down the many flights of stairs to the staff dining hall he got a message on his phone. As he expected—and yes, hoped—it was Carl.

> 13.00 Carl Kingson: I think You may be on Your break, Boss. If You can, please come to car park 4b. I have something for You.

After such a boring morning, Aq was pleased to feel that now-familiar tightness in his chest again; the anticipation and risk and excitement of the unknown. He ran back up the stairs and headed over to the car park. In 4b, Carl was standing next to a well-polished black car.

"Thank you for coming, Boss," he said meekly.

In the driver's seat, with the door open, sat a guy in a nice suit who Aq thought he vaguely recognised.

"What's this about... erm... *Mr. Kingson*? I need to be back with my assignation in an hour."

Aq stopped himself from saying 'sub' or even 'Carl'. He realised that this was the first time this roleplay had had an audience. Carl, he noticed, was still in role.

"Yes Boss, I'd like you to meet Beige."

The person stood up and shook Aq's hand. "Nice to meet you, sir."

An Oak Grove accent, Aq noticed and squirmed a little. He already felt awkward when someone called him 'sir'. He considered himself too young and far too poor.

At least until very recently.

"Beige and t' car are yours, Boss for as long as you need them," Carl was saying. "He came well-recommended and will take you anywhere You need to go."

"You bought me a chauffeur and a car?"

"Yes, Boss. But of course, he can pick you up and drop you off a short walk from work if it's a problem."

Aq thought it probably *would* be a problem having someone—someone who looked and sounded a lot like himself—driving him around. But he also realised, not for the first time in the last few days, that he was excited at the thought.

Is this okay? This is more than I signed up for. Calling me 'Boss' in front of a person I don't know. Is this still just a game?

Aq looked at the car. He knew very little about cars, but it certainly seemed new. It was black, extremely well-polished and was designed to look like it was made in the twentieth century.

One of t' latest bio-gas sauvite models, Aq guessed. *Just getting t' permit to drive a car in Espera must have cost a fortune.*

This is all so weird... I do hate t' solar trains though.

"Beige," he said softly, his voice almost breaking. "It's lunchtime. Could you take us downtown? To... T' Shadow-Tail's Table, for example?"

"Of course, sir."

Aq smiled and pushed his shoulders back.

Okay, let's do this.

"And make it fast, please. I don't have much time."

"Very good, sir," said Beige politely and opened the passenger door for him. "Anywhere you like."

"Get in Carl," Aq commanded. "You're coming with."

Chapter thirty-three

The argument began over lunch at the camp picnic table. Cyan had let slip that the place Teal had stayed was a resistance village and Jade, the only Esperan on their team, was not impressed.

"*T' villages* caused t' desert, not t' mines," he declared. "It was right there in t' documentary. Using too much water, growing t' wrong crops for t' soil..."

"Sorry Jade. I don't know about your *Esperan* documentary on *Esperan* TV, but I was right there, and maybe there's more to it than we know." Teal waved her fork in the air, her eyes wide. "What if t' resistance really *didn't* join t' Esperan state? What if t' stories that they told me are true?"

"They're not," said Jade flatly.

"It wouldn't be t' first time, you know. T' conservation industry got a long histo—"

"We talked about this already. It's not an industry. We are using science to save t' planet." Jade had his arms crossed again. "Something your so-called 'resistance' could learn a thing or two about."

Can he really be this naïve? Teal asked herself.

"I don't know, Teal," said Cyan diplomatically. "I mean what do we know about t' villages really?"

"But—"

"Without this park there would be nothing here..."

Where all this coming from?

"T' resistance fought t' State. They never fought Espera." Jade's voice was getting louder and higher. He was usually so detached, Teal had never seen him this angry. "Espera *liberated* t' State and there was no need for t' resistance anymore. We *are* t' resistance. We done so much for this land. T' reefs, t' forest..."

We. He's identifying with his state.

"Without everything Espera did for this place, people like *you* couldn't even live here!"

There was a moment of silence while Jade's words sunk in.

"People like *us*?"

Cyan put their hand on Teal's lap, but she pushed it away.

"What t' *fuck*?" Teal's voice was also getting louder.

"You know what I mean."

"Why don't you enlighten me, oh wise Esperan?" Teal was glaring at Jade. He glared right back.

"Trans women, for example," he said and turned to Cyan. "Non-binary people." He pointed at Indi, who flinched under his glare. "Bisexuals. Before Esperans came and freed this land, *protected* this land, you'd have all been killed. Now you get to run a research team in *our* forest, you get to—"

Cyan spoke at last, their voice as controlled as they could manage.

"Jade, you're stepping over a line. It's very important to t' continuation of our friendship and your place on this team that you shut t' fuck up right now and leave t' table."

"But I—"

"Right now, Jade. Get out of here."

"Yeah that make sense!" He slammed his fist down on the table. "Kick t' Esperan out. Send me away so you can have your little queer paradise!"

He stood up and pushed his chair out. It fell with a bang and he stormed out of the camp, mumbling in Esperan as he went.

"That was not okay." Cyan was shaking.

"Seriously." Teal tried to catch her breath. She looked over at Indi who was fiddling with a spoon. "You're very quiet. You don't agree with him, do you?"

Indi looked up.

"T' villages are resistance," she said confidently. "And Jade's an asshole."

Teal smiled.

"But you get that he's scared, right?

Teal stopped smiling.

"He's terrified of what you saw outside t' fence. His whole identity is based on his work—being a good little scientist and a good little Esperan. And right now, his work is t' park. You threaten one, you threaten t' other."

"That doesn't make it okay."

"No, I agree. And he should be strong enough to face reality. But he's not, clearly."

"He grew up in privilege," growled Cyan. "He went to t' best schools in Espera. What do he have to be so fragile about?"

"That's *why* he's so fragile. He hasn't lived yet."

"He's thirty-five!"

"I know, but he's kind of like a seedling grown in a greenhouse," Indi explained. "He's never been touched by wind so he isn't properly-formed. He's floppy like an over-grown seedling. He get his sense of self from work, science, Espera, anything to give him stability."

Teal laughed.

"A botanist and a psychologist!"

Indi smiled, glad that the tension was dissipating.

"Of course. But I'm pretty sure Jade isn't t' first fragile guy you've met." Indi stood up carefully. "Anyway, who want dessert?"

She crossed the camp to the kitchen tent and Teal watched her as if she was seeing her for the first time.

For someone so young, she certainly know something about people.

* * *

Aq was in heaven. Lunch was good. Amazing actually. Carl ate a little as well, to look less suspicious and because Aq told him to. The food was like nothing Aq had ever eaten in his life. Like nothing he had ever expected to eat in his life. Taking his lunchbreak at T' Shadow-Tail's Table eating monochromic delicacies, while his chauffeur waited outside, was outside of anything he could have imagined for his life.

But he wasn't completely comfortable. Looking around at the other diners, Aq began to feel like an imposter. Kingson had packed a spare shirt in the car so Aq wasn't wearing his uniform, but still he felt like they were watching him.

Like they can smell working class on me. Like any second now, they gonna tell me to leave and go back to t' staff burger joint.

Carl, presumably reading Aq's expression, leant towards him and offered him the dessert menu.

"Enjoy Yourself Boss. Everything You want."

Aq hesitated for a moment.

What t' hell. This might never happen again.

He took the menu.

An hour later Aq was back at work, accompanying a new assignation. Aq didn't pay attention to his name and knew in a week they would have both forgotten that the other even existed. He often gave his assignations nicknames to tell them apart. This one was Obnoxious Mining Guy. Aq was showing him around the Union complex and making sure all of his many needs were met. He already hated him.

What a dick. An hour ago I was treated like a king. Now I'm treated like nothing much at all.

Aq sighed as they turned the corridor.

I don't wanna do this anymore. And in all honesty, if Carl keep this going, keep serving me with money—without freaking out or becoming obsessive or running away—then pretty soon I'm not gonna need to. Like, ever.

His entire life, Aq had seen money as a question of survival, always having just enough to get by. Quitting his job would be a massive decision but he had a sense of new possibilities opening up before him.

I got a place to live—for now—and I kind of have a car, and access to more money than I can possibly use. What t' hell do rich people do with all their money anyway?

He knew who to ask.

They arrived at the main entrance to take Obnoxious Mining Guy back to his room and Aq paused to see if Moss was working on reception.

"Just one moment, sir," he said, "I want to check that your room has been cleaned for you."

"Well, I would assume that it has!" said Mining Guy in English. They could speak in Esperan but it seemed like he wanted to impress Aq with his knowledge of that exotic language. The fact that Aq also spoke perfect English was irrelevant. "But go ahead. I wait for you."

Of course you're gonna wait. You could never find your room in a month of Sundays.

Moss saw Aq coming over to the desk. He was talking on the phone but hung up as soon as his friend arrived.

"Hey, Aq!" Moss said loudly. "How's it going? You stinking rich yet?"

"Err—something like that. I'm at work."

Aq gestured towards the business man who already looked impatient standing next to the wall checking his phone.

"I see."

"You want to get something to drink. Maybe down on t' beach?"

"Hell, if you're paying, then sure. I finish in thirty minutes anyway."

"Perfect," said Aq. "Meet me at car park 4b in an hour?"

"T' car park?"

"Err. Yeah. I kind of have a car now."

"Real, man? Who *is* this guy?" Moss laughed. "I gonna be there. Run now, though. Your assignation don't look too happy."

Aq walked quickly back across the room.

"Well, that took long enough," said Mining Guy without looking up from his phone.

Aq smiled humbly.

"Sorry, boss—I mean sir—I mean...please follow me."

Chapter thirty-four

Jade was furious. After hitching a ride to Coral Beach with one of the Service jeeps heading back from the Control Tower, he decided to sit for a while on the beach to get his thoughts straight.

The weather by the coast was—as always—perfect. It seemed that no matter what rainstorms or humidity or chilling night winds might be passing over the forest, Union was always sunny, warm but with a cooling breeze, the perfect temperature all year round. Jade watched as a happy white family played in the water together, the kids screaming and splashing each other while their parents watched lovingly.

Jade didn't have kids. He'd thought about it, but he had yet to meet the right person to settle down with. For a while he had imagined he might have a chance with Cyan, before they had announced over breakfast that they were bringing their girlfriend to the project. He hadn't known how to respond to that.

They're both kind of hot. But three foreigners on a research project about Esperan ecology?

It was increasingly clear to Jade that the board was employing outsiders for prestige—they loved to brag about how many they had working for them.

Certainly isn't for their local knowledge. What Teal know about Espera anyway? Resistance villages, my ass.

Still, she *had* seen the Red Shadow-Tail, if that's what it was. And without Cyan, Jade doubted they'd have got their new funding at all. With the extension, they had three more months to produce conclusive evidence of Red Shadow-Tails living in the forest. The scans were good, but without recorded footage of their behaviour and—even better—a live animal, no-one was going to buy that they'd found a legendary beast just wandering around their camp.

Scans can be faked after all.

Jade sat back and dug his feet into the soft sand.

This project could be a real success. Could make me famous. A new Carl Kingson. I deserve that after putting up with these people for so long.

Aq's car pulled up at the beach's private car park. Beige opened the door for him and then opened the other door for Moss to get out as well.

"I message you," said Aq to Beige. "And here—" he held out a fifty "—get something to eat."

Beige nodded and thanked him. Aq and Moss crossed the car park towards the beach.

"What a trip!" said Moss when the driver was out of earshot.

"Yeah...I didn't ask for t' chauffeur obviously, just happened that way."

"No man, it's great. And he's just yours to order around and take you places?"

"Carl pay for his services for me."

"Awesome," said Moss with a smile. "Nice one."

Jade sipped from the can of organic beer he'd brought with him. It was warm and was doing nothing for his bad mood.

Barely twenty metres from him, two guys sat down. He could hear them laughing and joking. One of them was clearly loaded—Jade could see his designer shades and boots—and the other was apparently making his way through all the cocktails on the bar menu.

Those things cost a fortune. They must be real fucking rich.

A pigeon wondered too close and Jade absently threw a pebble at it. It flew away and re-joined its friends near the boardwalk.

How did I get to this point in my life still living off scraps of funding and working for outsiders? Why it not me *lazing around getting drunk with my friends and buying shit I don't need off t' internet?*

He heard the person with the nice shades talking on his phone. Apparently, he was ordering his driver to come pick them up from the beach.

This guy got a fucking chauffeur as well!

Jade hated them, and he hated himself. He opened another can of warm beer and drank half of it down without stopping.

Aq and Moss were spread out on a giant blue beach towel that Moss had produced from his backpack. A waitress came over and Aq ordered their drinks. Moss noticed that they were most expensive cocktails on the menu.

"I feel a bit weird about it all." Aq picked up some sand and let it run through his fingers. "I mean, Beige, he's obviously poor like us. I'm happy to order a rich Londoner about but one of us? That don't seem okay."

"It's cool. He's employed. He do a nice job with good tips. I bet your guy pay him a tonne and you can always have him pay him more after all."

"Yeah..."

"Everyone need a job. Just, you know, don't get too pushy is all. With this business guy on t' other hand, you can be as pushy as you like, no?"

"He seems to enjoy that."

"You fucking him yet?"

"No."

"Beating him?"

"No," Aq said thoughtfully. "He gave me a foot rub. And did my laundry. And made me breakfast..."

Moss laughed. "And paid you handsomely for t' pleasure!"

"Very. As much as I want. But that's t' other thing. What more do I want? I've already put some aside for me and my folks. He connected my phone to t' Union's internet service so I can shop any time I want. With t' money I got already I can pay rent on t' dorm for months and... and did I mention he's renting me a house over there—?" Aq gestured with his head east, towards the forest. "And talked about actually *buying* it for me?"

Moss made an impressed hissing sound through his front teeth.

"It's so quick, Moss."

"It *is* quick."

"What else could I want? What do rich people *do* with all their money anyway?"

"Milk it for all you can." Moss' voice became more serious. "Get t' house under your name in case he run. I know you don't have a lot of stuff but upgrade everything you own to t' best on t' market. And then get another one. That's what rich people do. We only need one bed, one bottle of perfume, one pair of running shoes so get t' best there is, and a spare. And get nice stuff that you don't need so you can sell it when this all come to an end."

"It's gonna come to an end, isn't it?" said Aq, a little sadly.

"Everything do, mate. So take what you can and run with it."

"Yeah. Do you need anything by t' way?" asked Aq, offering Moss his phone. It was already connected to the online store.

Moss' face lit up. "Well, *now* you're talking!"

Jade finished his beers and got up to leave the beach. He knew he should probably get supplies for the camp while he was in town, but he was still angry.

Why I'm always t' supply guy? Why they don't get their own tampons and razors for a change?

He left the beach and headed over to the perimeter road where he planned on hitching a ride back to camp. The Union budget had never stretched to giving them a camp vehicle, so they always had to hitch everywhere with the Service guys and take the solar trains across town. Unless of course Cyan applied for special permission to rent a car for the day.

It's annoying. I don't even care that I gotta travel with every random cleaner and nurse. Just want a bit of freedom, that's all.

He reached the road and stuck out his arm at the first vehicle he saw. It was a polished black car, and he saw through the open back window that it was the guys from the beach. Jade was furious.

This their frikking car? How these immigrants ever get so rich anyway?

He coughed on the dust the car left in its wake.

"Fuck this," Jade muttered to himself. "Fuck all of this."

Chapter thirty-five

After cleaning up the lunch table, Indi left the camp to go to a meeting. Cyan and Teal stayed behind to drink coffee.

"Should we be working?" asked Teal after a while, sitting down next to Cyan and pouring them both a second cup. "I feel like we should get something done today."

"Why should we? Indi's at yet another of her mysterious meetings—"

"She sure does have a lot of meetings."

Cyan nodded. "And Jade is off—wherever he is. Why should we do all t' work?"

Teal shrugged and finished her drink. The coffee was strong, and two cups was one too many. Her heart was beating fast and she felt herself getting agitated again.

"I still can't believe he said that! 'People like *us*.' What total bull."

Cyan took Teal's hands between their own.

"I know you're angry, hon. I don't completely disagree with him about t' fence, but he should never have said those things."

Teal gave them a strange look.

Since when are you diplomatic?

Cyan caught the look.

"We need him, Teal. I can't kick him of t' team if that's what you're thinking."

"Why? We only have him here to fix t' fucking scanners and analyse Shadow-Tail shit! He's so annoying! Always t' fucking expert on everything even when he got no idea what he's talking about."

"Breathe."

"Don't tell me to—" Teal stopped mid-flow to catch her breath. She noticed that Cyan had their hand on her thigh. "I—"

"Breathe."

She noticed then how close Cyan was. How familiar she found t' warmth and smell of their body. She caught her breath and found herself lost in Cyan's eyes, the green flecked with brown, sparkling in the sunlight.

"You're hot when you're angry."

Teal smiled and looked away. But Cyan's eyes drew hers back. Her chest was tight.

"Thank you."

Cyan tightened their grip on Teal's thigh.

"Do you want to kiss me?"

"I thought you'd never ask."

***

When Beige dropped Aq back at the villa, Carl was waiting for him outside the front door.

"Cheers, mate," said Aq to the driver. "See you tomorrow."

"Yes, sir."

The car sped away.

Carl stepped forward and handed Aq a chilled glass of rum.

"Welcome home, Boss. I missed you today."

"I bet you did, sub." Aq took the rum and drank it straight down. After the cocktails, he was already tipsy.

"Yes, Boss. How can I please you this afternoon, Boss?"

"About time you started using your imagination."

"Well, Boss. I have some ideas. Would you like to hear them?"

"Another rum," commanded Aq, stepping into the house. "Then you can tell me all about it."

***

"I want to please you," whispered Teal. "I want to make you happy."

Cyan rolled onto their back. Teal followed until she was perched just above their face again, her arms shaking a little as she supported her weight.

"I want to—"

"Lie down on me."

Teal allowed herself to drop.

"Kiss me."

She obeyed. As they kissed, Cyan grabbed a handful of Teal's long hair and tugged a little.

"Can I?" they asked.

"Please do."

They pulled harder. Teal moaned and released more of her weight onto her lover. The bed creaked beneath them. Teal was breathless. She couldn't remember when she'd felt this turned on. Arousal wasn't the same since the hormones. It was so much wider, more dispersed. A whole-body experience.

"Grind against me."

Teal did and was surprised to feel that she was hard against Cyan's jeans.

"I need you," she said and immediately wished she hadn't. Sex with Cyan always brought out her worst insecurities.

God, I sound pathetic. That's not what they want, they want someone independent, strong—

"I need you too." Cyan gave her a coy smile. "Inside me."

"Fuck…"

"Precisely."

"Now?"

"Now and tomorrow and every day."

Teal was already reaching for the box of condoms.

***

Carl was kneeling at the foot of the bed, waiting patiently.

Aq was drunk. He had finished off another two rums and had in his hand a massive, hand-rolled, organic cigar. He was trying to light it with a match, but his hands were clumsy from alcohol.

"Light this for me."

"Of course, Boss."

Carl had it lit in seconds and handed it back.

"Thanks. I mean…good boy."

A polite smile.

Shit, what's that? That never happened before.

Aq had never thanked Carl for anything and he liked it that way. He said that word every day to too many people.

"Anything to make You happy, Boss."

Aq lay back on the pillows that Carl had fluffed up for him and took a long drag.

"Rub my feet, boy—you know how I like it."

"Yes Boss."

Grabbing some organic beech oil from the cabinet, Carl got to work.

I need to fix that, thought Aq. *I don't want to hear 'yes, Boss' and 'right away, Boss' after every order. I just want him to obey.*

Aq thought about making that a new rule, but Carl was already working on his feet. It felt amazing and he took another drag on the cigar instead.

Sometimes that happen, he noticed.

Sometimes he wanted something but he didn't ask for it. Or order it. The pillows could be fluffed up again for example and his glass was nearly empty, but Aq didn't say anything. It was a block. Maybe it was too much of an adjustment to *really* get everything he wanted. Maybe he hadn't quite turned off that part of him that thought about Carl's desires and needs—that's what he was trained for after all—or maybe it was just too exposing.

And maybe before I demand it, I need to know what I really want.

* * *

Cyan was close to peaking. As ordered, Teal held them down, her hands on their wrists. She was inside. She could feel her whole body, every part of her nervous system, buzzing. Cyan was practically screaming, but Teal held her voice in. She loved this. She loved Cyan. She was afraid that if she allowed herself to speak, that's what she would say. That she would tell them how much she adored them and needed them and wanted them.

And that's not what they want. This is just sex. Beautiful, mind-blowing sex. Cyan could never love me how I want to be loved. But sex, well, that's something that work.

Teal bit her lip and pushed harder.

* * *

"Sub…"

"Yes, Boss."

"Come here."

Aq indicated the empty part of the bed next to him. Carl's face registered the slightest look of confusion.

"Yes, Boss."

Carl shuffled halfway up the bed. He was still kneeling. They had rarely been so physically close to each other.

Aq knew he was drunk, but he was in charge and he was supposed to get whatever he wanted.

What can go wrong?

He took Carl's hand and put it on his crotch. Carl's expression was something between surprise and joy.

"I don't wanna see your face," said Aq. He surprised himself. "You are here to serve me, and I don't wanna see your expression or know if you're having a good time or not."

There, I said it.

Carl's face showed that he understood.

"I may make a suggestion, Boss?"

"Mm."

"I have a mask in t' cupboard downstairs. That would help you to use me?"

Aq smiled.

Actually yes, that's exactly what I need.

"Get it, boy," he said.

"Yes Boss, thank you, Boss."

"Don't say 'Yes, Boss, thank you, Boss.' Just obey me."

Carl nodded and ran out of the room to get the mask. Aq took another drag on the cigar.

Fuck. Yes.

***

Cyan was orgasming, and Teal was just beginning to let go. They were kissing so hard that she couldn't feel her tongue anymore. There were things she wanted to scream, to shout, to let out. There were things she had never told Cyan. So many secrets. She pulled her head back just a little and saw then that Cyan was crying. Tears were running down their cheeks. Teal wanted to react somehow, but she was mid-orgasm, energy still flowing out of her. She took a breath, tried to speak.

And she was gone.

Chapter thirty-six

"No. No!" Teal shouted the words. "No!"

But she was already somewhere else. Standing, surrounded by the *cerezo* forest as far as she could see. It was dark, night-time dark. Her body still shivered in the wake of her orgasm.

Cyan, she thought. *Cyan.*

What's happening to me?

Then she heard the shouts and saw lights approaching. She heard thunder above her.

Wait, not thunder. A... helicopter?

Teal's heart jumped as she heard a shot ring out from deep in the forest. And another. And another. Teal dived to the forest floor and curled up in the leaves. She pushed her face into the dirt. She wanted to disappear.

"No!" she shouted again, and suddenly she was back in her tent on top of her lover, still holding them down by the wrists.

"Cyan," she whispered. But then she saw their face.

The angriest face she'd ever seen.

4. Communication

Prelude

A family sat eating breakfast together in a garden, surrounded by roses.

"Where's Daddy?" asked the little girl.

"He's at work, dear, like usual," her mother replied patiently, between sips of fair-trade espresso.

"What is Daddy's work?" asked the girl. She already knew the answer, but she always asked the question anyway.

"He helps the environment darling, you know that. He makes solar panels like the ones on our roof."

The little girl looked up.

"And what do they do?" she asked, already knowing the answer.

"They make electricity so we can put the lights on at night time and watch TV. It's clean energy, so it's good for the world."

"But—" began the little girl, finally thinking of a new question. "—What are they made of? Does it come from the ground? Who gets it out of the ground and how? What do the mines look like?"

The mother put down her cup.

"Eat your breakfast, darling."

Chapter thirty-seven

"Oh my god... wait..." said Teal, speaking very slowly as she tried to process. "What t' fuck... happened?"

"You spaced out on me again." Cyan could barely control their anger. "Get off me!"

Teal rolled off and stared in confusion.

She saw the condom hanging loosely off her.

"We were... fucking."

"What?" Cyan's voice was getting louder by the second. "What? Of course we were fucking! You spaced out, did your dissociation thing on me again. Right as I was coming!"

"My dissociation thing..." mumbled Teal. "But I didn't... and what's wrong with... oh god." She stood up suddenly and tried to run towards the sink, but it was too late. She threw up over the bedsheets—and Cyan.

Cyan stared at Teal. They couldn't speak. There was vomit on their leg. They stood up and released a sound somewhere between a scream of frustration and the crash of a falling tree.

Teal saw that she had puked in her own hair.

She said very slowly,

"Helicopter. Did you see t' helicopter too...?"

Cyan stared at her for a long minute.

"I can't take this anymore!" they screamed and stormed out.

"Cyan, listen to me. Cyan, wait for just a second, would you?" Teal begged as she chased after Cyan, hating herself for it.

Why does this happen? I didn't do anything wrong. Yes, I dissociated, or whatever t' fuck that was, but why is that my fault?

They just—

"Okay," said Cyan abruptly stopping and turning on their heels. "You want to fight? Let's fight!"

"No, I *don't* want to fight. What t' hell? I dissociated, fine. I wasn't in my body, big deal. That actually happen about ten times a day, and you know what? It isn't about you, Cyan. And it isn't a picnic for me either."

"Of course it's about me!" Cyan shouted "You were... *inside* me. I *let* you in."

"That was a big mistake."

"Yes, it was."

"But not only *my* mistake. Cyan, listen, there's something more to this. Something that happened to me in t' resistance village that I didn't tell you about. I'm going through some changes..."

"Enough with your village and your fucking changes! No-one want to hear about it anymore!"

Just then, Jade arrived on foot, back from his trip to the beach. He glared at Teal. Teal glared at Cyan. Cyan glared at them both.

Indi appeared from her tent, where she'd been taking a siesta. "What all this shouting about?" she asked, rubbing her eyes.

"Shut up Indi!" everyone shouted at once, and Cyan and Jade stormed off to their tents. Teal shrugged at her and walked off towards the platform.

Our team is falling apart. How long can we continue like this?

***

How long can he keep this up? This is fucking amazing.

Aq stretched and lay back on the pillow. Carl was still going down on him, where he had been for the last ninety minutes. Once in a while, Carl would splutter, change position or adjust his mask, but they both understood that, unless ordered otherwise, he was going to stay down there.

Aq was in no rush. The hour of massage, combined with the alcohol, had left him feeling more relaxed than he could ever remember being.

I had no idea my body could even feel like this.

Carl spluttered again and Aq could see that his eyes were watering.

"You okay, sub?" he asked.

Carl nodded and continued his work.

He's not, Aq realised somehow. *He need water.*

"Get yourself a drink," he commanded.

Even through the mask, Aq could see his relief. Carl wiped his mouth and left the room quickly.

Well, that's complicated. He's willing to push himself for me, which is great, but what if he push too far? How will I know?

Aq was beginning to realise that they would need a lot more communication.

Chapter thirty-eight

"Sub, I want you to work on my feet again for a while..."

Carl reached for the oil.

"And I want to establish some rules."

Carl didn't respond, but Aq could see he was waiting.

Even with t' mask, I can't switch it off. I barely know him, but somehow, I know what he's experiencing.

"What you've been doing tonight is good. Very good. And I want more."

Carl nodded as he warmed the beech oil in his hands and began rubbing it into Aq's skin.

"And I want to do more to you."

More oil.

"I want you to push yourself to please me, like you've been doing. But I also need to know that you're okay. Especially if I take it further."

Carl nodded, his fingers working around Aq's ankles, releasing tension.

And I do want to take it further. He talk about me using him. I like that. I wanna try it.

At some point, Carl had laid out a selection of whips and chains and some other implements—Aq could barely work out what some of them were meant for—on the counter across the room. They hadn't spoken about it, but Aq looked over at them now, curious.

It's pretty clear I can do more. And... I want to.

"I need to feel safe hurting you, sub. So I'm going to give you some words that you can use when it's too much."

I'm gonna be t' one giving pain, but I need to feel safe too.

"And I'm gonna make a list of things I want to try with you. And you're gonna tell me what is okay or not."

Carl looked up, nodded and continued his work.

I feel like this should have a name. I'm sure t' rich people in t' sex clubs have a whole system for it.

Carl made a sweeping motion on his calves that gave Aq a chill up his back. The rum had left his system now and he was thinking very clearly.

I can work this out. I want to. Then I can start really having some fun.

***

"Where is Teal?"

Jade looked up from his pile of papers. Cyan stood in the tent doorway with their hands on their hips.

"Not sure. I think she went to t' platform after you all had your big fight."

"We didn't have a fight... we..."

Cyan pushed their hands through their hair in frustration.

You got no idea what's going on Jade. You never do.

"But it's nearly dark already."

Jade shrugged and went over to the cool box to get a drink. He sat back down and looked longingly at his papers.

"Maybe she's sleeping up there," he suggested. "Or maybe she's going back to t' other side to join t' revolution. Seemed like she had a real good time with t' 'resistance'."

"Shut up, Jade."

T' other side. She wouldn't. But I wouldn't put it past her. She would do it just to punish me. Oh my god, what if she do?

Cyan left the tent, slamming down the flap behind them. They took off in the direction of the platform, and the fence.

Jade sighed and got back to his work.

"Babe, are you there? Hello?"

Cyan's voice was desperate. The sky was dark already. The birds had gone to roost, and the forest was silent. Cyan's neck hurt from trying to look up to the platform.

"If you're up there answer me! Are you there? Hello?

No reply.

"Fuck this," they mumbled, attaching the rope to their harness and pulling themself up into the trees.

They arrived at the platform panting and sweating, pulled themself onto the wooden structure, and unfastened the rope. The forest was nearly dark now and they opened their backpack to search for a headlight. But their eyes had already adjusted and they could make out a figure curled up at the other end of the platform. Cyan knew that sniffling anywhere.

"Teal, my love, I'm so sorry."

As Cyan got a little closer, they could see that Teal was sat with her back against a tree hugging her knees to her chest.

"I'm so sorry. I did it again, didn't I?"

Teal didn't respond. Cyan could hear her crying again.

"I know it's not fair, I'm sorry. My trauma isn't your responsibility. You obviously went through something too and I should have supported you. We should have supported each other. We both got triggered—"

"Cyan, please shut up. And stop analysing my feelings."

"Sorry," they paused. "Should I go?"

"Did you bring beer in that giant backpack of yours?"

"I think t' gin from last week is still up here somewhere..."

"Then sit t' fuck down and let's finish it."

***

"Your number, sub?"

"Two, Boss."

Good. So I can go much further.

He punched harder this time, just below the ribs, and Carl squealed.

"Still two, Boss." He squeezed the words out between his teeth.

"I don't want to hear you anymore, sub. If we get above seven, you're gonna tell me. Otherwise, no more words."

Carl nodded. Aq tightened the ropes around his sub's wrists. He stood back one step and pulled back his arm to get a wider shot.

Yep, this gonna work just fine.

***

"You gotta help me with t' rope. It's so dark. And I'm druuunk!" Cyan stood wobbling at the edge of the platform.

"Me too," laughed Teal. "Shall I radio Indi to come help us?"

"She gonna be asleep by now," replied Cyan, giggling for no reason. "Poor Indi, we're so bad to her!"

"Yes, poor Indi. Here let me help you with that before you fall off and break yourself..."

Cyan waved their arms up and down.

"I can fly down!"

"Stop that," laughed Teal, attaching the rope to Cyan's harness and adjusting their headlamp. "You're such a goofball."

"I love you!"

"No you don't."

"Pssst, *Teal*—"

"Yes, *Cyan*?"

"—I want you to take me to t' resistance village tomorrow."

Teal was shocked. Even in Cyan's drunken state, that was the last thing she expected to hear. Then she remembered that moment back near the gate. "We see you in two days," Azure had said. She had been so certain.

"Okay..."

Cyan giggled. "Promise?"

"Promise. Now get down before t' guards come over to arrest us for disturbing t' forest."

"I love t' forest! I love you! Wheeeeeeeee!!"

Cyan released the lock and went whizzing down the rope at break-neck speed to the forest floor. Teal watched from the platform in the dark as her favourite person in the world, as complicated and unpredictable as anyone she knew, landed on their ass in a fit of giggles.

Chapter thirty-nine

"I am dead?" Cyan asked, rolling over in bed. "This is hell?"
Teal was already awake and had been watching them sleep for a while. She smiled as Cyan held their head and groaned.
"You're not dead."
"What happened to me?"
"Gin happened."
"Gin..." Cyan said confused. "Gin?"
Teal chuckled. "Gin."
"Oh gin!" A look of recognition flashed across Cyan's face. "I remember now. And wait...we're going to t' village today!"
Teal's heart skipped. "You still want to? I mean we talked about it, but you were wasted."
"I want to!"
"Real?"
"Look Teal, I'm sorry. I haven't been supportive and I know that night was important to you." Cyan tried to sit up but lay back again. Their eyes were closed. "I want to meet this Azure person and hear about t' things you've been going through and I want to see what's happening out there with my own eyes. But mostly I want to be there for you."
Teal smiled.
Hot and cold.
"Okay, let's do it!"
Cyan tried to get up again, stood for a few seconds, wobbling, then collapsed back on the bed with a groan.
"I might need some water first though. And a shower."

Teal laughed and went off to the kitchen to fill a bottle. *Amazing*, she thought. *I'm going back.*

***

Aq was talking on the phone. Carl didn't mean to listen, but he couldn't help hearing most of Aq's side of the conversation.

"Moss, it's Aq, how you doing?... Good, good, a bit hungover... It's Pinar Day—you're free, no?... Wanna come over and have some drinks in t' pool?... Yeah, he's here, but it's no problem, if you don't mind getting served... Ha! Thought you wouldn't. I send Beige to pick you up. See you in a couple of hours?... I know right? See you soon, mate... Ciao."

Carl couldn't see. The mask itched his face but he couldn't scratch because his hands were above him in chains. The closet smelt slightly musty. He was grateful he could breathe at all. The mask his master had chosen only had nostril holes—that's all he got today. He had hesitated too long to bring the coffee. Had forgotten to buy new damiana cigarettes. Hadn't cleaned the pool in time. And this was his punishment.

His arms were tired. How long had he been standing for? He felt light-headed and tried to take a deeper breath through the mask. It didn't work. He had few options to make himself more comfortable. He tried to move his hips a little but was restrained on all sides by his master's suits and jackets. Something he couldn't even identify was pushing against his chest. There was the slightest flitter of panic, but he relaxed his muscles as best as he could. He deserved this. Secretly, he desired it. He was overwhelmed with gratitude.

"Thank You, Master," he whispered to no-one but himself. "I'm gonna do better next time, I promise."

The closet opened and Carl smelled the air as it rushed in, cool and fresh.

"Out now, boy. You got work to do."

Carl waited while the chains were untied and he could bring his arms down.

Oh, blissful relief.

He was desperate to rub his eyes and scratch the itches that had tormented him—not to mention the bruises from last night—but he held back.

My Master don't want to see that.

"Keep t' hood on. My mate's coming over and we'll need drinks, smokes and snacks. First though, I want to hear if you've learned from this punishment."

"I'm gonna do better, Boss. I'm gonna work faster and not forget things."

"Get to work then."

Carl went straight to the kitchen and made the most of a few seconds of privacy to scratch and rub and stretch his aching limbs. He couldn't believe his luck. This was just how he wanted his life to be. To have his decisions taken away from him—at least on his days off—to switch off his brain and just serve Aq's pleasure.

It's perfect. He's perfect. I want this to last forever.

* * *

"This is taking forever. Are you sure it's here?"

"That's what t' map says."

Following Azure's very rough map, Teal was driving Cyan and herself to the resistance village. It had been quite a while already since they left the familiar comfort of the city and the park and hit a dirt track out into the desert. The air was thick with pink dust.

"Anything look familiar yet?"

"I mean, it's a million miles of pink. How familiar could it look?"

"OK, well if this doesn't take us anywhere, we can double back and take t' left where we took t' right."

"But it's says right, no?"

"Yes dear." Cyan breathed deeply and tried to find patience. "But this map isn't very detailed and right now, this looks more like we landed on a big gay moon than a resistance village."

"It's close...t' map has to be right."

Teal was actually getting a little worried.

If t' map isn't good, no way we gonna find t' village. The car took a deep dip into a pothole and back out again. *And this road's for shit. But why would Azure give me this map if she didn't want me to come back? And she already knew I was gonna come back. How did that happen? Is this really a thing—seeing stuff before it happen? Maybe this is—"*

"Oh my god, there it is!"

Teal slammed on the brakes and they were both thrown violently forward against their seat belts. Through the dust she could just make out tents and there, in the middle of the road, looking completely unfazed, stood Azure and her daughter.

"I take it all back," said Cyan smiling. "Your map was perfect."

"Ready to meet t' resistance?"

Cyan pretended to check their very short hair in the mirror.

"Do I look okay?"

"You're beautiful."

Cyan blushed just a little, unlocked their door, and got out.

Chapter forty

Aq stood in the doorway and watched as the car pulled up in the long driveway. Beige got out and opened the passenger door. Moss unfurled his lanky body and grinned.

"Cheers, mate. Hey Aq!" he shouted. "Tip your guy, would you? I'd love to, but... you know..." He showed his empty pockets dramatically.

"Wait a second. Carl!"

Carl appeared immediately at the side of the house.

"Give Beige a hundred for me."

He did. Moss greeted Aq with a bear hug.

"You are out of control, mate," he laughed. "You don't even do your own tipping anymore."

Aq laughed too and led him to the grand entrance of the house. Moss took in the sweeping staircase and the chandeliers with an impressed whistle.

"Not too shabby, mate. Seriously, I need to get me one of these. Are you fucking him yet?"

"Pool's this way."

* * *

"This place is stunning!" Cyan said excitedly, as Azure invited them and Teal to sit down at the long communal table for tea. "I had no idea!"

"My father crafted t' central pole," said Azure as if that explained everything. She sat down and poured tea. "Teal, I'm glad to see you."

"Thank you! I really wasn't sure we'd see each other again."

"I had no doubt."

"How you knew?" Teal asked excitedly. "You saw it somehow, no?"

Azure threw a look at Cyan.

"That's a private conversation."

Teal was about to speak but Cyan interrupted.

"Oh, I mean I never asked if I could actually come out here. I just assumed, *we* just assumed that—"

"You are welcome here," Azure said flatly. She turned towards the door and shouted so loudly that Cyan physically jumped a bit.

"Rouge, order lau some petit-munjaree, duckie! Our guests have trolled far and they're hungry. And dowry bevoir—all t' soot is turning me thirsty."

Cyan gave Teal a look that said very clearly, *what t' heck was that?*

***

"Another plate of chips and cookies, sub, and another cocktail for me and my friend."

A silent nod and Carl ran off to serve.

Aq and Moss were floating on two inflatable mattresses in the pool in their swimming trunks. The sun was high and they were sipping from perfectly mixed Mai Tais. Moss always got drunk after one drink and he kept giggling uncontrollably.

"This is all too good to be true, Aq."

"It's okay, no? I mean, I'm making t' most of it."

Moss nearly dropped his drink in the pool and had another fit of giggles.

"Get everything you can," he said, then tried to sound a little more serious. "Mate, I seen a hundred subs come and go, but he look like he really enjoy serving you. He might even stay a while." Moss waved his hand indicating the house. "And this isn't bad neither. He's signed it over to you yet?"

"Not yet. It's been like five minutes."

"Five *good* minutes I bet," giggled his friend. "Five *real good* minutes!" Moss opened his arms to show how good the minutes must have been, but he overreached, wobbled, and capsized his mattress. He went straight under, his cocktail joining the pool water. He emerged a few seconds later, squealing and giggling.

Even Aq couldn't help laughing this time. But then in his drunken wisdom, Moss decided it was a good idea to capsize him too.

"No! Don't you dare! This cocktail cost as much as your shoes!"

"He can make us another one!"

"No, Moss, stop!"

But it was too late. With a splash, Aq was in the water too, and Moss was laughing so hard he thought he might actually throw up in the pool.

Carl knew he shouldn't be, but he was unhappy. From the kitchen he could hear the splashes and giggles of Aq and his friend.

Moss was it? What kind of name is that anyway? Sound more like a plant than a colour.

Carl added ice to the drinks he was preparing and gave them a good shake. He gave Aq's just a bit more sugar and Moss' an extra pinch of bitter herbs.

Who he think he is? Aq is my *Boss, he's* my *friend. Not this guy's. It shouldn't be like this,* he thought as he carried the tray through the corridor and passed the closet where he'd spent a good part of the morning. *I don't want Boss to have to punish me again.*

Adjusting his mask slightly, Carl pushed his shoulders back and walked out towards the pool carrying his head high.

* * *

"What's that weird language you're speaking?"

The long communal table was full of food, even though it didn't seem to be a planned mealtime. Villagers kept dropping in and grabbing a plate and getting back to whatever it was they were busy with. Cyan and Teal could hear crashes and grunts outside. It seemed as though at least one or two tents were being built or moved.

Azure was in conversation with her guests while simultaneously organising the village work, shouting instructions to the people passing in or out through the open door. Her voice was impressively powerful for someone who appeared to be in her sixties. She switched seamlessly between English and Polari.

"Polari," Azure replied to Cyan's question. "But it's a kind of slang not a language. A cant slang."

"Cant slang?"

"A form of slang used to speak secretly without outsiders understanding."

"But *we're* t' outsiders," said Cyan, slightly annoyed. "Why would you keep secrets from us?"

"Cyan is it?" Azure asked.

"Yes."

"Cyan. It is not all about you, dear."

Teal almost chuckled, but saw Cyan's face and held it in. They were not impressed.

"Teal?" asked Azure. "We gonna take a walk together, you and me."

Cyan looked even less impressed.

"Rouge!" Azure shouted suddenly. "Come in here and answer this person's questions about Polari, would you?"

"Yes, mom!" was the reply. "Two minutes!"

"My daughter will accompany you," she said to Cyan. "Teal, come."

She stood up and walked out.

"Okay?" asked Teal, looking at Cyan who sat pouting with their arms crossed.

"Do I have a choice?" asked Cyan.

Teal knew better than to engage. She ran out of the tent after Azure.

Chapter forty-one

"What a view!"

Azure had led Teal to the highest point of a hill overlooking the village. They could see for miles. The forest was bright green on the horizon against the pink of the desert. Above it, she could see that the village was beautifully arranged into spirals that connected the paths and tents. Herb and vegetable gardens formed smaller spirals and the occasional curl carved out of the soil which might have been art or a drainage system, Teal couldn't quite tell.

"Fractals..." she muttered to herself.

"Precisely. Tell me, Teal, did you journey again?"

"*Journey?* You mean, like... Ash? God, do you really think that's what this is?"

"It is."

"Wow, okay." Teal's heart was beating hard and her chest was tight—against her own will, she was remembering the events of yesterday.

"I see that you *did* journey again."

"Yes. Well, I think so... I was, well I have having sex—"

"—With Cyan?"

"Yes, with Cyan."

Azure tutted. Teal had no idea how to respond to that so continued talking. "So... yes, so we were *making love* and then I was out of my body again. Or like, in it, but somewhere else. Another place."

"And another time."

"If you say so."

"Tell me."

"I was in t' *cerezo* forest and it was night. I heard gunshots I guess. And there was, like, helicopters?"

"Helicopters."

Neither of them had seen a helicopter or a plane during their lifetimes. They were familiar with them from movies and pictures, but nothing flew above the skies of Espera now.

"I know, right? Maybe it was just a dream somehow, a hallucination."

"It wasn't."

"It's so weird. It's like I can almost understand it, but not quite," said Cyan, back at the camp.

Rouge nodded. She pointed at a bottle of Esperan gin on a shelf and said: "A bottle o' Vera."

"Why would anyone need a secret word for gin?"

"Polari came from t' UK, people drank a lot of gin."

"How did it develop?"

"You heard of cruising?" Rouge smiled.

Cyan was taken back.

She's what, sixteen?

"Erm, yes..."

"Well, *cruising* itself is a Polari word imported into English. Ships cruising from port to port like guys cruising from bathroom to... Anyway, you get t' idea."

Cyan crossed their arms. "I do."

"Polari developed out of criminalised gay culture—sailors, t' circus, all of that—when they needed to be able to speak without being understood. It was also big among criminals and sex workers for a while."

Cyan looked incredulous. "So, it's what? A secret queer sex language and now it's used by t' resistance?"

Rouge shrugged. "Mais oui."

"No way," said Cyan "I don't believe you. I would have heard of it."

Rouge poured some more tea.

"I believe you."

"You do?" Teal was amazed.

"You saw t' future, Teal. Ash told us this would happen."

"Ash. Wait... *Ash*-Ash?"

Azure nodded. "She told us you would come here and that you would share her curse."

Teal swallowed hard.

"You *knew* her?"

"I'm not *that* old, dear. She died before I was born, of course, but she passed on her wisdom through t' others including my parents. It's never been written down."

"Oral history..."

"Precisely. Much more secure than t' written word and continuously resculpted by those who pass it on."

"Is that why you use Polari as well...for security?"

"Precisely. And I got something I want to ask you and your team, but later. We gonna return to t' communal tent now."

"I'm sure Cyan is already impatient!"

"Cyan, yes," said Azure thoughtfully. "Teal, I'm sorry, but it won't work out with you two."

"I—sorry, what?"

"They're no good for you. They're wrong for you somehow, I can't say better than that. It's okay for now and you can probably continue to work together. But you can't trust them as a lover."

"I've known them *forever*, we went through so much together!"

"No good, Teal. Believe me."

Well, she hasn't been wrong yet. And I'm not sure Cyan treat me as well as they used to. But still—

"We go."

Azure, with Teal running after her, headed back down to the village.

"Hey! Good walk?" asked Cyan when Teal arrived back at the tent. "Rouge has been telling me so many things! Like, Teal, did you know Polari was actually a *cruising* language for criminal gay sex?"

Teal sat down and took a cookie.

"Oh my god, I hadn't put it together! I'd never heard it of course. So yeah, it came out of t' theatre and fish markets and stuff, right? A working-class slang of some kind. And, like, sailors bumming each other in public toilets?"

"Oh, so you heard of it?" Cyan's voice sounded disappointed.

"Of course! There was an art exhibition about it at t' Ash and Pinar museum once. We went, don't you remember?"

"I don't."

"You don't remember me complaining? It was all very clean and abstract and middle class, not very Polari at all."

"I don't remember that."

"Oh, well. It happened." She could see Cyan was annoyed about something but chose to ignore it. "Ooh, I have some *amazing* things to tell you. Azure said that Ash said that—"

Azure reappeared and sat down between them and interrupted.

"I have something I wish to discuss. Something I want to remain private." She signed to them in the so-called Universal Sign Language of the former State, 'Do you speak USL?'

Teal and Cyan's faces were blank.

"Is that a sign language?" asked Cyan.

Azure tutted.

"Then please switch off your phones and take out t' batteries."

Teal looked confused and took her phone out of her pocket.

"Like t' security thing? But they fixed that when Espera brought out t' sauvite phones." She showed her beaten phone to prove the point. "Total privacy, no-one can listen in."

"That's what they said of course," said Azure. "Please do it."

"Okay."

"Cyan?"

"Fine," they huffed. "But I'm not real okay with all this cloak and dagger, secret languages and phone security and whatever."

"Would you like to leave t' tent while we talk?" Azure asked.

Cyan shook their head. They already felt excluded enough.

Why these two get on so well? Azure's rude, bossy, but Teal seem to worship her. Look at her like she's so wise. She never look at me like that.

"No, I'm staying," they said, taking out their phone and dismantling it.

"Thank you, you need to hear this too." Azure was practically whispering and Teal and Cyan leaned towards her slightly. "So, as you know, we are resistance. Three generations live in this village including t' great-descendants of those who fled t' State."

Teal smiled and nodded.

"There are twelve more villages spread around t' desert..."

"Wow," Teal said, as quietly as she could.

"...And each year we come together and re-enter t' park. We visit t' graves of our ancestors and we collect t' herbs we need to help us survive another year. As you see, Espera make sure we don't get much medicine out here."

Cyan crossed their arms. "No-one go in t' park."

"No-one except your team and t' tourists and those rich enough to buy ecodevelopments," replied Azure. "And t' resistance. Once a year for t' last thirty years."

"Impossible."

"I promise you, it's possible. In fact, it's gonna happen again in three days."

Chapter forty-two

"Oh my god, this is t' best day off *of all time!*" shouted Moss to his friend, who was floating on the other mattress barely a metre away from him in the pool.

"You're shouting," laughed Aq. "You're totally drunk."

"Yes. I think you might be right! So, what's next? What else can we do with your hooded business man? I'm sure he's good for all sorts of things."

"Well..."

"I saw t' bruises. I know you've been having fun with him."

"I—"

"No judgement from me. This is class struggle or something..." Moss had a fit of giggles for no reason. "Class struggle... class strugggglle!"

"You can't breathe a word of this to anyone," said Aq, trying to get his friend to be serious. "As I told you, he's super well-known."

"Mate, I forgot his name instantly. I don't care. And no-one care if he's queer, this is Espera."

"We don't know if he's queer, Moss."

"Oh okay." Moss paddled his mattress closer. His arm brushed against Aq's. "And you, mate?"

"What do you mean?"

"Oh, never mind."

Shit.

Aq was getting hard.

"We should go in." He paddled towards the edge of the pool. "You know he's also good for a massage, that appeal?"

Moss' face lit up.

"Fuck, yes!"

"Give Moss a foot massage, sub. T' good ones like you give me."

Carl nodded and went to get towels and oil. He was grateful for the mask hiding his face today. The last thing he wanted to do was work on Moss' feet.

I want my Master and only him. When this guy gonna leave? Don't he have a home to go to?

Carl remembered the closet, remembered the pain of his arms tied above him.

Just do it, boy, stop complaining.

"Ah mate, that's awesome," said Moss. Aq was sat near him reading a comic book. "I would never get anything done if I had this guy around."

Aq felt odd.

It was one thing for him to objectify and 'use' Carl, or to joke in the pool when Carl was busy in the house, but it became very real to have both his friend and his sub in the same room together.

"I know, right?" he said as lightly as he could. "I'm gonna leave you two to it for a minute. I'm gonna—"

But actually where would I go? I don't wash dishes anymore, I don't cook or shop or clean.

"I'm gonna take a walk."

"Cool, see you soon," said Moss. "Thanks for this."

"No problem. I'll be back in twenty minutes. Enjoy yourself."

Beneath his mask, Carl was scowling. He watched Aq leave the room and then returned to his massaging.

I'm not okay with this. I didn't sign up for worshipping my Boss' friends too. I don't even know this guy, he's not beautiful like Aq.

"That's a bit rough actually, mate," said Moss. "A bit softer, would you?"

Carl secretly smiled and obeyed.

* * *

"Sadly, t' perimeter isn't really about conservation," said Azure softly. "And neither is t' park or t' research you're doing."

Cyan didn't respond. They glared at Azure instead.

"How so?" asked Teal.

"Did you hear of Brunel?"

"Isambard Kingdom Brunel?" said Cyan, brightening slightly. Architecture was one of their pet subjects. Azure nodded.

"An English engineer," Cyan said to Teal although she knew perfectly well who he was. "One of t' great architects of t' Industrial Revolution."

Teal sighed.

T' more insecure they get, t' more they need to prove themself.

"Okay."

"So you know about t' Clifton suspension bridge in Bristol," asked Azure patiently.

Cyan nodded. "I saw it once, it's magnificent."

Azure continued, "Then you also know that in 1831 it was due to be built on a site where a very rare plant called t' Autumn Squill grew. T' wife of Brunel's assistant warned him that construction would destroy its habitat, so Brunel had t' plants relocated."

Cyan seemed surprised.

"Now note, although some bulbs were moved and t' plant survived, what this man did effectively was build a bridge on top of t' habitat of a rare species." Azure sat very still as she told her story, but her eyes were bright. "But he was branded a conservationist. T' Bristol zoo even put a plaque by t' bridge declaring it 'one of t' first recorded examples of plant conservation.'

"And who get t' credit? *Not* t' indigenous people who protected their lands for tens of thousands of years. *Not* t' resistance movements worldwide resisting English colonialism. A very famous and eventually rich, white man, built a bridge, destroyed a precious habitat and became t' first conservationist."

Cyan was glaring again.

"And that isn't t' end of t' story..." Azure continued.

"Go on," said Teal, hanging on her every word.

"In 1831, after a bill for greater representation in t' parliament was rejected, protesters took over Queen Square—a central area of Bristol made rich from slavery—and rioted for three days. T' riots disturbed construction of Brunel's precious bridge and he was sworn in as a special constable. T' cavalry charged with swords, eighty-six people were injured and four people were hanged, despite a petition of ten thousand Bristolians to stop it."

Azure paused for breath.

"Brunel of course later returned to construction and finished t' bridge—"

"—and helped conserve t' Autumn Squill by destroying its home," said Teal. "Wow, it's a fucked up story. Right, Cyan?"

"Bullshit," they said, suddenly standing up. "I don't believe a word of this. Besides, what it got to do with t' park? *Of course* we're conserving t' forest. I mean look around you—" their voice was getting louder and they opened their arms wide "—it would all be desert without t' perimeter. Without our research. And without t' money from tourism to pay for it all. *This* is conservation. Without *us* there'd be nothing."

"Cyan, sit down," commanded Teal, louder than she meant to. "You sound like Jade! It is actually possible for there to be more than one perspective. Sometimes things are complic—"

"Like Jade?! How dare you?!"

Cyan stormed out of the tent, pushing over a chair as they went.

There was a moment of silence. "Sorry, I don't know why they reacted like that," Teal said, very quietly.

Azure shrugged and smiled. "Quite normal. Like most people, Cyan is completely invested in keeping things t' way they are."

Teal nodded but couldn't keep eye contact.

"They can only imagine life within capitalism so when they see t' effects for themselves—this desert of dust created from t' sauvite in your phones and solar panels and lightbulbs—they look to Big Conservation for t' answers. Green capitalism, ethical consumerism, eco-tourism, habitats without t' very people who created them. Throw in some queer liberalism and a reformed police state and you have—"

"Espera."

Chapter forty-three

Moss and Aq were having fun. Pool and cocktails. Jacuzzi and cocktails. A massage followed by a rowdy game of table tennis and yet more cocktails. Eventually though, the time came for Moss to get back to reality. Beige came to pick him up and take him back to Union. Moss gave Aq a big bear hug and couldn't stop saying thank you.

"No mate, I mean it, this was t' best day off—"

"Ever!" Aq laughed. "You may have mentioned it."

"See you at work tomorrow?"

"Of course."

"Unless you decide to quit and get worshipped all day?"

"See you at work, Moss."

"Thanks mate! Ooh and Happy Pinar Day!"

"You too."

Moss got into the car. Beige closed his door for him, got into the driver's seat and drove them off into the forest.

Aq closed the gate and walked back into the house. He was aware of coming back to reality.

I almost miss t' dorm, he thought as he walked up the grand staircase. *Not really, but, like, I miss t' guys a bit. Or something. Maybe I miss things being familiar.*

He passed Carl on the landing ironing his shirt for tomorrow. Carl paused and put the iron down. "Permission to speak, Boss?"

"Not now, boy."

He went to his bedroom to read and closed the door.

***

Cyan was driving over the speed limit—if there even was one out in the desert—and the car kept bumping violently in and out of potholes.

"Hon," said Teal carefully. "Maybe we could slow down a bit?"

Cyan ignored her and maybe even sped up a bit more.

"Hello? Cyan?"

"Yes, what is it?"

"Please slow down. This is a rented car remember?"

"Fine." They braked and swerved around an especially large pothole.

"Is everything okay?"

"Not particularly," said Cyan staring straight ahead. "I don't want to talk about it."

"But—"

"I said I don't want to talk about it."

Teal stopped speaking. She knew she would cry if she said anything else.

***

Carl finished ironing, tidied away the board and hung up Aq's shirt. He lifted the mask and scratched his nose. He was feeling less and less comfortable.

I need to say something about Moss. I want to set a limit. I'm gonna serve Aq so well, give him everything I have. But not his friends. Just him.

He stood thinking on the landing for a while, then took a deep breath and knocked on the door.

"What is it?"

"Permission to speak, Boss?"

Again? Aq thought, not looking up from his comic book. "Yes?"

"A personal matter, Boss."

Aq made eye contact. "Do you *have* personal matters, boy?"

"I apologise, Boss. I just wanted to ask if I'm gonna go to work tomorrow."

Aq hadn't thought about it.

I guess he gotta work sometime. Me too for that matter.

"Sure, boy. You're gonna work."

"And Boss...may I prepare my things for tomorrow? My suit for example and I have some messages to respond to."

"Sure. Do that."

"Thank you, Boss. And, Boss...?"

Aq was getting impatient and put down his comic book. "What, boy? What is it?"

"Sorry, Boss. Can I bring you something, Boss?"

"I'm gonna be hungry soon."

"Of course, Boss. Enjoy your comic."

Carl shuffled out of the room, closing the door as gently as he could.

Aq continued reading, but he couldn't concentrate. He scratched his head. He read the same page three times.

No. I can't ignore this. That wasn't okay. He obviously wanted to ask me something or to discuss something. I mean, yes, I'm t' boss and yes, I decide. But I do need to deal with it.

He put down his comic, stretched and shouted, "Sub, get back up here!"

Carl ran so fast he slipped on the staircase and banged his knee. He pushed through the pain and re-joined Aq in the bedroom.

"Yes, Boss?" he gasped.

"What did you want to tell me?"

"Oh...sorry, Boss." Carl stared at the carpet. Then at the pile of whips and chains on the desk. Then out of the window. "It was about your friend..."

"You don't want to serve him—only me. Right?"

Carl looked at the carpet again.

"I shouldn't make demands, Boss."

"It's no problem, sub. As long as you work twice as hard to please me."

Carl looked up and Aq could see the excitement in his eyes.

"Now, Boss?"

Aq lay back and unfastened his belt.

"Now."

* * *

When they arrived back at camp, Cyan went straight to bed without a word. After their time together, Teal was half expecting them to ask her to sleep over again. She went to the kitchen tent to catch up with Indi, but she was nowhere to be seen.

Probably gone into town to party on her day off. Or another of her mysterious meetings.

Teal felt suddenly lonely. She wanted to be excited. Everything that Azure had told her had been so big and life-changing. Ash. The resistance. The park.

And of course, t' Red Shadow-Tail.

She walked past a table covered in scanners, beamers and field guides. In all the events of the last days, she'd almost forgotten about their incredible discovery.

But as she got to her tent and curled up alone under a blanket, Teal shivered a little despite the summer heat. It was all so big. All so new. She wished she wasn't doing it alone.

She lay for a while listening to blackbirds declaring their availability and a pair of foxes from the den to the east fucking as loudly as only foxes can.

"No," she said to herself out loud, suddenly energised. She threw off the blanket and got out of bed. "No. I'm too young for this!"

She ran out of her tent, grabbed the rental car keys and her phone and got in the car.

I'm going out tonight.

Chapter forty-four

Teal parked up at the out-of-town car park and took the train into the city centre. Driving a car was a source of shame in Espera and she didn't want to be seen parking near the party.

Besides, I got no clue how I'm gonna get home tonight. Can't drive home if I drink. And I definitely wanna drink.

The train pulled up at T' Old Mall station and Teal got out. She always found it a strange name now that there were no more malls. In fact, Esperan law only allowed small businesses in the city, so every street—at least in the wealthy centre—was lined with local shops. Organic bakeries were already preparing a batch for the next day, small, brightly lit shops sold recycled books and wooden toys. Teal passed at least three vegan pet food stores. But definitely no malls.

She passed a white family; mom, dad and kids on the sidewalk. They were all holding hands and carrying cotton shopping bags and smiling big smiles. Teal had a sense of how surreal the city felt to her today.

This is all nothing like t' resistance village, she noticed. *More like, what they called it? Disneyland or something.*

A crowd of young people passed her, cycling and singing the Esperan anthem.

This is not t' desert.

Teal arrived at the party venue, where she knew Indi would probably already be curled up drunk in a corner and Jade would be making out with some random person. She had noticed that people of all genders seemed to be magnetically attracted to him.

I have no idea why. All that Esperan arrogance maybe? They really think that they're t' best people in t' world. T' purest, t' cleanest, t' most inclusive. They really believe—

Enough of that. I'm here to have fun.

Teal stepped inside.

***

Aq sat on the sofa watching a soap opera, an extra-strong drink in his hand. Carl was working on his feet again, careful not to block Aq's view of the TV. After their conversation about Moss, he felt closer to Carl than ever.

He was also aware that he didn't really *want* to feel so close to him. He wanted to lose control more. To give more pain. The more they played, the more secret desires seemed to surface for him—locking Carl in the closet had given him such a rush. Aq had meant it as a punishment, but the total control was unlike anything he had felt before.

Carl has a way of coaxing these things out of me, he noticed looking down briefly to where the hooded sub was hard at work. *And it just make me want more.*

"Stop now, sub."

Carl stopped.

"Did you finish putting t' ceiling hooks and chains up in t' bedroom?"

Carl nodded.

"And you laid out t' clothes I told you to?"

Another nod.

I barely need to check, he never disobey me.

"Bring me t' list."

Carl presented his sauvite tablet, which displayed a long list of activities he had written up for Aq. They were divided into various categories: Interesting, Not Interesting, Tried, Not Tried, Possible, Impossible, With Encouragement.

As Carl kneeled at his feet patiently, Aq spent some time moving activities from one category to another on the screen.

"These?" he asked showing the list to Carl.

His sub read and nodded eagerly.

"Good. Go up and get ready for me. I'm gonna be there in five minutes."

Carl ran up the stairs so fast he nearly slipped again.

***

"Best party ever!" Teal shouted despite herself.

One hour in and she was quite tipsy. All drinks were sold on a sliding scale at the bar and all profits went to a fox sanctuary in Oak Grove so Teal had allowed herself four organic gins.

Or was it five? Who care?

She had dragged Indi away from the sofa she was sleeping on and onto the dancefloor. She was awkward in her body but danced with total abandon. In that moment, Teal was overwhelmed with love for this most geeky and mild-mannered member of their team. They had both been to this party before. It was well known for the organic herbal highs they mixed into the drinks and Teal was beyond happy.

A person in a high femme red dress and sexy black heels rolled their wheelchair over to join the pair. Indi seemed to vaguely know them, and the three of them danced beautifully together for a while. The music kept building to crescendo after crescendo and Teal was euphoric, her arms raised to the ceiling. She was almost crying with joy. She felt nauseous for a moment and thought she might journey again. But she felt her feet, breathed deep, and she stayed.

Now she was definitely crying and she hugged Indi hard.

"I love this!" she shouted in her ear. "Best party ever!"

"Oh my god, that was so good!" shouted Teal, standing with Indi outside and watching the partiers go home.

"Ow, I'm right here, you don't need to shout!" Indi protested, laughing. "It was awesome, right?"

"So, so good. What's next?"

"I, well, I already have a plan for tonight."

"Real? Who's t' lucky human?" Teal was still shouting.

"You already met them actually. Verde, in t' red dress?"

"Ohhh..." Teal grinned. "They are fucking beautiful."

"Right? We've been dating for t' last few months. We met in a meeting."

"How is it possible that I didn't know you had such a beautiful lover all this time?"

"You never asked I guess."

"I never asked...and Jade? Where he is by t' way?"

"No clue. We came together, but he left early with his girlfriend."

"Jade has a girlfriend?"

"You really are caught up in your Cyan drama, no?" Indi laughed.

"I guess I am."

"Hey Indi," said a voice. Teal turned and saw Verde coming down the ramp. If it was possible, they looked even more beautiful in the subtle streetlight.

Their foundation and highlighter game is so good. And those heels...

"Coming?" Verde asked, tapping Indi's thigh.

"Hell yes!"

Indi turned and gave Teal a polite cheek kiss.

"See you at t' camp," she said, and ran after her lover.

Teal wasn't sure what to do next. She definitely wasn't in a state to drive yet and the first trains out to where she had parked didn't run for another hour or two.

Well, t' beach is nice, she thought, and she hopped on a tram heading to Dignity.

Teal arrived and took the stairs past the cactus garden and down to the beach. The sun was just rising and the soft waves of the sea were illuminated in orange and red. The air was crisp. The sound of the water on the sand made her feel calmer than she had been in weeks.

I love this place, Teal thought drowsily as she lay back on the sand. Within seconds she was asleep.

***

Carl was exhausted. Lying back on the massive bed, Aq was more relaxed than he had felt for a long time.

"You're gonna sleep at t' bottom of t' bed tonight."

Beneath his mask, Carl smiled and nodded.

"Now, Boss?"

"Now."

Fully-clothed, and without a word, Carl curled up like a cat near Aq's feet and fell asleep.

Chapter forty-five

On the soft sand down below Dignity station, Teal was having the strangest dream. Above her, the station was a park. A city park, all grass and benches and ornamental shrubberies. There was screaming all around her. The sky was white. She couldn't breathe.

Tear gas, she realised.

She moved across the park in that strange way people do in dreams; she imagined being somewhere and then suddenly she was there. She saw an older woman was running across the grass followed by hundreds of other people.

"To the hotel," the woman shouted. "To the tunnels!"

Teal looked at her hands. Her fingers were blurred. She had too many.

So this is a dream. I'm asleep.

She woke with a jump, feeling disconnected. She had fallen asleep in an awkward position and one of her legs was numb. She shifted and shook her leg but still felt cold inside.

What kind of dream was that? It was almost like what they tell us t' Battle for Dignity looked like. It was almost as though—

She was interrupted from her thoughts by an oystercatcher; the bird had landed just a few metres from where she lay and poked its beak into the sand. It walked a few centimetres and poked again. It came so close that Teal could have touched it with her feet, but she didn't move. She was enraptured.

It was then that she realised all the connections around her that she had been ignoring. A line of dunlins walking along the water's edge and the sound of the water itself. A murmuration of starlings above her. The blueness of the sky. The sand beneath her, the stones of the cliff. She was immersed in a world of complex and unfathomable beauty. She had connected.

I am not alone, she realised then. *I am never alone.*

Chapter forty-six

Teal pulled up in the camp and parked the car. She looked at the sun low in the sky.

Still morning. Cyan won't be too pissed. I really can't face any drama today.

"Hey everyone!" she called as she opened the flap to the communal tent. "Good morning!"

Cyan was in one of their tidying frenzies and barely noticed Teal's arrival. Indi and Jade were at a desk lost in their papers.

"Good morning," Teal repeated.

Indi looked up and smiled.

"You have fun last night?" she asked.

"Totally, I slept on t' beach!"

Cyan looked up from their cleaning for the first time, shook their head and tutted. Teal was in too good a mood and ignored them.

"And you, Indi?"

"*So* good," she said with a wink.

"I bet. Hey, what time are t' tourists arriving?"

"In an hour," said Cyan. "I'm taking a shift at t' platform and you and Jade are gonna meet them at t' Ash and Pinar Museum. We really don't need any more bullshit insect counts, to be honest."

Despite Cyan's sullen mood, Teal was actually excited. She hadn't been to the museum in years. She looked over at Jade who was scribbling something on his pad and pointedly not acknowledging her presence.

"Fine for me," she said cheerfully. "Okay with you, Jade?"

He muttered something she couldn't quite hear.

She ignored him.

"Awesome... so I'm gonna wash up and meet you at t' car in half an hour."

"Can't wait."

Teal continued to ignore him.

I have bigger things to think about.

The museum was almost empty and Teal was glad they hadn't come the day before. On Pinar Day the museum was always packed with performances and live enactments of various mythological scenes of Pinar's life but the day after was wonderfully quiet.

Teal went to pick up the 'conservation volunteers' from their bus. She saw them waiting impatiently for her in the car park. Everyone looked under the age of twenty-three, mostly middle-class students from Espera University getting eco-credit for their degrees. Some were as young as twelve, probably sent by their parents. They were all beyond excited.

The Ash and Pinar Museum was famous across the Five Nations for its holographic displays and the interactive recreations of resistance life. As they left the grassy car park, the first building they came to was the cabin itself. Partially rebuilt after the Exodus fires, the cabin was designed to be as authentically cramped as possible.

The volunteers filed in one by one to see the shelves filled with jars of herbs, some of which were even said to be the original herbs dried by Pinar herself. There was the table where Ash had treated Jason's injuries. There was even the bed that Ash and Pinar had slept in together. Staff had been told to never answer that most common of questions: were Ash and Pinar really lovers?

Teal stepped in but decided to wait outside instead. She had seen the cabin many times growing up. She had loved it as a child but somehow, after her journey beyond the park boundaries and her experiences at the resistance villages, none of it seemed as real to her anymore.

Jade returned from wherever he had skulked off to.

"Boring, right?" he said, leaning against the cabin wall. "All this resistance bullshit."

Teal was about to respond when the volunteers appeared from the little cabin door, wide grins on their faces.

"What next? What next?" they demanded.

"T' main building, I guess?" said Teal without much enthusiasm.

"You're gonna love it," Jade said to her with an odd note in his voice. "They have a temporary display all about your favourite subject."

"Which is what, exactly?"

"T' *genders*, of course."

"As we all know, Ash, t' great leader of t' resistance, was transgender. Do you know what that is?"

Teal rolled her eyes. In the room in front of her, a group of school children were sat in a circle around a holographic figure, which kept changing shape to keep the children's attention. For now, it was a frog.

"I know, I know!" said one of the children.

Who t' hell don't know? Teal thought to herself.

Since the Liberation, Espera had had at least one trans president, possibly more, and some of the most successful business leaders were rumoured to be trans. Gone were the days when trans folks lived in fear or even had to come out in public. Trans rights were a central tenant of Esperan law and things were only getting better. At least that's what Teal had always been told. She was beginning to doubt things were so simple.

Is it really progress to have trans presidents and trans capitalists exploiting a trans underclass? Is that actually what Ash would have wanted? I guess I'm never gonna know.

On a wall, a documentary about the Exodus was playing on a loop. *Not t' good one,* Teal noticed.

Not the one that she kept on her micro-beamer and had seen at least a hundred times, the one made by a black trans woman with hardly any budget even though she did all the archival research.

This was the Hollywood version. Made by a cis guy—*wealthy and white, of course*—with a big focus on Danny; how beautiful and strong he was and how he always seemed to be throwing the first stone. There was almost no mention of Ash or Kit at all. Teal yawned and tried not to watch. She looked around, suddenly realising that the volunteers had wandered off while she had been lost in her daydream. She ran down the museum corridor after them.

* * *

Aq sat in his blue silk boxers by the pool, watching the water. The sun was warm on his skin. The coffee Carl had made him was fresh and rich, and from the kitchen he could hear the sounds of his breakfast being prepared.

This is too good to be true.

Aq put down his coffee and looked at his phone.

An hour until work.

He sighed and took another sip. He stared into space for a while, listening to bird song and taking in the peaceful morning. His mind was full of images from the previous night. Of all the new things he had experienced.

"You know what?" he said to himself as he took his phone again and typed a message to the Staff Department. "Screw it."

10.00 Aq Hass: Sorry. I'm feeling hyper sick today and can't make it to work. I'm gonna be in tomorrow for my next shift.

An automatic message came back immediately.

10.01 Staff Dept: Your shift today has been cancelled and given to another member of staff. Your salary gonna be adjusted accordingly. You have used three of your possible cancellations this year, please complete t' proper paperwork upon your return.

Aq put down his phone.

Love you too.

Carl arrived on the patio carrying a large tray filled with all of Aq's favourite breakfast foods.

"Shall I prepare your work clothes, Boss?"

"I'm staying here today, sub. And you too. Cancel your meetings."

Carl nodded and left to do just that.

This is a slippery slope, thought Aq as he started eating. *But to hell with it.*

Chapter forty-seven

Teal found her volunteers in a wide-open display room, gathered around another hologram—this time a metre-long clownfish. They were sat cross-legged on a luxurious mauve carpet listening intently as the clownfish taught them about Queer Ecology. Teal secretly hated this kind of learning—'edutainment' as she called it—but it was clear that her volunteers were having a good time and weren't going anywhere fast.

Oh, what t' hell, she thought and joined them on the carpet.

The clownfish was speaking.

"Me, for example, I can change sex twice during my lifetime!" said the perky hologram.

The display morphed into an anemone, tentacles waving in the holographic seawater. Several clownfish swam around the audience. One of Teal's volunteers laughed as a large female flitted around her head before returning to the centre of the room.

"A single female and male live together in this poisonous anemone with a few babies that are neither male nor female…"

A larger fish—a barracuda—appeared from the edge of the room. To dramatic music, it swam straight over to the anemone, grabbed the female in its long mouth and swam away. Teal's volunteer squealed and looked like she might cry.

"Sometimes, as you see, a female sadly dies. When this happens, *amazingly,* t' male gains weight and… becomes female to take her place!"

The little holographic male before them did just that.

"Then, even *more* amazingly, one of t' juveniles sexually matures and becomes male. And together they create a happy new partnership!"

The two newly gendered fish swam happily around the room together.

"And so, we see how easily some animals can change sex." The room suddenly filled with holographic fish of many colours that swam around the audience. "And it's not only clownfish. Also parrotfish, cleaner wrasse, in fact a quarter of reef species change their sex at some point during their life."

The audience gasped. Teal rolled her eyes.

Everyone know this stuff.

The display changed and a new lesson began. Her volunteers were enraptured. Teal shifted uncomfortably on the scratchy carpet.

I'm ready to get out of here.

***

"Ready, sub?"

Carl couldn't reply even if he wanted to. He was gagged and hooded and his arms were above him chained to a hook in the ceiling. He tried to nod, but with the hood and the thick leather collar around his neck, he wasn't sure if Aq saw it. He made a thumbs up sign with his right hand.

I'm ready Boss, he said in his head. *I'm ready for everything you want to give me.*

"Just as we discussed, boy. No noise this time. I don't want to know how much it hurt you, I want to hit you, punch you and kick you and I don't want you to react."

Yes Master.

Aq finished strapping the boxing gloves on. He decided to let go a bit more this time. To give up control. That was becoming his fantasy, he realised, to let everything slide and just take what he wanted. He had gotten so close in the previous sessions and he wanted more.

Money is one thing, Aq thought. *But sex—and whatever this is? Kink, I guess. I had no idea this is what I wanted.*

But as Aq spent more time in the villa, enveloped in this new environment of luxury and service, it was fast becoming everything to him.

And apparently, it's what Carl want too.

"Questions, sub?"

Carl shook his head, braced himself and planted his feet.

Aq began.

* * *

"Time now for your questions," said the holographic teacher, which was now a Whip-Tail lizard.

Gay, Teal remembered. *A whole species of only females that fuck and nest together. Lesbian lizards. I loved those as a kid.*

One of Teal's youngest volunteers raised his hand.

"Go ahead," said the recorded voice of the lesbian Whip-Tail.

"Thank you, um... mister lizard," said the twelve-year-old boy. "I want to know... like, why are there only two genders?"

The lizard morphed into a red deer.

"That's a great question!" said the red deer. "But actually, there are more than two genders. Me, I'm a red deer for example. My species has at least four different genders—males with antlers, females with antlers, females without and males without. We all have different lives. And of course, humans have many, many more."

"Okay," said the boy, gaining confidence. "But like, maybe I mean sexes. Isn't everything a male or a female?"

"Another great question!" said the red deer. "In fact, you're more or less right. It's all about gamete size. Do you know what a gamete is?"

The teenage boy blushed a bit. "Sperm?"

"That's right!" the deer announced enthusiastically. "Sperm and eggs. Sperm are small gametes. Eggs are large. And pretty much every sexually reproducing plant and animal species on t' planet, minus maybe one or two, divide into these two groups—big gamete and small gamete, female and male."

"I thought so..." said the boy proudly.

"But of course, it's more complicated than different individuals being a single sex for their whole life..."

The room filled with fish and Teal tutted.

Not t' clownfish again.

"Some species have individuals who change sex during their lifetime, like these clownfish. Or for example, nearly all plants are both male and female at t' same time. And some, like this tropical ginger—" the figure turned into a talking ginger plant "—change sex every day. I make pollen in t' morning, and eggs at night!"

The boy looked unimpressed. He was interested in sex, not plants.

"And of course, many, many animals are intersex..."

The figure became a massive grizzly bear and a spotted hyena that filled the room.

"We are partly male and partly female. In some populations of bears, up to twenty percent of female bears are intersex—they have a clitoris-penis. They mate with it and give birth through t' tip of it. And *every* single female spotted hyena—" the hyena stepped forward dramatically "—has a penis almost exactly t' same as males, they can pee with them and they can get erections."

The teenage boy blushed again.

Teal was hungry. The display was impressive, she had to admit, but this information was all very basic. She had grown up watching Queer Ecology documentaries on TV. None of this was new. Jade appeared and sat next to her.

"Amazing, right?" he said in his usual sarcastic tone. "Have you seen t' clownfish yet?"

Teal ignored him. Being in a room of probably mostly cisgender people learning about sex and gender, she felt uncomfortably visible and was impatient to leave.

"And that's just animals and plants!" announced the hologram, suddenly becoming a giant magnified fungus, spreading its mycelia all over the floor and the ceiling. "T' *Schizophyllum commune* fungus for example has 32,328 different sexes! Can you imagine?"

Teal could imagine.

"Can we leave now, please?" she said to Jade. "Surely it's time to send these children back to school?"

Jade chuckled.

"T' bus is already waiting for them, I just wanted to see how long you'd last."

He stood up and the holographic fungus wrapped round his legs.

"That's all t' time we have for now kids," he announced.

They let out a collective moan but got up and obediently followed him out of the room. Teal dragged along after. Her good mood was definitely over.

When the last volunteer was back on the bus, Teal checked her phone and saw that she had a message from Cyan.

12.45 Cyan Tylor: Hey you. Me and Jade decided to take t' afternoon off. Come with him and meet me at your favourite café in town?

Just like that they take t' day off? Imagine t' drama if I did that. And since when are we hanging out with Jade?

Teal waved goodbye to the bus and typed her reply.

12.50 Teal Moore: On my way.

COMMUNICATION

Chapter forty-eight

Aq's phone was ringing on the balcony. It was the fourth call he'd received—and ignored—in an hour. He went outside and looked at the display. It was work. *What they want from me? I already cancelled.*

He looked at the flashing screen for a moment.

I should probably answer, it must be important.

Aq paused for a moment and looked at his gloves, shiny with various body fluids. He thought of taking them off but heard Carl's muffled sounds of pain in the other room and changed his mind. He pushed his phone under a cushion and turned back to his sub.

"Right, where were we?" he growled.

***

"These cupcakes are amazing!"

"Told you."

Teal had been complaining about the museum for the last twenty minutes. Cyan nodded vaguely while they ate their way through three cupcakes. Jade had got bored and gone to the eco-store down the road to pick up some supplies.

"It's just so commercial now. I mean every display is sponsored by Rak Industries or some other shit. It wasn't like that before, was it? There was literally a recruitment poster for Perimeter Security in t' bathroom that said, 'Ash and Pinar protected t' planet, you can too.' I mean, they did, obviously. Everyone know how much they loved t' forest, but like, would they have wanted t' park to be protected by eighteen-year-olds with rifles? Would they want t' resistance to be evicted?"

"We work for t' park," mumbled Cyan, their mouth full of cake. "You real don't think we're protecting t' forest?"

"I guess…" said Teal vaguely. But the truth was she was less and less sure.

Suddenly Jade came running in, slamming the café door behind him.

"We've gotta get out of here!" he shouted "There's a riot and it's coming up this street. I nearly got caught in it outside t' store!"

Cyan looked unfazed. "Sit down, Jade. There's a demo here every week, you know that."

It was Esperan policy to allow a large demonstration every week in the city centre; all the major non-profits took advantage of the opportunity to promote their work.

"No, it's something else. There were police chasing people."

"So then it's one of t' small 'counter' demos." Cyan said patiently between bites of cupcake. "They're not as official—but they also kind of are. I think Espera allow them to let t' radicals to let off some steam without doing any real damage."

Jade was losing patience.

"No, would you *listen* to me please? T' police… I think they shot someone. We need to leave *right now*."

"Esperan police don't carry weapons," said Cyan wrapping up their cake in a napkin in case they needed to make a quick exit. "Only t' Perimeter Security do."

"I'm telling you, they just shot someone. We need to leave."

Teal stood up, but hesitated. "I want to see. T' police can't just go around shooting people. I want to see what happened."

"Up to you," said Jade coldly. "But I'm not gonna stay around to get shot."

Cyan shrugged and, grabbing their cupcake, followed Jade to the door. They left the café and turned right.

From the other direction, Teal could hear screams. She stepped out of the door and defiantly turned left.

Standing in the street, it took a while for Teal to get her bearings. On Progress Avenue, one of Espera City's most beautiful planted streets—filled with palm trees and rosemary bushes—everything looked wrong. All the usual families and cyclists and dog-walkers were gone.

What t' fuck's happening here?

There was a tight group of people in the centre of the road, surrounded by a line of Esperan cops. Unlike the usual street cops who wore beige, organic hemp uniforms, Teal could see these were riot police in full military garb. Of course, they still wore the mandatory rainbow stripes on their helmets.

More police arrived. Teal watched as they erected some kind of mobile fence around themselves and the protestors. She recognised the banner that covered it—the same as the ones put around new eco-developments—printed cotton with a shiny Espera logo and the words 'Protect and Improve' in deep green.

Teal got closer but couldn't see anything of what was happening inside.

Cyan said they shot someone, could it be true? What can they be doing in there? This can't be okay. Not in Espera.

A woman in an expensive hat rushed past her.

"Wait, stop. Do you know what's happening here?"

The woman turned her head but barely paused.

"No-one know! They said it was resistance, but that's crazy! There's no resistance. Espera *is* t' resistance! Terrorists, if you ask me."

She ran on and disappeared into a boutique down the road. Teal looked around her and realised that she was the only person still standing in the street who wasn't inside the fence ring. Everyone else had gone back to their shops and houses.

What is this? I never saw something like this. Could it really have been a resistance demonstration? *She said they don't exist, but I know better. God, I want to do something. I gotta help.*

But the fence was four metres high and there was no-one to talk to. Everything in the street was quiet.

This is so fucking surreal.

Teal felt powerless. She turned to leave, but suddenly another crowd of people appeared around a corner. They were running and screaming. Teal could see the fear in their eyes. More riot cops chased after them and something—*yes, shots*—were fired. The sky turned white. Teal flashed back to her dream on the beach.

Tear gas. I gotta get out of here.

She ran. She was already partially blinded and held her shirt up over her mouth. Her eyes felt like they were bleeding and she couldn't catch her breath. She turned a corner and ran, with no sense of where she was going. She just knew she had to get to fresh air.

She turned another corner and suddenly, incredibly, she was out of it. She stood in a perfectly normal Esperan street. People carried cotton shopping bags and their babies on their backs. There were bicycles and a man was whistling.

Full of adrenalin, Teal shouted,

"Fuck this. Fuck all of this. How can you not know what's happening two streets away? People are being attacked over there!"

She was still catching her breath when a man stopped next to her.

"Excuse me, would you have time for a quick chat?" he asked her politely. "And would you be interested in supporting t' orphaned hedgehogs?"

Teal pushed him away and, following the tramline, started making her way to the next platform. She couldn't breathe, she couldn't think. Her world was no longer the same. *Nothing* was the same.

Chapter forty-nine

Aq paused a moment to catch his breath.

I didn't know it could feel like this.

This morning's session had been their most intense yet. Each time Aq released himself into his sub, he felt it more deeply. He was learning to channel his anger through kicks, slaps, spit and sweat. He was experimenting with his own limits with every punch. He still hadn't taken Carl above a seven.

There's so much more I can do.

As each hour passed, Aq became aware of something strange, something like another presence in the room—a bond that was sealing around Carl and himself and holding them together for the length of each session.

Afterwards, when they both collapsed on the bed in a chaos of sticky body parts, toys and assorted clothing, this seal broke and an ambiguous distance opened up between them. A thinning of veils, during which one of them had only to say a certain string of words and the entire fiction would fall apart.

But it never did. The moment closed each time and they retreated back into the protection of their roles. Aq knew they were bonded—tighter each day—and neither wanted to pull at the stitches.

"Master," gasped Carl, trying to catch his breath. "May... I?"

"Get washed up, sub. And wear your best suit this evening to serve Me My evening meal."

Carl nodded and removed himself from their play room.

Master, Aq noticed. *When did that happen?*

COMMUNICATION

* * *

Teal arrived back to the camp exhausted and filthy. Her hair was in knots. Cyan ran over to her, panicked.

"What happened to you? Are you okay? I was so worried about you. Were you in t' riot? T' demo or whatever it was? Are you okay?"

Teal didn't respond and walked past them to the bathroom without a word.

"Teal?" Cyan's voice was getting louder and higher. "Teal! Don't ignore me!"

Teal closed the door and locked it behind her. She emerged from the bathroom trailer an hour later. Her hair was perfect again, her make-up subtle but carefully done.

She passed the park bench where Cyan and Jade sat together surrounded by research papers, books on Shadow-Tails and a flask of tea.

"I'm going out," she declared. "I'm gonna take t' car back to t' rental place before closing tonight. I'll get a lift back with t' soldiers."

"No," said Cyan, standing up and knocking a map onto the ground. "Wait." Their hands on their hips, they were furious. "Sit down, Teal, we need to talk. It's not okay that you..."

Teal kept walking, got in the car and drove away.

As she pulled into the resistance village, Azure appeared standing in the road, like a vision emerging out of the dust. This time Teal wasn't surprised to see her.

I expected you to be expecting me.

"Come in, my dear," said Azure, offering her hand. "We have a lot to talk about."

Teal took her hand and followed her to the communal tent. Her face was already wet with tears.

"It was awful," said Teal, blowing her nose into a tissue. "I never saw something like that. I had no idea..."

"Drink your tea, dear."

Teal did.

"Now, listen. You got caught up in a resistance demonstration, yes. And it was as violently attacked as all resistance demonstrations are. T' miners are on strike and, trust me, what happened at t' mine today was a hundred times worse than what you saw in Espera City."

Teal sipped her drink silently, taking in the words.

"I gotta show you something. Are you okay now?" Azure stood. Teal nodded and got to her feet as well.

"Come."

Leaving the communal tent and crossing the central square of the village, Azure led the way to a large, round tent that Teal hadn't noticed before. It was covered in pink dust and barely stood out from the desert. Above the door, there was an image of a sage leaf in a circle. Teal recognised it as a healing sign, a hospital.

Azure pulled opened the door. Teal heard screaming.

***

Carl, wearing his best suit, served Aq his meal on the balcony. Aq nodded distantly as the tray arrived on the table and dismissed his servant with a wave. Grey Shadow-Tails were chasing each other in the trees near the villa and Aq vaguely recognised some birds that sang loud, proud melodies in the highest branches.

Perfect.

Every day the food became more elaborate, and every day Carl would slip something onto the tray as a gift. Aq opened the little box and found a bright, sauvite ring. He slipped it on his right pinky finger.

Just t' right size, of course.

The ring caught a sunbeam and refracted it into a thousand colours.

A good choice. A perfect choice.

Carl shuffled onto the balcony to serve Aq some red wine. He poured him a glass and turned to leave.

"You've spilled some on your suit, sub," said Aq, pointing at a red stain spreading on Carl's left side.

"Oh, Master. I'm very sorry. I think I'm bleeding."

And without another word, Aq's sub rushed off to the bathroom to redress his bandage.

Fuck. Did I take it too far? We need to talk.

***

There was blood everywhere. The room was a chaos of bruises, bandages and IV lines. Teal didn't know where to look.

"What t'…?"

"From t' demonstration at t' mine today," said Azure calmly. "It's not t' first time."

Teal watched silently as people ran back and forth applying dressings and poultices. The tent was thick with the stench of panic cut with the crisp, clean scent of comfrey leaves. Teal recognised Rouge, Azure's daughter, lying in a bed to the side. She had a dressing on her head and was unconscious, hooked up to an IV bag.

"Your daughter…" she said.

"Yes. T' company has been withholding workers' pay until they get greater yields of sauvite. But t' sauvite is running out. She stood up to t' commander and got hit with t' blunt end of a rifle for her trouble."

Her voice was a mixture of pride and anger.

"T' company carry rifles?" Teal asked. "Is it *that* bad?"

"You can't even imagine."

"But—" Teal knew how naïve she sounded as the words left her mouth. "—This is Espera."

"Not out here it isn't," said Azure, with a bitter tone that Teal had never heard her use before. "We don't exist. T' mines don't exist. Espera's precious solar panels are made out of magic and their sustainable economy is made out of miracles. And—" she paused for a moment "—you already got an idea of what happen if we bring our protest to t' city."

Teal thought back to the scenes in the city centre just a few hours before: the tear gas filling the air, the fence concealing whatever horrors were taking place inside. The dark green slogan. 'Protect and Improve.'

Azure looked at her face and said sadly, "You're beginning to see it, aren't you?"

Teal nodded.

Yes, I think I am.

Chapter fifty

"Are you okay, sub?"

"Yes, Master."

"Boss…"

"Yes, Boss."

"Did I injure you?"

"Only a little, Boss. An eight, but only an eight. It's fixed now."

"Can you take more?"

"Yes, Boss. Unless you'd like a swim while I fill t' jacuzzi?"

Aq took the hint.

"Do it."

"Hey Moss, how's you, mate? Sorry I didn't see you today. I…well I didn't come to work again."

"Aq, are you okay?"

"What? Yeah, I'm fine. I'm at t' villa, like I say. Just had a swim and my sub's running me a bath. I'm sitting by t' pool with a cigar as we speak. I decided to stay home—"

"—Aq shut up for a second. You really didn't hear?"

"Didn't hear what?"

"There was a demo today, in t' city centre."

Aq was distracted by a grey heron flying over the villa, its wings picked out in orange from the setting sun. "So what? There's always a demo."

"No, like a *riot*. Not t' A to B thing that happen every week. A bunch of our people were called in to protect t' city. It got really out of hand."

Aq remembered the missed calls he'd seen earlier.

They must have sent Perimeter Security in to control t' crowd.

"Shit," he said, shivering a little from a cool breeze coming in from the forest. "Was anyone hurt?"

"None of *us*, luckily. T' rioters got smashed up, though. They did t' surrounding-fence thing but there were too many to hide. It was all over Esperan news this evening."

"What were they rioting about?"

"Who know?" replied Moss. "Who care? This don't happen in Espera. And, Aq, t' weird thing was—" Moss paused for effect. "They said they were *resistance*... Aq? Aq, hello?"

Aq had a coughing fit.

"Yes...sorry. What? Resistance—that a *joke*?"

"That's what they told us."

"But don't these people know history? Espera *is* t' resistance."

"I know, right?"

"I mean, it's not perfect—we know that better than anyone. And there's Oak Grove... but, I don't know, this is so weird. Guess I better come to work after all."

"Yes, you should. Don't you have an evening shift at t' fence tomorrow?"

Aq could hear that his bath water had stopped running and Carl was back in the kitchen preparing him a drink.

"Yeah," he said. "I called in sick."

Moss laughed. "You sound very sick."

"*So* sick."

"Don't leave us, eh? With all your new-found wealth. Your dorm-mates already miss you."

"I'm sure they do."

Aq could sense Carl standing behind him, hovering near the door waiting to bring him his drink.

"Hey, mate, I gotta go. Take care okay? And don't get caught in any riots."

"I'll try, mate. See you tomorrow?"

For a second, the question hung in the air. Aq took in the still pool in front of him, reflecting a vibrant orange sky. The last thing he wanted to do was to go to work. He took a deep breath in and could smell jasmine in the evening air.

"Yes mate. See you then."

* * *

Teal was making her first herbal preparation and her nostrils burned from the smell. She had no idea what she was doing, but she was a fast learner.

And after all these years with Cyan, I know how to follow orders.

"Stir it faster and take it off t' heat before it burn. That's right, bona, like that. Now add more leaves."

She was happy just to be helpful. She was still shocked by what she saw. Fifteen patients—kids and adults—half of whom were unconscious, all beaten by security guards at the mine.

Esperan security, she reminded herself. *T' Green State did this.*

"Now, wrap it up in a bandage," one of the nurses instructed her. "*Bona*. Now use this tape to fix it to his knee... *Hey!*" he shouted at someone bringing candles. "Dowry sparkle ajax, please. She can't vada a thing in here!"

Outside the hospital tent, the sky was getting dark. Teal remembered that she was supposed to return the rental car before sundown.

Cyan won't be pleased if I—

Her patient woke suddenly and cried out in pain.

"Not so tight," said the nurse. "You gonna cut off his blood supply."

"Sorry," Teal whispered and returned to her work.

***

The jacuzzi water was so hot that Aq could feel his whole body. His heart raced, his skin broke out in goosebumps, and he let out an involuntary sigh as let go of the sides and slipped into the bubbles.

"Sub!" Aq shouted, once he had caught his breath.

Carl appeared on the deck and set down a gin cocktail and a bowl of olives on a small table within Aq's reach.

"Yes, Boss?"

"This is awesome."

Carl's face lit up.

"Anything else I can bring you, Boss?"

"Not for now. Go prepare your work stuff if you need to."

"Yes, Boss."

Carl silently disappeared back into the villa. Alone again, Aq took a sip of gin and slipped down deeper. Jets of water were massaging him from every side. He felt almost dizzy from pleasure.

Even if this end tomorrow, I'm never gonna forget this feeling.

***

"That's all we can do for tonight," said Azure, washing her hands in the sink. "We're all exhausted."

Teal was too tired to agree. She just nodded.

"Your bed is made up for you already. You remember where it is, no?"

Another nod.

"Bona nochey, Teal. And thank you for your help today."

"Bona noch-ey," she replied and stumbled her way over to the guest tent. She passed the rental car on her way and had a vague memory of how angry Cyan had been the last time they got fined for the car, but she was too tired to care. She climbed into bed with her clothes on and was out in seconds.

Outside the hospital tent, one of the nurses, a non-binary person with their hair in braids, came to stand with Azure and share a herbal cigarette in the cool breeze.

"Long night," said the nurse.

"Yes."

"Is Rouge okay?"

"She's gonna be okay."

"Fucking bastards."

Azure took a drag and exhaled. In the light from the tent, the passionflower smoke wrapped around them both in beautiful curls. Azure was exhausted and worried, but the herbs were already helping. She passed the cigarette to her friend.

"Teal with us now then?"

"Not yet. She's beginning to understand though."

"She still don't know how important she is, no?"

"How could she?" said Azure. "She work for Espera and she think her journeys are just weird dreams. She didn't even know about t' mines."

"Her life about to become a lot more interesting."

"That's certainly true." Azure finished the cigarette and stubbed it out in the sand. "Tomorrow gonna be a big day for her."

"Tomorrow already?"

"Yes."

"She's ready?"

"She's gotta be."

"Are you?"

"Everything that's gonna happen already happened," said Azure philosophically.

She left and went to her tent. She sat for a while in an old chair outside, watching the sky. It was fairly clear, the breeze was slight and hadn't picked up too much dust, and the moon rising on the horizon seemed exceptionally bright.

Tomorrow... don't know if I'm ever gonna be ready for this.
Azure put her hands together, said a silent prayer, and went to bed.

Chapter fifty-one

Aq lay in the jacuzzi and watched the moon rise over the forest. He was somewhere between entranced and dazed. As the hot water relaxed his muscles, he absently replayed the sessions from that day. He wasn't even sure how many there had been.

When do one session finish and t' next start? We've kind of been in one big session for a week already.

That afternoon there had been tears. There had been a fit of laughter during which Aq had had to remove himself from the scene until he could get himself under control. There had been several minor medical emergencies.

What a fucking day.

Aq realised he hadn't thought about money since that morning. He knew that Carl was drawing up a contract to give Aq greater control over his income.

I don't even suggest these things. T' house, t' money, this is all his big fantasy.

The moon was above the trees now. It was bright and full, and Aq could almost feel its light on his naked skin.

And tomorrow, work again.

He could feel Carl's presence behind him near the sliding balcony doors.

"Yes?"

"Sorry Boss. T' bed is ready for your massage now."

Aq leaned back and stretched. He took one last look at the moon and went in to be served. He lay on his front, a pillow beneath his chest and his forehead resting on his hands, as Carl massaged his feet and legs, his back, his neck. Even his ears.

I didn't even know that was a thing.

As much as Aq was allowing himself to relax, to play, this level of touch and intimacy was still new to him. He had never received a massage in his life before this week. In Espera, massage was still very much associated with spas and luxury, things that Aq knew little about. Luckily, Carl knew a lot. Aq had only to point at a region of his body—his lower back for example, which was always painful—and Carl would warm up some oil in his hands and make magic happen.

The feeling that came after the massage almost scared Aq sometimes. He panicked the first time, when he felt like his muscles didn't work properly. He felt like he was falling.

I'm relaxed, he had realised. *This is what that feel like.*

He rolled onto his back and looked up at the ceiling, carefully avoiding Carl's masked face. He found it much easier to enjoy being served when he got no clues at all about his sub's state of being. He tried not to listen to the grunts of exhaustion or the squeals of pleasure-pain during a session.

The mask his sub was currently wearing didn't even have eye holes, just a gap for his mouth. Aq liked that even more. He didn't want to humanise him, he had realised. When he did, he felt his training kick in—to take care of *Carl*, to serve *him*. To make sure he was happy and to put his own needs last.

Now that they had their consent system in place, Aq wanted to leave as much of that behind as possible.

His head was so deep in the fluffy pillows he almost missed that Carl was whispering something to him.

"What, boy? What are you saying?"

"Sorry Boss. I was suggesting something new for Your massage."

"Yes?"

"I asked if you'd like me to massage your prostate, Boss."

Aq paused for a moment. The word wasn't totally unfamiliar, but he wasn't sure.

That a muscle somewhere? Why would he be so specific?

"Sure, boy," said Aq looking at his sub. Behind the mask, he thought he caught the glimpse of a smile. "Do whatever give me pleasure."

Aq lay back and his head got lost again in the pillow. He vaguely heard a snap of some kind and figured it was Carl's knees, which often popped when he was working. Then he felt a cold wetness, just where he wasn't expecting it.

"Hey!" Aq shouted louder than he meant to. "Are you touching my ass?"

Carl froze. "Erm... yes Boss. I'm so sorry, I thought you..."

"I didn't say you could do that."

"But Boss. Sorry. Your prostate is inside."

"*Inside* my ass?"

"Yes, Boss."

No-one has ever touched my ass before, Aq thought. *That isn't a thing that men like me do.*

Men like me.

He rolled the words over in his head for a second while Carl waited silently. Until a week ago Aq had never so much as kissed a guy. Now, for all intents and purposes, he controlled one twenty-four hours a day. And they had fucked and played, in ways that Aq didn't know he desired. But *getting* fucked?

Bottoming, Moss call it.

That was something else.

That felt dangerous. And the idea of it, of Carl touching his prostate—apparently some mysterious pleasurable thing inside his ass—scared and excited Aq in equal measures.

Excited him, because it was one more new thing from a week of new things. And scared him, because when he thought about his asshole, and he thought about being fucked, it reminded him of the dream he'd had too many times from which he woke scared and aroused. The dream with the guy inside him. The dream with the beautiful, green dress.

"You can do it, boy," said Aq, almost despite himself. Releasing the words felt surreal. "But I'm in total control. You tell me what you're going to do and you obey me completely."

Carl nodded. "Always, Boss."

Aq lay back and they began.

Chapter fifty-two

Teal was on the research platform. It was hotter and more humid than she'd ever known it and she was trying to work, but she couldn't focus. Equipment kept moving away from her, she could never find what she needed. She thought she heard another Red Shadow-Tail above her—and jumped up to scan it—but it was just a magpie. Ten magpies. A world of magpies.

This is like a dream, she thought to herself. *But no, I don't dream about magpies.*

A voice called her from the ground below. She knew without looking that it was Jade and she realised that she hated his voice. She didn't trust him. He wasn't right. Cyan was there too somewhere, their voice was calling her. Teal. Teal.

"*Teal!* Wake up for god's sake!"

Teal opened her eyes. Cyan was really there, standing over her, hands on their hips. Teal saw the tent ceiling above them.

I'm in t' village, she thought slowly.

She lifted her hand slowly to count her fingers.

"You're not dreaming," said Cyan impatiently. "Something's happened."

Teal was still half in the dream. She mumbled "Jade..."

Cyan was taken aback.

"Yes," they said. "Fucking Jade."

* * *

Aq had the sense that he was dreaming as he walked down the carpeted corridors of the Union building to meet his assignment of the day.

Such an ugly purple, what do they even call that colour anyway?

The flashing recruitment screen in the elevator. The smell of organic lemon essential oil used by the cleaners. None of it seemed real to him. Not after what he had lived this week.

This is t' unreal version of life, he thought. *Working my ass off every day. Being insulted and patronised just to get enough money to survive. This is a dream. A nightmare.*

He turned the corner and saw his assignment waiting for him at reception surrounded by her luggage. She had just arrived from Paris. Her arms were crossed, and she looked very impatient.

"Sorry for t' delay, Ma'am," he said. "Let me take your luggage for you."

The businesswoman tutted and followed Aq with a sweep of her impractically long coat.

This has to be a dream.

∗ ∗ ∗

"What did Jade do?"

"Sit down and I'll tell you," ordered Cyan, pointing at a chair next to the bed. Teal had only just got out of bed and really wanted some coffee, but she sat.

Why do I do that? she thought vaguely. *I have no will of my own.*

"Well," said Cyan, still standing with their arms crossed. "You know he's been dating this Esperan nurse downtown."

Teal knew no such thing. In fact, she made a point of knowing as little as possible about Jade's personal life.

"Okay..."

"Well, she—t' nurse—turned up at t' camp late last night in a cab.

She wanted to warn us about him. And I think she just didn't know where else to go."

"Warn us about him?"

Cyan sighed.

"He *beat* her, Teal. She turned up bleeding."

"Fuck."

"Yes."

"Where is she now? Jade's girlfriend?"

"Her name is Maroon. She's here, having tea with Azure."

Teal rubbed her eyes.

"Here, in t' village?"

"Yes. Where else could I take her? You were gone and Indi's hopeless."

Teal stared at them.

"I guessed you might be here even though obviously you didn't bother to tell me, and your fucking phone don't work. I had to rent another car. That's coming out of your wages by t' way…"

"You brought Maroon here? Why?"

"I just told you."

Bringing her here make no sense, thought Teal. *Cyan must have panicked.*

"And Jade?"

"In town I guess. I called t' police." A momentary look of panic crossed Cyan's face. "Did I do t' right thing?"

Teal could see they hadn't slept much, if at all. She thought they might even cry.

"What do we do next, Teal? This is fucked up."

Teal stood and touched their shoulder lightly.

"I'm gonna go get us some coffee and we can make a plan."

She left the tent with an overwhelming sense of things unravelling around her. The Shadow-Tail, the resistance, the riots, and now Jade. Her life was changing fast and she wasn't in control. Cyan looked like they were falling apart.

It's going to be a hell of a day, she thought.

She stood for a moment outside the tent in the dusty morning air.

It's more than all that. There's something else.

Teal reached up and stretched. She bent to the sides and touched her toes. It didn't help.

Something isn't right. Something...

She pushed the thought away and went to get coffee.

***

Aq felt like it had been the longest morning of his life. His assignment was everything he had imagined. She was incredibly rude, demanding, and insisted on calling him 'boy'. He finally got her off to her meeting—'Very important, you know. Crucial to your little Esperan economy...'—and he now had twenty minutes to run errands for her.

Twenty minutes to get back to the delegate's room, make sure room service had done their job, collect her complementary spa tickets from reception—'I've spent *quite* enough time waiting there thank you very much. Really, t' bureaucracy of this place!'—and get back to take her to the delegate lounge for drinks.

He already knew he wasn't getting a tip from this person. He wasn't going to get it all done in time unless he ran, and she was definitely the kind to make a complaint. Aq picked up his pace, turned the corner at the end of the corridor at a run, and collided with a cleaner's trolley, knocking lemon-scented hemp fibre towels all over the floor.

I'm ready to wake up now.
Wake up, Aq. Wake up.

Chapter fifty-three

I'm to wait outside apparently," said Cyan, standing by the door of the communal tent, their arms crossed as usual. "Even though *I'm t'* one who brought Maroon. Even though *I'm t'* one who—"

"I'm sure Azure has her reasons," said Teal as she stepped into the communal tent, leaving Cyan outside kicking their foot into the dust. Azure sat next to the table pouring tea. A young person was curled up under a blanket in the corner in floods of tears.

This isn't right, thought Teal, casting a glance over towards the hospital tent. *I feel bad for this Maroon person, but t' village has enough going on right now.*

Azure looked surprisingly calm and offered her tea as she sat down.

"Azure," said Teal softly. "I'm really sorry to bring more drama to your door just as you..."

Azure shook her head. "Nonsense. Maroon gonna stay here for a while. I was expecting her. And we need another nurse."

Teal looked surprised. "You *knew* this was coming?"

Azure smiled.

"Didn't you?"

Teal had to think for a moment as she sipped her tea. She had never trusted her precognition. She always felt like she was supposed to—trusting her feminine intuition or something—but she never had the confidence. And besides, Cyan had always told her it was nonsense, that no-one could see the future and why did Teal think she was so special?

But Azure didn't talk to her like that. Quite the opposite, she even seemed to assume that Teal would see things coming or relive what had already been. She had even called it *journeying*, the same word that people used when they talked about Ash's legendary abilities.

But I'm not like that, thought Teal. *I'm not special.*

She flashed back suddenly to her dream earlier that morning. The noise of the helicopter and what she could have sworn had seemed to be the Femme Riots. Teal had that feeling again deep in her gut.

Certainty, she realised. *A message.*

* * *

Aq received the message just as his assignment was eating her six-star meal.

> 12.49 Carl Kingson: Boss. I miss You. I am at a meeting now, but I want You to know that I wish I was serving You right now. You were perfect last night, Boss. I have sent Beige to deliver a gift—he'll be in t' car park at one PM, I hope that's okay. Please don't work too hard. You deserve only t' best. Your sub.

Aq looked at the time: 12.50. He wasn't supposed to take his break until two because one of his colleagues was off sick and he needed to take care of her assignment as well as his own.

Fuck that, he thought. And headed down to the car park, where Beige was waiting for him with an envelope.

"Thanks Beige. Did he tip you already?"

"Generously, sir."

"You don't need to call me 'sir', you know."

"It's in my contract, sir."

"You have a contract, mate?"

"Of course, sir. For t' next six months."

Aq touched the envelope. 'To be opened in private' was written in

Carl's careful handwriting.

"Would you like me to take you somewhere for your lunch, sir?" asked Beige, holding the passenger door open.

Aq thought about it for a moment. He had three more hours at Union and then he was on Perimeter duty that evening. Getting out for an hour seemed like a very good idea. He took out his phone.

"Moss? Are you on your lunch yet mate? Oh already? Okay. No, nothing. Just was gonna take you out in t' car if you wanted. Sure mate. Yeah, you have a good day too."

Aq hung up and paused.

He realised that he was feeling something deep inside that he couldn't place. *Stomach pain? No, a different kind of feeling.*

Is it loneliness? Do I miss Carl? Is that what's happening?

But that didn't seem quite right.

It's just a really weird day.

"Take me to T' Shadow-Tail's Table," he commanded, throwing the envelope in the back of the car and getting in the passenger seat. "And call ahead. I want t' best table in t' house."

***

"Did you know?"

Azure repeated her question, her voice intense. Curled up in her blanket, Maroon had stopped crying and was wiping her eyes.

"About Jade?" Teal replied.

"Yes."

"I guess I... I don't know... I had a feeling about him?"

"You never liked him?"

"I never liked him. We've fought a few times."

"And you didn't feel he could be trusted."

Maroon sniffled again but still didn't speak.

"That's true. I never felt completely safe with him," said Teal.

Where is she going with this?

"So, you knew."

"I knew that he was going to beat up his lover?" she said, looking at Maroon who was picking at the table. "Of course not."

"We don't always know t' details," said Azure patiently. "But we know."

"Okay."

"What's gonna happen tonight, for example. What does your instinct tell you?"

"Erm... I don't know. I guess me and Cyan gonna go back to t' camp at some point. And, I don't know, dinner? Bed?"

"You know."

Teal took a deep breath and realised that she *did* know. That feeling deep in her gut that had been with her since last night. She knew. She was certain.

"Something is coming."

Azure looked deadly serious and nodded.

"Precisely."

Chapter fifty-four

Teal was daydreaming; staring at the central pole of the tent, trying to assimilate.

Azure looked thoughtful and spoke softly.

"It's not about you, you know? It's not about being special or magic."

Teal's felt a touch of disappointment. "Okay."

Maybe it's like Cyan say. I'm not important.

"It's not about you being alone, disconnected, I mean. That's just what individualism has taught you."

Teal avoided eye contact and played with a strand of carpet. Azure continued.

"T' world *is* special though—t' blackbirds and t' woodlice and t' clouds and t' dust. Shadow-Tails and *cerezo* trees. So when you know things, and you see how things are gonna be, you're just connecting, reclaiming your place in that bigger picture."

Teal looked up.

"It's about t' greater fabric of life," Azure concluded. "It's not us as individuals. We're all part of it. We're *all* special."

Teal nodded and smiled.

"You look freaked out," said Cyan when Teal came out of the communal tent a while later. "What happened in there? What's t' plan with Maroon?"

Teal wasn't ready to talk about it yet. She walked past Cyan in a dream and headed for the sink to get some water.

"Hey! Can you even *hear* me? Come back here, stop fucking

ignoring me!"

Teal kept walking. Cyan chased after her.

"We gotta get ready," said Teal when she put down her empty glass.

"Ready, ready for what?" Cyan's voice was getting louder again. "Look, I don't really understand what this thing is you have with Azure, all your riddles and nonsense—"

"It's not nonsense."

"You *real* believe that you were in t' Femme Riots?"

Teal looked shocked.

"Yes, your *friend* in there told me about your hallucination this morning. Apparently *she* believes it was real too. Like Ash or something."

"I think it *was* re—"

"It's *not*, Teal. I'm sorry. But you're just not that special."

"I—" Teal's voice almost broke. She took a deep breath and it steadied. "Go home, Cyan."

"Excuse me? What t' f—"

"No-one invited you here. We don't need you. Go home."

Cyan was about to start yelling again, but Teal walked right past them. Her heart pounding, she went back into the communal tent and without a word she sat down and poured herself another cup of tea. Maroon had stopped crying and sat with Azure in a gentle silence. They all heard the car pulling away, turning hard in the dust and screeching out of the village.

"We have work to do," said Azure softly. "It's time."

* * *

Back to work, thought Aq, as Beige pulled them into the Union car park. *But I haven't open my gift yet.*

He read the envelope again: 'To be opened in private'.

So mysterious.

"Catch ya later, mate," said Aq as he got out.

"Yes, sir."

Aq checked his watch. He was late. He left Beige polishing the car's bonnet and walked over to the car park bathroom. He let himself into a stall and looked at the envelope. He had that feeling again. He was hard, but he had been hard each and every time Carl had given him a gift.

It's not that.

He felt strange, a bit sick even.

Fuck it.

Aq opened the envelope and took out a carefully folded letter. He read it. He read it again. Then he ran out of the toilet, shouting.

***

"Come with me, please."

In silence, Teal followed Azure back up to the hill that overlooked the village, back to where she had first learned about Azure's family.

"Maroon is in t' hospital tent," announced Azure. "Already keeping herself busy."

"She okay?" asked Teal.

"She's gonna be. We gotta deal with your workmate too at some point—if t' police didn't already—but not today."

Azure sat in the dust and said "Sit."

Teal sat.

"No talking for a minute please. Just slow down and listen to t' wind."

Teal listened.

"Taste t' dust on your tongue."

Teal could taste it. It was acrid, metallic.

"Feel your body."

Teal tried, but her thoughts were wondering. She wasn't present. She felt herself move although she sat perfectly still. The world was spinning.

"Don't worry, my love, we're gonna go together this time." Azure squeezed Teal's hand. "I'm with you."

Above them a crow was calling, and another called back. The desert was peaceful.

But Teal could only hear screaming.

They were in the forest. That much she could tell. The humidity and the smell of American cherry bark and eucalyptus were as familiar to her now as her own hands.

We're in t' forest. And it's night. It should be quiet, should be that peaceful time when everyone is asleep.

But as Teal and Azure stood between the dark trees, the screaming surrounding them was growing louder.

* * *

"Wait! Wait! Beige, stop t' car!"

Aq's voice echoed through the car park as he ran back to the car. Beige was just pulling out. He parked and rolled down the window.

"Yes, sir?"

"Take me to Dignity station, right now!"

"Of course, sir," said Beige, getting out and opening the passenger door for him. "Anything wrong, sir?"

"Yes!" said Aq as he got in and slammed the door. "Carl is fucking leaving me!"

* * *

"Azure," said Teal very slowly. "Where are we? What's happening?"

Azure didn't respond. She grabbed Teal's hand, and suddenly they were running. Teal didn't recognise this part of the forest. She had certainly never lived this moment before. The screams behind them were unforgettable.

"We're in t' future?" Teal gasped as Azure took her around a particularly thick tree. She didn't respond and didn't slow down. Teal felt sick with confusion but kept running.

"Here," Azure whispered, suddenly dragging Teal down behind a giant bush of brambles. Teal got down as small as she could and asked again.

"We're in t' fut—"

Azure's eyes flashed. She put her hand over Teal's mouth. They could hear the people behind them coming closer. Azure pointed with her chin beyond the bramble bush out to a break in the forest.

A gated driveway, Teal realised. And some sort of massive villa at the end of it.

Azure indicated for her to get down lower behind the bush, just as a screaming crowd erupted from the forest all around them, running towards the house.

* * *

Aq read the letter again, his hands shaking:

Master, Boss.

I'm so sorry, but I gotta leave. It isn't about You, You are perfect. I got scared and I need to be alone for a while. I will explain one day, Master, and I hope You forgive Me.

You gave me everything I ever wanted, and so much more.

I wish I could please You more,

Your sub.

Aq ran onto the platform, but he was too late. He saw Carl already sitting in the solar train next to the window and the doors were closed. He looked like he might be crying.

Aq was waving the envelope in the air and managed to get Carl's attention. He mouthed the words, "What t' fuck?"

Carl looked confused for a moment and then made a turn-the-page gesture with his left hand. Just then, with a piercing whistle, the train pulled away.

Aq stood frozen for a moment in disbelief. He pulled the letter out of the envelope again. He turned it over this time and saw that there was something printed on the back in very small letters.

> T' villa and its contents are Yours now, Boss. You're gonna find a contract at t' house and an address to send t' completed forms to. I'm sorry.
> Your sub.

Aq couldn't move his feet. He wanted to, but he couldn't. Something was inside him, pulling him away from himself, away from his own body.

He felt a shiver run slowly down every vertebra of his spine and then, as quick as a flash of understanding or a decision made, Aq was gone.

Chapter fifty-five

All the lights of the villa flashed on. Teal saw two figures running out towards them. One of the people she had never seen before, a skinny guy in a security uniform, and someone else with long hair and heels.

As they arrived and unlocked the massive gate, letting it swing open, she realised that she definitely knew the person with long hair. Teal could see—clear as day—that it was her. Herself. She looked tired, scared. But it was definitely her.

She watched as the future Teal held the gate open for the crowd of people. They rushed in and Teal locked the gate behind them. She and the security guy ran back into the villa as a thunderous sound appeared above them.

A helicopter, she realised. *Another one.*

She looked at Azure for confirmation, but her friend was looking all around like she was taking in every detail. Like this would all be useful one day. Like this was a crucial moment in time that might change everything.

Then Azure pointed behind them, into the darkness of the forest. Teal saw nothing—just trees, the footprints in the mud left by the crowd, nothing special.

Someone was there. He stepped out of the gloom and Teal could see that it was that same guy—the skinny one in the security uniform. He was looking straight at her, his eyes wide with fear. Teal looked back over towards the villa. He was there too running back towards the house.

But I... Who t'...

Then Azure grabbed her hand, looked her straight in the eyes and said:

"It's time."

On the hill overlooking the resistance village, Teal was on her knees throwing up.

On the platform, Aq was on his knees throwing up.

This is all happening too fast, they thought. *What t' fuck just happened? Wait... Who are you? Who are you?*

Then it was broken, and time moved on.

"Let it out, my love. It's gonna be over soon."

Teal could hear Azure's voice and feel her hand on her lower back, but she couldn't stop. She couldn't process what she had just lived, she couldn't think, she just had to get it out. Her head hurt. Her body was in spasms. She had to let it out.

"Sir? Sir? Are you okay? Sir, what happened?"

Aq couldn't speak. He took the handkerchief from Beige, wiped his mouth with it and looked at the vomit on the platform in front of him with disbelief.

Where... When?

"Here, sir. Let me get you back to t' car. I'm gonna have station staff sort this out for you. That's it, this way."

"It's over now. Here's a glass of water."
"Don't worry, you're gonna feel better soon."
"Let's go back to t' village."
"Where would you like to go, sir?"

5. Connections

Prelude

"Now take a deep breath. And imagine a beam of pure, white light emanating from your crown chakra. Good. Another breath. Breathe out the darkness, breathe in the light. Dark out. Light in. Good. And take your client into the stretch. Very good. Now a short rest—any questions?"

"I'm confused," declared one of the students. "Isn't yoga a Hindu practice?"

"Of course," replied the teacher, tucking her blond hair behind an ear.

"But you talked about energy meridians and acupressure points. Isn't that Traditional Chinese Medicine?"

"Yes." The teacher's voice was defensive. "I also have a certificate in acupuncture."

"Great. But I guess I'm confused about the term, 'Thai Yoga massage' then. I mean, Thailand and India are pretty different. And isn't Thai massage Buddhist?"

"I have been to Thailand."

"I'm sure it was lovely."

"*And* India."

"Well done. I'm just concerned that we might be mixing things here. Don't these different practices ultimately come from different cultures? I know cultures have always mixed—and of course there are connections between Thai massage and India—but how respectful is it for us as white people to blend them all together? Isn't Thai massage, well, Thai?"

The teacher smiled patiently.

"I understand now. And I see your confusion. I was unsure as well, but last summer I went on retreat learning about American Indian spirituality." The teacher touched her gold dreamcatcher necklace lovingly. "And I came to a great realisation."

"Okay..."

"Despite our differences, all of our cultures are truthfully just one great culture of humanity."

"But—"

"We are one."

"But—"

"Thank you everyone, have a peaceful weekend."

Chapter fifty-six

Moss was at work behind the Union reception. Since the large conference—'Sauvite Technology Beyond Espera'—had finished, the building was almost empty. He preferred it this way. At least he could catch up on his reading. He leaned back in his very comfortable, hand-woven rattan chair, surrounded by oxygenating house-plants, and turned another page.

No-one had checked in for over an hour, the phones were silent. Moss was getting sleepy. He could see from the sun streaming through the windows that it was late afternoon. His book wasn't that good, and he decided he should probably order some coffee. His friend Amar down in the café usually ran him up a cup if she wasn't busy. He'd been caught napping at his desk too many times already.

Moss was warm and his eyes were almost closed. His book slid off his lap and landed on the floor with a thump.

Right, coffee.

He reached for the phone, but it started ringing before he touched it. Then the secondary phone started ringing. And his cell phone in his pocket.

What t' fuck?

He answered the phone.

"Reception here," he said as calmly as he could.

"Moss is that you?"

"Of course it's me—"

"This is Vi, down at operations. We need you at t' fence, every security guard is getting called up. There was some kind of incursion."

"I—shit, okay. Who's gonna take over reception?"

"One of t' cleaners can do it. A monkey could do your job."

"Well, thanks Vi-down-at-operations, I really appreci—"

Moss heard the beep-beep-beep of a disconnected call. He put the phone back down.

Racist, classist, fucki—

All the phones started ringing at once again.

"Okay, okay! I'm going, I'm going!"

Moss left the reception to get his security uniform from the dorm. He ran to the lift, but then caught himself and slowed down.

What do I care? he thought.

He turned and, walking as slowly as he could, he took the stairs.

***

"Azure, Azure, it's happening!"

The runner was out of breath.

"So soon?"

"Yes, t' first villages are already at t' fence."

"We're coming."

The runner headed back down the hill.

Azure turned to Teal who was still on all fours recovering. "No more time to rest I'm afraid. Things are moving faster than I expected."

"What—" Teal tried to clear her head. "What's going on?"

"Some of t' villages have an action planned. A visibility demo for t' miners, at t' fence. Come, we need to get back down."

Azure led the way back down, her feet kicking up pink dust.

Teal followed and asked in a tight voice, "Are they going to breach t' fence?"

She was already certain.

Sometime soon, t' resistance gonna breach t' fence and enter t' park. And there's gonna be helicopters, a villa and that mysterious security guard. But I'm not ready for that yet. There's so much I don't understand.

"Not today," said Azure firmly. "That's not t' plan."

But things don't always go according to plan.

They arrived back at the central square of the village. Teal realised that it was already afternoon.

How long were we gone?

She swallowed and pushed her shoulders back.

"What do you want me to do?"

"It's not time yet," said Azure calmly. "Please assist Maroon in t' hospital tent."

Teal was relieved. Stirring herbal mixes and changing bandages sounded much more doable than breaching the fence. She wasn't quite ready for the revolution.

"Are you sure?"

"This is where t' revolution needs you today."

It's like she read my mind.

"Okay, are you gonna be alright?"

"What's gonna happen has already happened," said Azure mysteriously. She abruptly turned her back and walked away.

I'm never gonna get used to that.

Teal took a deep breath to calm her heart and stepped into the hospital tent.

* * *

As Aq sat in the car he turned his phone on. He had twenty missed calls. Half were from work and half were from Moss. He dialled Moss first.

"Mate, where were you?"

"I—"

"We've been called up t' fence, some kind of incursion apparently? Where are you?"

Aq swallowed hard.

"Nearly at t' Union Building. You're still there?"

"Yeah, I'm waiting for you at transport. Grab your gun and get down here mate, we're gonna go together."

"Be there in ten minutes." Aq hung up the phone and turned to his driver. "Go faster. Much faster."

Chapter fifty-seven

"Where were you, mate?" Moss asked as Aq arrived panting. "I mean, I'm not in any great rush to protect t' fucking park, but our commander's not too happy."

"It's complicated." Aq poked his friend in the arm. "You look very handsome in green."

Unlike Aq, who worked for both security and the Protection service, Moss rarely left the Union Building. Aq hadn't seen him in his Protection uniform since they trained together five years before.

"I look good in everything!" Moss adjusted the gun on his shoulder. "But I hope I don't gotta use this thing. It's been years."

"Please don't shoot anyone, Moss."

"All right mate," he laughed. "I do my best. Transport's here. Let's go protect t' world or something."

Aq laughed for the first time that day.

"Yes. You and me, Moss, we are just that important."

"*So* important."

"T' *most*."

A fog of adrenaline and testosterone hit them as they got into the service bus. It reminded Aq of his dorm.

How do these guys smell so bad? he wondered to himself. *Carl don't smell like that.*

Carl...

He pushed the thought out of his head. He had no way to process everything that had happened in the last hours. He took a seat next to Moss.

"I bet you missed that smell out in your fancy villa, no?" said Moss laughing.

Aq smiled but didn't answer. He was looking out the window at the other service buses passing them on the road, all full of his workmates in uniform.

This is half t' service in Espera, he thought. *This shit must be serious.*

* * *

The atmosphere in the hospital tent was heavier than the day before. Although there were fewer injured to be taken care of and an extra nurse, everyone seemed more serious and barely anyone spoke. Even the patients were quiet.

Teal wanted to ask for details. About the riots at the mines and if anyone knew what was happening at the fence today. But the room was so quiet, she couldn't bring herself to speak. She saw that the comfrey mix was running low and sat next to Maroon, who was preparing more.

Teal offered her a weak smile and got to work.

* * *

Cyan and Indi were sat at the camp picnic table eating lunch when the soldiers started driving by.

"Perimeter's busy today," said Indi between mouthfuls.

"What's that?" Cyan was distracted. They were a little scared that Jade might turn up at the camp.

Unless t' police took him away. Who t' hell know? We're falling apart here and as usual, I'm t' one who has to hold it all together.

"Look, another one," said Indi putting down her fork. "That's t' fifth Service bus that's gone by in t' last hour! Is there something happening at t' fence?"

Cyan came back to the present. "That *is* a lot of buses. Let's go to t' platform and see what's happening."

"I don't know," said Indi, stroking the back of her neck nervously. "It's also a lot of guns..."

Cyan pushed away their plate and stood up. "Let's go."

***

A leader stood up at the front of the bus and announced,

"Right. So, as you heard, we got an incursion at t' perimeter, near one of t' research posts. A large group of people from beyond t' park is protesting—about t' mines or some such nonsense—and they seem to be trying to get t' attention of Esperan media. There are at least three TV channels already set up filming. They can't breach t' fence of course, but there are a lot of important diplomats around this month for conferences, so we've been sent in as a show of strength. 'T' park is sacred' and all that."

There was a hum of laughter among the soldiers. This was one of the most ridiculed of Union slogans.

"As long as they don't do anything crazy, don't do anything at all. You're just there to look impressive. Am I clear?"

"Yes, leader," said the soldiers.

"And guys?" the leader looked over the bus-load of young and untrained window cleaners and spa masseurs. "Please don't shoot anyone, okay?"

More laughter. Aq didn't laugh. He looked out of the window and watched the endless miles of trees and fence pass by. Then they passed a clearing. Two people walking near a park bench. Tents and a bathroom wagon.

T' research camp, he realised. *We're nearly there.*

As they got out of their bus, Aq saw another six unloading soldiers. Some were professional Perimeter service, but a lot of them were on-call service, like Moss. Aq recognised Mag the cleaner and Purple who sorted out wages.

"It's so weird seeing everyone in green," he said to Moss. "We never even have drills anymore. There's just no point."

"Right?" said Moss. "This never happen."

He paused and looked thoughtful.

"Because this is Espera."

After a few minutes, their shoal—the Union carefully avoided words like 'unit' or 'squadron'—were ordered towards the fence. Aq and Moss followed behind at the back. Neither of them were particularly interested in getting involved if they could avoid it.

They walked for five minutes through the *cerezo* forest, their shoal marching loosely with almost everyone either checking their sauvite phones, taking selfies—twenty-first-century style—or chatting to their colleagues as they went.

We look nothing like an army, thought Aq watching them.

They soon arrived at the fence and Moss let out a gasp of surprise.

"Fucking hell."

Chapter fifty-eight

Cyan arrived at the platform and unhooked their rope for Indi to follow.

"My god, look," they whispered as Indi arrived and unhooked herself.

Where there were usually only one of two bored security staff patrolling while the other would wandered off into the forest to pee, there were now at least a hundred soldiers lined up in front of the fence. Another fifty stood above them leaning out of the watchtowers.

"So many guns," replied Indi breathlessly. "I don't like this at all."

Cyan pulled a scanner out of their bag.

"Creepy, right? But it's gonna make a great picture for t' research paper."

* * *

As he and Moss took up position on the forest floor, Aq could see the TV camera crews a hundred metres away, filming through the fence. Compared to the military presence, the demonstration itself was smaller than he had expected—barely thirty or forty people with banners standing in a clearing among the trees, illuminated by afternoon sunlight.

"Hardly worth all this fuss, right?" he said to his friend.

Moss shrugged. "Don't these people have homes to go to? I sure have better things to do than stand here sweating in these boots."

"Falling asleep in reception?" said Aq with a wink.

"Precisely."

There was some kind of movement from the crowd on the other side. There was a chatter of voices and an older woman stepped out with a megaphone. Soldiers levelled their guns at her nervously.

Aq flashed back to what he had seen at the station. The forest. The villa. The helicopter. The two people huddled down behind the bramble bush.

"Listen up!" Aq heard her say. "My name is Azure. Yesterday at one PM, workers at t' sauvite mine Harmony were attacked by security staff for refusing to work. They haven't been paid for over two weeks and were defending their right to peacefully protest."

Moss rolled his eyes and sighed, but Aq leaned forward. He wanted to hear what this was all about.

"As we know, t' Union allow protest when it suit them, when it boost their reputation. But t' Union and Espera are also built on sauvite and nothing get in t' way of profit. So we were attacked."

Azure's voice broke a little. She swallowed and continued even louder.

"My daughter, Rouge, was among those injured. She has a concussion and possibly brain damage. We can't even take her to get proper medical attention because she's on Esperan lists and they won't let her in t' hospital. *This* is what your great Green State do to its workers. *This* is what your precious eco-democracy look like."

Azure's words rang through the trees. The protesters waited. The soldiers, their guns levelled at the crowd, waited. The TV crews were filming everything and streaming it live back to screens across the city.

Aq had the sense of time slowing down around him. To the right, Moss and so many others had their guns pointed, fingers shaking near their triggers. Ahead, the protesters, banners held high in the clearing. Fuck your Union. No Pride in t' Perimeter. Environment not Eviction. Aq could hear a bird calling somewhere behind them. A crow. Then it happened.

One of the protesters pointed up to the canopy above them. Aq saw something dark jumping from one branch to another across the fence and into the park.

"A Red Shadow-Tail!" someone shouted.

The lines of soldiers leaned forward to get a better look. The crowd of protestors pointed, shouting. Someone panicked. A shot rang out, a warning, stay back. There was a moment of stunned silence, and then the protesters pulsed. Towards the fence, towards their park.

Azure was at the front, walking stick in hand and she locked eyes with Aq.

I know her. I know her.

Another shot rang out, so close that it left Aq's ears ringing.

Moss...

The woman swayed, and dropped.

Chapter fifty-nine

Cyan dropped the scanner. With a crash it bounced off the wooden platform and down into a thick bush of brambles and ivy.

Indi dove down, flattening herself.

"It's fine, get up, I just dropped something is all," said Cyan, their voice tight with anger and fear.

Indi sat back up, looking ashamed.

"What happened out there?"

"I don't know. I can't see any more than you can."

"But we heard gunshots. Did they shoot someone?"

"I don't know."

"Did they—"

"Indi! I don't know! And I don't real want to be so close to those trigger-happy eighteen-year-olds anymore. Let's get back to t' camp, okay? We can listen to t' radio and find out—"

Indi was attaching the harness before Cyan had finished speaking.

* * *

Aq stood frozen. He thought for a moment he was going to throw up again. Blood on trees and blood on the fence. Panicked voices and TV cameras. Moss, barely a metre to his right, was still pointing his gun.

"Enough," said Aq with a calm he didn't feel. "Put it down now, Moss."

He took the gun from his friend and laid it on the ground.

"I didn't mean to, I didn't—"

"I know, mate."

The leader from the bus arrived with five thick-set guys in security uniforms.

"Moss," he said. "Was it you?"

Moss stood and turned away from the blood and Azure's body in the dirt. "Take me away from this place."

Aq watched on as they handcuffed his best friend in the world and walked him away from the scene.

Chapter sixty

Teal could hear voices outside the hospital tent. People were terrified. That much she could tell.

"What are they saying?" asked Maroon, looking up from the bandage she was changing. "What is that language?"

"Polari," replied Teal.

"Do you understand it?"

"Just bits and pieces. Hold on, I find out what's t' problem."

Teal put down the dressings she was folding and stepped out of the tent. Three people were standing in the central square. They were shouting and waving their arms. Teal couldn't understand them, but she knew fear when she saw it.

"Hey, sorry," she said approaching them. "But people are injured inside, could you take this somewhere else?"

One of the people gave her a look and another spoke "Teal, is it?"

"Yes."

"I—I don't know how to say this. The demonstration at t' fence was attacked. People are on their way back now."

"Oh fuck, sorry. I didn't mean to—are people injured?"

"Yes..." the person looked away from her, out onto the horizon. "Azure was shot."

"Fuck. Fuck." Teal felt sick. "Is she okay?"

"They killed her, Teal. Azure is dead."

Teal's head spun. She sat down in the dust and hugged her legs to her chest.

"No," she said. "No, no, no..."

***

Aq got out of the car and closed the door without saying a word to his driver. He walked up the driveway and dug in his pocket for the key.

I've never opened it myself before, he realised.

He stepped inside. The house was still and quiet. Aq went to the kitchen. It was pristine just as Carl always left it. He opened the fridge and took out a pot of leftovers from the night before. He put them on the biogas stove, but he realised he didn't know how to light it.

Is it automatic? he wondered.

He looked for a spark button but couldn't find it. He looked for a match, a lighter, anything.

"Where are you when I fucking need you Carl!" he shouted and hit out, knocking the pot onto the floor and spilling food all over the clean white floor.

"Fuck this!" he shouted, and he fell to his knees. "Fuck all of this. Fuck all of this. Fuck—"

Aq cried then for the first time in as long as he could remember. He curled up on the food-splattered floor and cried.

***

What's gonna happen has already happened.

Teal was sure now that Azure had known but hadn't wanted to tell her. And on some level, Teal had known too. That feeling she'd had in her stomach for days. She shook her head, but it wouldn't clear. The tears came then. She lay down in the dust and tried to make herself very, very small.

***

Hours went by. Night came, but Aq only vaguely noticed the change. He could hear owls calling in the backyard, hunting under cover of darkness. A ray of moonlight came through the window and illuminated his body, still curled up on the floor. He couldn't move. He didn't know how.

Carl is gone. Just like that. And my best friend in t' world...killed someone who I know from a vision of t' future—or something. Outside this house that Carl bought me.

Carl.

Aq's stomach hurt when he thought of him.

Do I miss him, is that what this feeling is?

Aq curled up smaller and covered his face to block out the moonlight.

Fuck all of this. I'm never gonna leave this place.

Poor Moss, where are you now?

***

Moss sat in his cell staring at the screen on the opposite wall showing twenty-four-hour news cut with documentaries. He had seen himself shooting that woman at least thirty times already.

Azure, they said her name was, though no-one seem to know where she came from.

More than anything he wished he could switch off the screen and get some sleep, but apparently 'learning about t' world' was part of Espera's restorative justice programme for prisoners and being put in front of a TV was considered a cheap form of education.

Moss couldn't close his eyes without seeing the same scene anyway, so it made little difference.

He lay back on the organic cotton bed and stared up at the ceiling. The programme had changed to a documentary about the Esperan reefs now, which wasn't much better. For the next morning he had been given a list of activities to choose from. Yoga. Pilates. Bonsai. He had selected Bonsai, but he had no idea what it was.

They want me to feel like I'm in a fucking hotel. Maximum Humanity Prison they call this place. But this has nothing to do with restorative justice. I'm still locked in a box.

Besides, I don't deserve justice.

Moss kicked the wall absently.

Why was I even holding a gun at all? I'm a receptionist. A lazy one at that. They had no right giving me a gun and putting me there.

He sat up and watched the screen for a while. Pretty fish and Esperan flags.

Well, it's better than blood.

In the middle of the night, the door to Moss' suite opened.

Not cell, not even room, fucking suite they call it. Apparently mine's called Avocet, whatever that is.

"A new roommate for you, Mr. Hiyat," said the guard, all muscles and beige cotton. "So you won't be lonely."

Sure, that's why.

The new 'guest' was let in and sat on the other bed below the screen. The guard locked the door and left.

This guy look like he's having an even worse day than I am.

On the screen, Moss saw himself holding a gun once again. The fence. The crowd. The dead woman on the forest floor.

Please distract me from all this.

"Hey mate," he said as cheerfully as he could. "My name's Moss. Late arrival, eh?"

The new guest grunted.

"What's your name?" Moss tried again.

Another grunt.

"Sorry, I didn't hear you?"

"My name's *Jade*, okay? Can we not talk? This is bad enough as it is."

Moss lay back on his hemp pillow. He was exhausted. He wanted to cry but wouldn't let himself. The screen was back to documentaries again. Esperan security building the fence. A stuffed Red Shadow-tail in a museum. Proud guards protecting the perimeter.

Perfect. That's just great.

Chapter sixty-one

The next morning, just as the first sunlight was coming through a very tiny window in the ceiling, the muscled guard came back to Moss' cell accompanied by a smiling guy in a suit.

"Mr. Jade Kramer?"

Jade grunted.

"You've been cleared of all charges," said the lawyer with a grin. "They couldn't find t' person who charged you apparently. Of course, t' Esperan state take domestic violence *very seriously*—we are a *feminist* state of course—but without evidence, our hands are tied."

Jade smiled.

"But," said the lawyer with a wink. "I'm sure you've learned something from this and aren't gonna do it again, no?"

Jade smiled wider.

"Of course not," he said standing up.

Next time I'm gonna finish t' job.

He nodded to Moss on the way out.

"See ya later. Hope you get off as easily...*mate*."

An hour later, Moss was taken to his bonsai class. He was led down a long corridor, at the end of which he and the guard turned a corner and stepped out of an emergency door. Suddenly Moss was outside the building on a high enclosed catwalk between buildings. Below him, and all around the island, the sea was a bright blue. Gulls flew above, calling. Moss paused to take it in. From this vantage point he could see Espera city a few kilometres away, the beach at Dignity, even a little ferry boat bringing prison visitors back and forth.

Like a holiday resort, Moss noticed. *But this catwalk is in a cage for a reason.*

The guard hurried him along. Moss crossed to the other building and took one last look over the sea. Dark clouds were coming in, he noticed. A storm.

He entered the communal hall and saw that he was the last to arrive. In the bright, open room, complete with pine floors and skylights, at least a hundred prisoners sat at tidy little desks trimming miniature trees.

"Welcome to hell."

The guard gave Moss a push and locked the door behind him. Moss took a chair. He had no idea what he was doing. He picked up the scissors— bright blue, very blunt, children's scissors—and noticed the projection of a smiling white woman at the front of the room. Apparently, he was supposed to follow her instructions and, as everyone else was doing, trim his little tree into beautiful shapes.

What is this? Who t' fuck need a miniature tree?

His mind was still replaying the forest, the screams. He tried to focus on what the white woman was saying, but he didn't care.

This is bullshit.

He looked around and noticed a young person standing in the corner filming the class. The camera they held was emblazoned with the Espera media logo. They looked nervous and were flanked by two very large security men.

This is all just advertising, a publicity stunt. A prison is still a prison. How did this happen? How long I'm gonna be here?

Moss felt a pain in his chest. *I miss Aq.*

He tried to focus again on the instructions and, as delicately as he could, he made the first cut with his children's scissors. Moss watched in dismay as his little tree collapsed in half on the desk.

Well, fuck.

A sudden voice behind him made him jump.

"Moss Hiyat?" Moss turned around. It was the smiling lawyer again.

"Yes?"

"Come please, I take you back to your suite. You can leave your, ah... little botanical wonder here. We have a very special offer to make you."

"Wait...what? But she *wasn't* armed, was she?"

"Possibly."

"You really think she was going to attack t' fence and shoot someone?"

"Potentially."

"No mate, I don't understand. She was. Or she wasn't."

"That's not really how things work, Mr. Hiyat."

"It's just Moss."

"Fine. This is an opportunity for you, Moss. This Azure and her band of anarchists were attacking our sacred park. They are enemies of conservation. They are enemies of t' environment. You saw her reach for a gun. You protected yourself and your...*comrades*. You protected t' park and Espera."

"But—"

"You're gonna be a real hero, Moss."

"But did she real—"

"Or..." The lawyer indicated the TV-illuminated cell with his right hand. "...You can stay in this suite until you stand trial for manslaughter and we can move you downstairs where t' refugees are. I assure you that conditions down there are much more, shall we say humanitarian and restorative."

Moss knew when he was beaten. He was too tired to think anymore.

"Where do I sign?" he asked in defeat.

I miss Aq.

Chapter sixty-two

Aq had slept the night on the floor. He still felt broken. He dragged himself to the jacuzzi and sat in it for a while. He couldn't find the button for the bubbles so he sat in the lukewarm water and stared into space. Afterwards, he dug around in a closet until he found a towel. He dried off but didn't bother to get dressed again.

Naked, he walked back to the kitchen and, carefully ignoring the mess on the floor, found some organic breakfast cereal in a cupboard, went to the lounge and sat on the enormous sofa to eat straight from the box. He looked around for a remote control for the TV but couldn't see anything.

"TV on," he tried, and the screen flashed on.

"Maybe I should have tried that with t' jacuzzi," he mumbled to himself. "Fuck, I don't even know how this house work."

And it's mine now. Which is, like, t' best thing that ever happened to me. But without anyone to share it with, what's t' point?

"I'm not ready," he said out loud.

The TV was on the Esperan news channel and Aq saw soldiers lined up along the fence.

That's my arm, he realised as the camera panned from his gun onto Moss' face. *Fuck. I don't want to see this.*

He was about to say 'TV off' when the image changed and there was Moss again, standing on a stage with a microphone and a crowd of journalists. Aq's heart skipped a beat.

"Volume up."

The camera zoomed in on Moss' face. He looked exhausted.

"...I'm not a hero," he was saying to the press. "I just did my job. To protect Espera from terrorists. To protect our sacred forest from those who hate our freedom."

Moss took a breath and looked out over the crowd.

"I work on reception at t' Union Building," he continued. "I'm just a normal guy, but I wanted to do my part. I'm not a hero." He paused and then raised his voice "I just love Espera!"

The journalists were applauding. The news commentator was euphoric. Aq let out a big breath.

"Wow," he said out loud. "That's quite a spin."

The TV went to commercials.

Still naked, Aq went back out to the patio to think.

"Jacuzzi on, hot water."

He climbed in.

Of course, he was glad that his friend was out of jail and free. Moss might even become famous if the Espera PR machine had anything to do with it.

But that woman—t' same one I saw by t' bramble bush—she died yesterday. She wasn't a terrorist. She said her daughter had been attacked by security at t' mine. I didn't even know there were sauvite mines. And seeing how well they treat me—and I work in t' frikking Union Building—I don't want to think what life in a mine looks like.

"This isn't right. None of this is right."

Aq's phone started ringing. It was Moss.

"Mate, finally! Are you okay? I left you, like, a hundred messages."

"I was locked up on t' island for t' night—I mean, *in restoration* or whatever—"

"I just saw you on TV!"

"Right, yeah. So they made a deal."

"Come over and tell me about it?"

"God, I want to so bad. I have another press conference in an hour. They're like trying to make me a hero or something. But Aq, I fucking kill—"

The phone hung up.

"Moss? Moss?"

Aq dialled back but the call wouldn't connect. He dialled again. Nothing.

"Fuck!"

He threw his phone away in frustration and it bounced off a palm tree next to the patio. He lay still for a few minutes and tried to calm himself down.

What's gonna happen to Moss now? And what about t' woman from t' other side?

Aq looked out to the forest beyond the villa walls.

And what did I see, that night, at t' station, at t' gate? Who were those people—t' woman that Moss killed? Was that real? How do all these things fit together?

Aq noticed vaguely that it was beginning to rain, little drops of cool water were falling into the tub and bounced off the plants around him.

"More bubbles," he commanded.

Chapter sixty-three

Teal woke with a start. For a moment, things were still okay. For a moment her memory was blank and there was only the warmth of the bed and the sound of raindrops falling on the tent.

Then it came back. The demo. The shooting.

Azure is dead.

Teal rolled over in the bed. The rain was getting louder. Somehow, she felt the inexorable pull of time on her.

Everything that's gonna happen, already happened. That's how she said it. I'm gonna be in t' forest again, with t' resistance. But is that how time work? Everything laid out ahead with no escape?

Teal stared at the ceiling listening to the rain.

But no, said a voice inside her. *It's more like a circle. Days and seasons and years. And t' details aren't certain, just general strokes. An intuition of how things work out, of how t' dust tend to settle.*

"Okay," Teal said to herself. "So what do that mean really?"

It mean you have a choice to make.

Teal got out of bed, got dressed and left the tent. Someone she hadn't met before was running past with two shovels. They paused for a second and shouted,

"T' hospital tent is flooding! We need to dig a trench to reroute t' water! You can help us?"

Teal got to work.

***

The drainage ditches around the research camp were already full. The rain showed no signs of stopping and Cyan was running back and forth across the camp, shouting. They couldn't find Indi anywhere.

"Indi! I need your help out here! T' camp's going to flood and we need to reroute t' water!"

Cyan checked her tent, the kitchen, the bathroom, but there was no sign of the botanist anywhere.

"Indi? Where t' *fuck* are you?"

They checked the research tent. The seat where Indi always sat hunched over her papers was empty. On the little desk, Cyan saw a note with their name on it. They picked it up and tore it open.

Sorry, Cyan, I needed to go into town today. Verde is having a hard time. I tried to call, but your phone don't seem to connect. Did you go to t' other side? Call if you need me, Indi.

Cyan tore up the letter and threw it down on Indi's pile of papers.

"Fine!" they shouted. "I do it all myself! No problem Indi, go fuck your lover, go off and join t' resistance with Teal, sure, why not? Leave me here to run t' camp and collect five million samples myself in t' rain. Fuck off then. Leave me here alone. I do everything anyway!"

Cyan stood for a moment, hands on their hips, exhausted. There was no response to their shouting but the thunder of the rain on the tent.

It's not them I'm angry at. It's me. Jade betrayed us. He's a fucking monster. And he's been here in our camp all this time. What if he had hurt Teal or Indi?

I chose him to join t' team, this is my fault.

They heard something crash outside.

Just a branch. God I'm jumpy. What if he come back? We can hardly expect t' police to deal with it.

"I need to get out of here."

Cyan grabbed their bag and keys and left the camp.

***

Aq couldn't eat. He couldn't get anything done. He had managed to leave the jacuzzi for ten seconds to retrieve his phone but then he had got back in and he hadn't moved since. The rain was cold now. He had to sink deeper into the bubbles to stay warm.

He couldn't see how things would move on from here. Normally his life was predictable. Work too much, have some drinks with Moss, eat dinner with his family. Repeat. Repeat. Repeat. At least the cycle was familiar.

In a single week his life had turned upside down. And he couldn't understand what he was feeling.

A lack of some kind. An emptiness.

Aq looked around the decadent patio, the palm trees and hanging baskets and delicate cactus-pebble displays that he didn't have a name for.

It don't make sense. I got more now than I ever had before. But I feel...lonely. Somehow, I had a connection with Carl. Or was it just a distraction?

"Fuck if I know."

Aq kicked the side of the tub for no reason.

Or is it Moss that I'm upset about? I miss him, but I've often gone weeks without seeing him. Why would I miss him now? None of this make sense.

Aq's stomach grumbled.

I wonder if pizzas deliver out this far?

***

Teal worked for a solid hour digging trenches. She was soaked through and covered in pink mud. Riverlets ran all through the village, but for now they had got the water more or less under control.

Most importantly the hospital wasn't flooding anymore. After a short break, leaning on the side of a tent to catch her breath, Teal peeked into the hospital tent to see how things were. She wanted to check in on Azure's daughter.

She was still asleep but came to every now and then to drink water. The gash on her head had stopped bleeding, but for the few moments that she was awake, she seems confused and disoriented and soon fell back unconscious. No-one had told her about her mother yet.

Teal checked her bandages.

How she's gonna deal with this?

She had a sudden thought, a moment of doubt.

Unless she knew? If her mother could journey, then maybe Rouge can too? I mean who can and who can't? I thought Ash was t' only one, and even that seemed more like a legend.

Rouge mumbled something, turned a little and fell silent again.

And t' security guard? Apparently he can journey, although he seemed as surprised about it as I was. What do all this mean really?

Her head full of thoughts, Teal went back outside into the rain to finish digging.

"Teal, thank you for your work this morning. Are you gonna join us for t' meeting?"

Teal wasn't sure if she had met the person speaking to her or not. Three other villages had joined them and more injured people had arrived. She was socially overwhelmed, knee-deep in a trench, and she really wanted a shower.

"Sure, thank you. Is it in t' communal tent?"

"Isn't everything?"

The person smiled and left her to her digging.

Teal wiped her brow with her shirt sleeve and pushed her hair out of her eyes.

Is this what t' revolution looks like? Digging and bandages and meetings?

She looked over at a new group that had just arrived. Without pausing, half picked up shovels and came over to help the trench team. The other half, chatting in Polari, took great plates of food to the communal tent.

Well, sign me up.

Chapter sixty-four

Half an hour later, Teal was crammed into the back of the communal tent between a bale of hay, a knot of friends gossiping and eating, and another person cuddling a wet dog. She had never seen the tent so busy.

Rouge, she knew, was still sleeping in the hospital, but Teal recognised some of the other patients spread out in the room, sitting in wheelchairs or on the ground. She counted fifty people, probably double the population of the village itself.

The atmosphere was abuzz. People talked seriously in small groups. Kids, excited to see their friends from the other villages ran in and out trailing mud behind them. The pounding of the rain was magnified by the fabric of the tent. Everyone was talking all at once in a loud slang she could barely understand. Teal felt herself getting dizzy.

"Hi," said the person next to her with the dog. "I heard you don't speak Polari."

"Err, hi, yes that's right," said Teal with a weak smile. "Sorry, it's kind of hectic in here. I'm a bit—"

"—overwhelmed?"

"Yes."

"It is busy, no? Even more than usual. And with what happened yesterday... you heard about it?"

Teal looked for a moment at the beautiful central pole that Azure's father had made. It was covered in various wet jackets and umbrellas. She nodded sadly.

"I did."

"If you need to catch up on anything, let me know. Did you eat?"

"Thank you, that's kind. No, not yet."

Truthfully, she was starving after a morning of digging, but hadn't found the courage to climb through all the people to get to the table.

"I get some food now. Shall I grab you a plate?"

Teal smiled.

"Thank you."

"Super welcome."

***

The pizza was completely tasteless. Aq ate it on the sofa, spilling crumbs over himself, and threw the crusts onto the floor. He was wet. At least he'd had the forethought to put some pants on when the pizza delivery guy arrived. A fifty-shell tip was required just for coming out this far, and it had taken an hour. Apparently, there was a special delivery service from Espera city just for the villas out in the park. And it was expensive.

Because not everyone got a house servant to cook for them. And sometimes you just need junk food.

Aq flicked another crust onto the floor. He was feeling self-destructive and he could feel his mood getting worse. He had stopped caring about anything. As he got up to pee, he paused by a mirror. He was unshaven, his hair was unwashed, and he had pizza sauce on his chin.

I'm a fucking mess.

He decided the bathroom was too far and he peed into a flowerpot instead.

***

The village food was simple and delicious. Teal had no idea where they grew their vegetables out in the mud, but everything was fresh and lovingly prepared. She had barely finished eating when a person she recognised as Azure's sibling stood up to speak.

They sure look like her.

Everyone, even the children, stopped speaking at once. The speaker's eyes were red and they looked like they hadn't slept. Teal saw that, despite their sadness and exhaustion, this person's face was filled with rage. They pushed their shoulders back and addressed the meeting.

"Boyno everyone. Its bona to vada your dolly old eeks here again. She wishes we mollied together without t' National Weapon having to kill one of our own. Let's begin."

Fuck, of course it's all in Polari, thought Teal. *I'm not going to understand a word.*

A gentle voice to her side whispered, "Please let me know if you need translation."

Teal smiled, and whispered back, "You are awesome."

* * *

"Mate, it's me again."

"Moss! Where you were?"

Aq was so relieved his eyes were watering.

"Sorry, they kept me real busy here. I'm gonna be free in an hour though. Can I come see you? I got so much to tell you."

Aq looked around the living room, the floor was slippery with his wet footprints. Seven towels were strewn over various pieces of furniture, not to mention the fallout from his pizza.

"I gotta clean first but come over!"

"Get your guy to do it."

"Oh yeah, I didn't tell you yet... anyway, it's a long story. Shall I send Beige to pick you up?"

"Erm... no need, mate. I kind of got my own driver now."

Aq made an impressed sound. "Well, we certainly got a lot to catch up on, see you soon."

"Bye, mate."

Aq hung up and smiled.

Okay, good. Things are getting better.

He picked up a towel.

Now where t' hell is t' washing machine?

Chapter sixty-five

Four hours in, the meeting showed no signs of ending. Teal was finding it increasingly hard to concentrate the more tired she became, and following the translation was complicated.

Sometimes when she could just about understand the words of the speakers directly she would stop listening to the translation. Then it would get difficult again, and she ended up between languages, not able to concentrate fully on either one. Her translator had to leave a few times to take care of their baby but was instantly replaced with volunteer after volunteer.

"Sorry," she said to the newest person translating as they struggled to keep up with the speaker. "I didn't catch everything. I understood that there's gonna be some kind of action connected with t' funeral. And like, a general strike in t' city was that it?"

"Yes... and t' thing we do every year."

Teal remembered sitting in that same tent with Azure, barely three days earlier, hearing about the annual break-in at the park. She nodded.

"Azure told me."

"I thought she might have."

"One thing I didn't quite understand. When t' strike gonna start?"

The translator smiled.

"We been infiltrating t' city for a very long time. It already began this morning."

"Wow. Thank you."

Teal's heart fluttered with excitement.

Have I ever even seen a strike before? Actions, strikes, protests. I gotta decide what I'm ready for.

Looking around the room at the three generations gathered, crammed in close, Teal felt honoured to be a part of this. Almost no-one even knew her, but their kindness was touching. She had the sense of being somewhere important, doing something worthwhile. She was part of something much larger than herself.

And she hadn't thought about Cyan all day.

* * *

At that moment Cyan was sat by themselves, silent, and in the dark. The movie was supposed to have begun twenty minutes earlier. But there was nothing—they were staring at a blank screen. With a frustrated sigh, they turned around in the chair. They could see that a few other people from the audience had already got up and left.

They looked up to the booth near the ceiling where the holo-beamer should have been projecting the latest blockbuster onto the screen. It was empty and the lights were switched off.

What is this? I paid good money to be here—well t' research budget did. Where's my fucking movie?

They stood up and took the stairs two at a time up and out of the hall. They went straight to the ticket office to find someone to complain to, but that was empty as well.

What is this? Where everyone go?

Huffing dramatically, Cyan stormed out of the cinema and into the street.

They froze in panic.

* * *

Azure's sibling came to where Teal was still sat at the back of the tent.

"Hi, you're Teal, no?" they asked, putting out their calloused hand with a smile. Teal shook it.

"Yes, I'm sorry, I don't know your name."

"Rosa. I want to talk to you about Azure."

Just as abrupt as their sister.

"I'm so sorry for your loss," said Teal weakly. In truth she had no idea what to say. She was still processing Azure's death herself. Although they'd only known each other a few days, Teal had felt an intimate connection and couldn't imagine moving forward without Azure in her life. The work and the meeting had been a good distraction, but deep inside she was in pain.

"Thank you. She gave me something to give to you."

"Oh, wow, okay... What—?"

"I can't show it to you here. Come."

Rosa walked out of the tent.

Teal stood and, climbing over a dusty hay bale and nearly stepping on someone's baby, she ran after them. The pair ran through the rain to the guest tent where Teal had slept the previous night. They both wiped their feet as they went in, but it was hopeless, there was pink mud everywhere. It was getting dark inside, but Teal could just make out six or seven forms on the ground

Sleeping bags, she realised. *From t' other villagers. I'm gonna have roommates today.*

She thought of her own little tent back at the research camp.

Cyan. Sex. Helicopters. What a week.

Rosa was in the corner of the tent pushing some buttons. Suddenly a holo-beamer switched on and a hologram of a person illuminated the room. The person stood tall with her hair in a tight bun, her left hand grasping a walking stick. Teal would know that proud posture anywhere.

"Azure," she said softly, her eyes already filling with tears.

Chapter sixty-six

"Teal, it's good to see you."

"Erm... hello?"

"T' interactivity of this technology still isn't great," announced the Azure hologram. "But it's enough for me to explain a few things. Is Rosa with you?"

Teal looked over to where Rosa stood adjusting the beamer controls.

"Yes."

The hologram turned to look, but apparently couldn't turn that far.

"Come sit with Teal, would you love?"

Rosa came over and sat down in front of the flickering hologram. The image of Azure sat too and they were all silent for a moment.

"So t' vision came to pass as I foresaw it?" asked Azure.

Rosa nodded. Teal was silent, but another tear fell from her cheek.

"Then there is a lot of work to do."

"Teal, I created this hologram four days ago. We have only just met. But I know that we are already close, already bonded."

Teal nodded. She realised it was difficult to keep eye contact with the hologram, just as it had been difficult with the living Azure.

"I need you to move forward for me. I need you to help t' group when they arrive in t' park. Only someone on t' inside can help us this time and it's gonna be you. What's gonna happen, already happened."

"I..." Teal felt inevitability pulling at her heart. "Okay."

"This is gonna be bigger than anything you've seen, my young friend. Wider than replacing a bad state with a less bad one, deeper than reforms and creating more ethical options within capitalism. That in itself is a paradox that cannot be resolved."

Teal felt her heart beating. She was momentarily aware of everything around her, every shadow and corner, every breath.

"Change is more difficult than building bigger fences against poachers, putting up reefs against rising sea levels. T' land cannot be bought, but we tell ourselves the myth that everything has a price, even life itself. My life was given a price and it was worth less than a patriotic Esperan, or a cisgender woman, or a politician. They took it without a thought."

Teal looked at Rosa and saw that though they sat tall and proud as their sister, their face was wet with silent tears.

"This is bigger than just an economic system. For as long as cities have existed they have depended on t' importation of resources from outside. For as long as there have been Esperas there have been sauvite mines and agriculture destroying t' soil. Every Rome had its Egypt. Every Europe had its colonised world. Civilisation itself is not sustainable. It has destroyed almost everything living in its wake and its hunger cannot be assuaged."

Teal was silent. She was used to Azure's political monologues and this felt important.

"Traditional indigenous people t' world over have known this and have resisted. And *we* know this and we resist too. What we're starting today is gonna take decades to complete, but everything *is* changing. And everything's *gotta* change. You're a part of that now, Teal. Are you ready?"

Am I? Really?

She heard that voice again. *You have a decision to make.* Pushing her shoulders back and sitting taller, she said as confidently as she could, "I'm ready. But I don't know how—"

"Ash is gonna show you."

"Ash—"

"She passed me a message. When you meet her, you're gonna travel together, like we did. Three times. But she can only come with you two out of three. Is that clear? Two out of three."

Teal didn't understand but nodded.

"But for now you need to find t' guy from your journey. T' guy in t' Union security uniform."

Teal nodded again and the hologram turned to Rosa.

"My love, take care of Rouge for me. She's yours now to guide. She's becoming a brave and gentle woman. I couldn't be prouder."

Rosa smiled just slightly.

"I love you," said the hologram and abruptly disappeared.

"That's it?" said Teal despite herself.

"That's it." Rosa stood up, switched off the beamer and left the tent just as suddenly.

"Wow," said Teal to herself. "Just wow."

***

"Aq!"

Moss ran up the driveway and grabbed his friend in a bear hug. Aq was squeezed so tight he couldn't respond.

"So good to see you!"

Aq squeaked a reply.

"Ah mate..." Moss finally released Aq and let him breathe again. "Could you tip my driver? I got nothing." He showed his empty pockets. "I did bring some beers though."

"Some things never change," said Aq, rolling his eyes. He gave the driver a fifty. She drove off and Aq closed the gate behind.

"Want to drink something?" Aq asked as he re-joined his friend at the house and waved inside the front door.

"Mind if we take a walk?" asked Moss. "I've been inside way too much. And it look like t' rain's stopped for a while."

Aq looked at the pizza boxes sticking out of a recycling container half-hidden by a giant cactus.

"Yeah, me too actually. Let's go."

Aq opened the heavy gate again, they left the villa compound and walked out into the *cerezo* forest together. A chorus of blackbirds and robins sang above them. Eucalyptus leaves rustled all around in a faint breeze. They followed a path through a thick patch of forest—still dripping from the downpour—and out onto the river. In some places trees grew along the riverbanks, in others, there were wide-open meadows and they could just make out the perimeter fence on the horizon.

They sat for a while on a tree trunk looking out over the river and the meadows, which were full of blue and red flowers although spring was long gone. Moss told Aq about the rehabilitation centre. Aq told Moss about Carl. They shared stories and beers and Aq felt that familiar connection again. His best friend. His mate, his colleague, his—

"Aq?"

"Yes, mate?"

"You're staring at me."

"Oh, right, sorry."

Fuck, what was that?

"Everything alright?"

"Erm, yeah. It's fine. All good. Just been a wild few days you know? So tell me more about t' TV thing?"

Aq took a sip of beer. His heart was racing. *What just happened? Is that how I see him? Do I really want to—?*

"So yeah," said Moss, scratching his boyish stubble, stretching and opening another bottle. "They offered me two choices. It was stay in prison and murder innocent little trees for t' rest of my life or tell t' world that that woman—whoever she was—was an enemy of conservation and I was a hero for shooting her."

"But she wasn't, no? Armed I mean?"

"No mate. Of course not. We were t' ones armed to t' teeth. All us janitors and spa cleaners and receptionists with no idea what we were doing."

"Fuck Espera."

"Yeah, I guess." Moss' voice was quiet and he picked at the label on his beer. "I mean t' prison sucked obviously. And like, maybe t' fence system isn't perfect. But I still believe in Espera. I mean, remember t' State?"

"No, and neither do you."

"What they told us at school I mean."

"Yeah, sure. Very bad. Evil State or whatever."

"Well, it was certainly no picnic for queers like us..."

Aq gave him a look. "I'm not queer, Moss."

"Oh right, yeah sorry. Just you know, with your delegate and everything..."

"It's not t' same thing."

"Oh right. Sure mate. I get it."

Aq thought he heard the slightest disappointment in Moss' voice. He flashed back to their time in the pool. Moss paddling close to him. Aq's embarrassment when he got hard.

But he's my best friend. Sure, there was that time when we were twelve—after history class, behind t' school building when we were supposed to be smoking. We never talked about that, but it was obvious we were just kids, fooling around or whatever.

They both stared out at the flowers and butterflies for a while. Aq had a sudden feeling, a familiar sense of being too high and looking off a ledge. The same feeling he'd felt after his first session with Carl.

Unless I am.

Aq watched a bright yellow butterfly pass by, a world of opportunities opening up before him.

I could be. And if I'm queer then I don't need to hide anymore. My fantasies. That part of myself that I've been too scared to think about.

Then anything's possible. Even me and Moss could—

"I should get back, mate. My driver's coming to pick me up in an hour. I've got like another hundred interviews lined up before I can sleep tonight."

"Erm, sure." Aq stood up and brushed himself off. "Let's get going then. Must be hard work being an Esperan superhero and all."

Moss punched Aq in the arm. Aq punched him back. They walked back together to the quiet little trail through the forest.

Chapter sixty-seven

The road in front of Cyan was completely blocked. A biofuel bus was parked horizontally across three lanes of traffic and the road was a chaos of honking cars, biovans and angry cyclists.

"What's happening here?" Cyan shouted at the first person they saw, an elderly man with a walking stick.

"Didn't you hear? It's a general strike! First I've seen since I was young lad. I remember it as if it was yesterday, I was on my way home from work…"

Cyan ignored him and walked out into the street. *What a mess. How can this be allowed to happen?*

"Get out of t' way!" shouted a person on a bike, racing past them and up onto the sidewalk to avoid the road-block. Cyan turned and stepped back into the safety of the cinema. Shaking, they leaned against the wall of the empty ticket booth and stared for a while at the publicity projection—part poster, part trailer—of an upcoming kids' movie about climate change and the brave cats with Esperan accents who were stopping it. Outside Cyan could hear shouts and yells and what might have been firecrackers.

"This is no good," they said to themself. "This could get dangerous."

I wish Teal was here.

They took out their phone and checked their messages for the hundredth time that afternoon. Nothing. They called Teal's phone again. It went straight to voicemail.

Still outside t' fence, they thought to themself. *Still out there with those—*

Just then the hologram of cats in superhero capes flickered and disappeared. The lights of the ticket booth also went out, followed by all the lights in the cinema. Cyan looked out through the glass doors. All of the electricity had gone out in the block.

"This can't be happening."

* * *

The delegate from Paris was not happy. She stood at the Union reception holding a pillowcase in one hand and a half-empty bottle of water in the other. She was practically screaming at Amar, who had been working reception since Moss' sudden departure.

"Yes ma'am," said Amar, as patiently as she could. "I'm very sorry to hear that. Right away ma'am, of course I'm gonna replace everything and find you a better room. Yes ma'am. So sorry."

"And another thing—!"

Amar turned and opened a little drawer full of keys. They were in a disorganised mess—just as Moss always left it—and it took her a while to find the key for the best suite in the building. Breathing deeply, she tried to find patience, but she was beginning to lose her temper.

Who do these people think they are really? My son broke his back cleaning their frikking jacuzzis. My grandma died without ever staying a night in a hotel as nice as this one.

She found the key at last and held it in her shaking hand. Behind her the Parisian was still shouting.

I'm so fucking tired of this.

Amar put out her hand to pass the key when suddenly all the lights flickered out. Except for the light coming in through the windows, the whole building went dark. Amar smiled for the first time that day.

"It really happened," she whispered. "This is it."

She gently placed the key back down on the polished surface. The delegate stared at her, looking terrified. Without another word, Amar walked past her to the door and stepped out into the sunlight.

***

When they arrived back at the villa, the driver was waiting for them outside the gate.

"This is me, mate," said Moss as the driver opened the door for him. "Time to be famous."

"Don't forget about us little people, okay?"

Moss laughed. "Wait, who are you again?"

Aq stuck out his tongue.

"Be in touch."

"I call you tomorrow," replied his friend. "Are you, like, ever going to Union again?"

Aq sighed and unconsciously glanced at the villa. "I need to think about it. I kind of don't need to, but how would I explain it to my family?"

The driver coughed impatiently.

"Gotta run mate. Espera wait for no man."

"See you, Moss."

The car drove away and left Aq standing at the gate.

He went in to order another pizza.

***

The pizza delivery place was on fire. Two of their mopeds had been thrown on top of a barricade in the road to block the tramlines. Cyan saw fireworks being thrown out of windows.

That's probably what started t' fire, they thought to themself, carefully crossing to the other side of the street. *Fucking kids.*

Esperans considered themselves 'a nation of animal-lovers' and as fireworks scared dogs and cats, they were illegal in the city. But one day a year, they were allowed in carefully controlled displays in public parks.

Apparently, someone has been stocking up.

Cyan knew they were in some kind of shock. They had never seen anything like the chaos that filled the street in that moment. The looting and burning of stores. The broken windows and the barricades. What had started as a general strike had become something much bigger. Just behind them, some adolescents threw a brick through a window. Cyan stood and watched numbly as the young people climbed into the store and left with their hands full of cardboard boxes of fair-trade sneakers.

Cyan couldn't understand.

Esperans have a good life. After all this isn't t' State. Sure, there are poorer neighbourhoods, but in general, there's equality here, there's peace.

And if people wanted change, then Cyan was certain that this wasn't the way to go about getting it.

This is just kids stealing sneakers. People letting off steam. Mob mentality. Mindless violence...

But somehow, they knew that that wasn't the whole story. A firework exploded a few metres from their feet.

"Right! Enough!"

They ran away from the chaos, around another barricade and past a burning security vehicle. Down towards the beach.

***

"What's next?" asked Teal, standing outside the tent once more with Rosa, who was impatient to get back to the meeting.

"My sister told you," they said. "You need to go to t' city—"

"—To find t' random Union security guy."

"Yes."

"Just like that."

"If you saw him in a journey of t' future, then it's gonna happen either way." Rosa gave her an intense look that reminded Teal suddenly so much of Azure that she felt a pang of loss deep in her belly. "That's how these things work."

"Always?"

"Often enough."

"Do you also—?"

Rosa shook their head.

"T' meeting's started again. Good luck."

"When I'm gonna see you again?" asked Teal.

She heard her own tone and hated herself for being so needy, but without Azure, without Cyan, most likely without her job, she felt suddenly insecure.

"In t' forest," said Rosa. "Tomorrow."

God, so soon.

"Okay. Until tomorrow then—" said Teal, but Rosa was already gone.

Teal walked over to the rental car.

How many days is this thing overdue now?

She got in, turned around and headed off back towards the city.

Chapter sixty-eight

"This is so creepy," said Moss, although there was no-one to hear him. His driver had left him just in front of the Union Building and he stood outside waiting. There wasn't a single person anywhere.

Moss could see through the windows that the building was dark inside. Outside was getting darker too, and he could see more oily black clouds coming in from the west. Moss was supposed to be giving an interview outside the building for Esperan radio. In fact, he was already late.

Where they are? He felt a shiver run down his spine. *This isn't right at all, I should go check inside.*

A heavy drop of rain fell on his shoulder as he pushed through the revolving doors. Inside, reception was calmer than he'd ever known it. It was evening and there should have been delegates arriving, phones ringing, companions picking up suitcases, a cleaner somewhere in the shadows polishing the brass handrails or wiping a window. There was no-one. A cleaning cart lay overturned near the entrance. All the lights were out.

It's like a museum or something. He smiled. *What would I know about museums?*

He looked at the reception where he normally sat dozing in the afternoons, ignoring the chaos around him. He longed for those days of normality. Moss knew his life wasn't exciting, and he knew it could be much better than it was, but he missed the routine, missed always knowing what came next. Work all day, meet Aq at the bar in the evening. Maybe catch a movie once a month if they got enough tips.

He went around the reception desk and sat down in his usual place. The key drawer had been left open, and he pushed it shut. Outside, the wind was picking up again and Moss could see the palm trees being blown around. There was a silent flash of lightning from somewhere beyond.

"This is so creepy," he repeated as he leaned back in his favourite chair. Despite the strangeness of the situation, exhausted from a sleepless night behind bars, Moss fell fast asleep.

***

Cyan arrived at the cliff overlooking the beach. They already felt better. Although they could smell smoke on their clothes, the fresh wind blowing in from the sea felt wonderful. They entered the cactus garden and walked down the narrow little steps that led to the beach, pausing for a moment in the garden to take in the giant saguaros towering over spherical echinocacti and prickly pears. Radiant birds of paradise were in full bloom, and the air tasted of sand and sea salt.

Cyan paused at a holographic information sign, apparently solar-powered and still working despite the electricity cuts. They had read the sign many times before but stopped to read it again. History always made them feel calmer.

> A hundred years ago this area was a squatted community garden serving t' local neighbourhood which had been poor for as long as anyone could remember. Later, despite a ten-year battle to save t' garden, t' State tragically destroyed t' whole project during a single night of t' Improvement. Twenty people were injured and one older person from t' neighbourhood died from a heart-attack. Two hundred trees were felled and replaced with sushi bars, coffee shops and a tourist information centre.
>
> Later, Esperan land improvement reclaimed t' land and began

to cultivate cacti that would survive both t' warming climate and t' sandy soils, giving us t' beautiful garden we enjoy today.

Cyan loved it in the garden. It was their favourite place to be alone in the entire city. They sat on a bench and looked out over the sea, past the reefs, out over to the rehabilitation island.

T' island.

They saw black smoke spiralling up into the sky and at least thirty small boats heading towards the mainland.

Fuck. How big is this thing gonna get? Is there no stopping it?

They reached into their pocket to check their phone again.

Maybe Teal has deigned to reply to my five million messages.

Their hand was shaking. They felt panic rising in their chest. Then they heard the chanting. Out past a bank of saguaros, they picked up voices almost lost in the wind. They breathed deeper.

I know that mantra. Some collective love is just what I need.

They headed over to check it out. Twenty people sat amongst the aloes chanting for peace. Cyan quietly sat down to join in. They looked around at the happy smiles facing out towards the sea. They all wore the same t-shirt, Cyan noticed. It was beige and printed with 'Be t' change you want to see.'

A little cliché, Cyan thought. *But okay. Better than smashing windows and burning police cars for sure.*

They closed their eyes, diving into the chant and the sound of the wind rushing through saguaros. They felt better now, safer.

Shouts cut through the calm of the chant. Cyan's heart skipped a beat. A group of people dressed in black had appeared and were making their way down through the garden. Cyan heard shouting down below and saw that the beach was full of boats. A second group were climbing up through the gravel and plants. They wore a uniform that Cyan didn't recognise.

Wait, not a uniform. They're prisoners. And refugees from t' island.

The two groups met and embraced each other barely a hundred metres from where Cyan's circle sat. Cyan could hear the excitement and fear in the prisoners' voices. United, the prisoners, refugees and their friends began to head up towards the city when a wailing siren sounded out from above. They froze. It was Union Security.

The figures ducked for cover, hiding down behind boulders and cacti and a giant sculpture of some fallen hero. From their position, Cyan could see them all, silent and terrified, as a line of security cops appeared at the cliff and started climbing down, guns in hand.

"You down there!" one of the officers shouted to Cyan's group of chanters. "Have you seen anyone come through here?"

Wordlessly, one by one, the chanters pointed at the people hiding behind rocks and cacti. The officers arrived, arrested each one and dragged them away. They screamed as they were taken.

The garden became quiet again.

"Don't worry," said the group leader calmly. "They were violent people and violence is not t' way. Be t' change."

"Be t' change," his group repeated back to him and they picked up the chant again. Instinctively Cyan tried to join in, but their throat was closed.

They couldn't make a sound.

Chapter sixty-nine

"Mate, wake up!"

"Hmmm who—?"

"It's me," said Aq, shaking his friend's shoulder. "Only *you* could take a nap at a time like this!"

"Aq!" Moss rubbed his eyes and looked around, remembering where he was. "Oh, I fell asleep."

"In reception. Huge surprise."

Moss grinned. "What are you doing here?"

"I had Beige drive me over. I couldn't order food for some reason and obviously without Carl around, t' kitchen's totally empty." Aq sat down in the other chair next to his friend. "When I saw what happened to t' city I came here to find you. Are you alright?"

Moss gave him a confused look. "Did something happen?"

"You didn't notice that Union is abandoned?"

"Well, yes, it *is* pretty quiet."

"Even t' delegates have left town. There's a general strike, t' city is burning!"

Moss rubbed his eyes.

"Real mate?"

"Real."

"Fuck." Moss looked thoughtful for a moment. "Although... I mean it's kind of time, no?"

"To have some decent working conditions, yeah. But I'm surprised you'd support it."

"Maybe. I don't know. Things have been pretty bad recently. I mean I *killed* someone, Aq. Someone's mum, someone's sister. I..."

Moss stared into the distance for a moment. "Actually, I can't deal with that right now. Can we do something?"

"Go out and join t' riots?"

Moss looked around him at the empty building.

"I mean, we could..."

"Or?"

"Or we could make t' most of an empty hotel and go jump on some beds."

"Real?"

Moss smiled. "Haven't you always wanted to. I know you have. And I bet t' sauna's still hot too."

Aq laughed. "If it help you feel better, let's do it."

"Class war!" shouted Moss, bouncing so high on the mattress that he nearly hit the ceiling. The bottle of champagne in his hands had erupted over the both of them and they were soaked and sticky. "Revolution!"

Aq was dizzy. Moss was shirtless, and he could barely keep his eyes off him as he bounced up and down, squealing. He was caught by another burst of champagne from the bottle and he got off the bed giggling.

"Ah mate, we're supposed to drink this stuff not wear it!"

"So?" shouted Moss, already totally drunk on three sips. "There's plenty for both!"

Aq smiled at his friend. "You're ridiculous. Let's go to t' sauna and get washed off. If there's still hot water."

With a final jubilant bounce, Moss arrived next to his friend on the soaked carpet.

"Can't wait to get me naked?"

Aq blushed.

"No, I... it's just I—"

Moss rushed out of the suite and shouted back,

"Come on then!"

In the spa, the water was still hot. Wearing just towels—the fluffy, thick organic ones from the suites, nothing like the scratchy things they had in the dorms—they got into the sauna and sat down. Moss opened the little valve and the room filled with steam.

"Yes!" he said. "Now this is what I'm talking about."

Aq was uncomfortable. He hated being shirtless, even around Moss. He had always felt that way and he'd never quite worked out where it came from. As a man, he was allowed—even expected—to bare his chest anytime he wanted to. But he'd always been the last in the park on a sunny day to take off his shirt. Even on the beach he preferred swimming with his t-shirt on.

"You look awkward mate. Have some more champagne."

Aq took the bottle and downed a big gulp. The bubbles were helping, it was true.

"You make me do t' stupidest things," he said, slurring slightly. "I love that."

"Yeah!" said Moss, "We have fun together! I'm sorry, though, about your guy leaving."

Aq hadn't thought about Carl in several hours. It felt strange to think about him now, when he was with Moss.

"Thanks. It's okay," he stared off into the steam for a minute. "I mean I still got t' villa, right?"

"Totally!" Moss raised the bottle. "Cheers to that!" he said and took a long sip, half of it running down his chest.

It was too much. Something about the bubbles on his bottom lip, the steam and sweat and champagne running over his hairy chest pushed Aq over the edge.

"Mate..."

Moss looked him back, straight in the eye.

"I know."

"You know?"

"Of course. Always have."

Through the steam, Aq felt something brush against his leg. It was

Moss' hand. He couldn't respond, but his friend gave him a little squeeze. Aq felt dizzy again. He leaned forward just a little bit. Moss leaned just the same amount, no more.

Aq's heart hurt in his chest, but he knew he was ready. He leaned forward and paused barely a centimetre from his best friend's champagne-covered lips.

That's when they heard the banging at the door.

Chapter seventy

"Hi, hello, my name's Teal. Oh my gosh, I'm so sorry to disturb you. I couldn't find anyone in t' building. I'm sorry I didn't know you were…"

"Who are you?" Aq resisted the urge to cross his arms because he knew for sure he'd lose his towel. Without looking, he knew he was visibly aroused. "Wait…" he said, as he took in Teal's face.

"Wait…" repeated Teal and they stared at each for a good thirty seconds without speaking.

Moss appeared out of the steam.

"Who is it? Are we in trouble?"

"I—" Aq tried to speak. "It's you, isn't it?"

"Yes," said Teal. "I came to find you. I can't believe you're real."

"But who? How—?"

Moss stood next to them and poked his friend in the arm.

"Who is this? You two know each other?"

"From a dream…" said Aq distantly.

"From a *journey*, actually." Teal handed Aq a dry towel. "We have a lot to talk about. And we need to get moving."

"To t' villa?" Aq asked.

"Yes."

"Fuck."

* * *

Cyan stumbled back up the steps through the cactus garden. They needed to get as far away as possible. To be alone to process. To never again hear white people chanting about peace one minute after refugees had been dragged over gravel by police.

On impulse, they pulled out their phone and called Teal. They had done the same thing so many times that day that the action was automatic. This time the call connected. They nearly dropped the phone in shock and sat abruptly on a wet step, listening intently to the call tone. No-one picked up. They called again. Nothing. One more time. And Teal answered.

"Oh my fucking *god*! Where t' *fuck* have you been?!"

"Hi Cyan. Are you okay? Oh, you called me. Just saw your messages, sorry."

"Like a *thousand* times! Where were you?"

"In t' village, obviously. Wow, so much has happened since then."

"Since you sent me away, you mean? You know they shot someone at t' fence? I was right there with Indi."

"Yes, I knew her. You too. Hey wait a second, would you?" Cyan heard Teal cover the phone but could just make out what she was saying. She was talking to someone, a guy, telling him to put his clothes on. He seemed annoyed that she was talking on the phone.

"Teal? What's going on there? Where are you?"

"I need to go actually, Cyan. I have stuff to do. Let's chat later okay?"

Cyan swallowed hard.

"Wait, hon. I'm sorry, okay? Please just tell me where you are, tell me you're okay."

"I'm at t' Union Building. I'm fine."

"T' Union Building? Who's that you're with? Why did you tell him to put his clothes on?"

"Bye, Cyan. Thanks for checking up on me."

Teal hung up.

Cyan stared at their phone for a long time, their hands shaking.

They threw it on the ground and smashed the screen with their heel. Swallowing tears, they stood up and ran back up the steps to the city.

"I'm so fucking stupid…"

An alarm was going off and a large protest passed by. Cyan crossed straight through, pushing people out of the way. Over to the side, people in black hoodies were burning something. The 'Save t' Orphaned Hedgehogs' people were hiding behind their banner and retreating from the fire as fast as they could. Cyan ignored them all.

"T' Union," they said to themself. "I gotta find Teal. I gotta fix this."

*　*　*

"So wait, *how* do you two know each other?"

Moss was sobering up but was still confused. He reached for another towel and wrapped it around his chest. He had only gotten top surgery last year and wasn't comfortable with strangers seeing his scars yet.

"You took a journey together? Where to?"

"It's hard to explain, Moss. We just know each other."

Aq looked into Teal's eyes.

"We have a connection."

"Oh, okay," said Moss, looking down at the floor.

Aq knew that sound of disappointment anywhere.

"Not like that."

"No, it's fine," said Moss. "I get it."

"You don't. Really."

"It's all good. I leave you two to catch up or whatever and I'm gonna go raid t' kitchen, I bet t' ice-cream's melting or something."

"Okay Moss," said Aq softly. "We come find you there soon, okay?"

"Sure."

Moss walked away, shuffling in his fluffy towels.

"I like your friend," said Teal smiling.

"He's awesome."

"Or more than a friend?"

"Moss is awesome."

"Got it." Teal winked. "So, you do remember me?"

Aq nodded.

"Do you know where we were actually? During t' journey?"

"It was my villa, in t' forest. What do you mean *journey*? What happened to us? Was that real somehow? What was that?"

"Wait, you have a villa?"

Teal looked at Aq's floppy hair and remembered the security uniform she'd seen him in before. Unless he was very high up in the service, she found it extremely unlikely.

"I do. It's complicated."

"We need to go there."

"To t' park? But why?"

"Because what already happened, gonna happen again."

"Mmm?"

"I'm gonna explain on t' way. But that's where we need to be—at your place when t' resistance reaches t' park."

"Resistance? Oh my god, *who are you?* What are you even talking about?"

"Okay, it's too much, I get that. Let's go find your mate—Moss, was it? Eat some ice cream, and I explain everything."

Aq nodded and led the way to the kitchen. They passed the sauna and he glanced at the open door on the way.

This is without a doubt t' weirdest day of my life.

"Let me just put on a shirt, okay?"

Aq and Moss had shed their clothes into a big pile on the floor and after a minute of digging around, Aq gave up looking for his own t-shirt and slipped on Moss' security uniform shirt instead. They were about the same size anyway.

It smell like him.

Teal gave Aq a strange look when she saw the shirt.

"Okay?" he asked.

Teal smiled. "Sure."

Chapter seventy-one

"I feel like this happened in one of t' old movies," said Moss as he ate another spoonful of melting ice-cream. He had given up with a bowl and was eating straight out of the metal tub. "Like, really old. Something about dinosaurs?"

Aq rolled his eyes a little.

"You and your dinosaurs," he laughed sitting down, and picked up a spoon. "How can you even watch those archaic movies? They were so slow—and flat."

"I like it, it makes me feel like I'm revisiting history somehow."

Teal, her mouth full of cherry cheesecake banana ice-cream said: "Speaking of which... Aq—"

"Okay, okay. So tell me again? You and me are time-travellers and we travelled to t' future. Everything they said about Ash was true and t' resistance is coming to take over t' park."

Moss stared at them.

"Well not everything," replied Teal calmly. "But yes, in a nutshell..."

"Real?"

"I don't need you to believe it. But we're going to t' villa either way. What's gonna happen—"

"Already happened." Aq put down his spoon. "Got it."

"Mate..." said Moss tentatively. "With all due respect, *what t' fuck*? Time-travel? Ash?"

"It's hard to explain. A thing happened that involved t' two of us—"

Moss looked sad again.

"Okay."

He scooped out another giant spoonful.

"Well, actually not just t' two of us, right Teal?"

"Right."

"You were there with someone, hiding down in t' brambles. An older woman maybe, with a walking stick. Who was that and how is she involved?"

Teal looked distant for a moment and poked the table with her spoon. "A friend of mine. She was killed."

"Oh, I'm sorry…"

"Her name was Azure."

Moss choked, dropped his spoon and started coughing loudly.

"Moss? Are you okay?"

Aq patted him on the back, but Moss kept choking. Eventually he caught his breath and was about to speak but fell silent as someone new arrived in the kitchen. Someone with their hands on their hips, shouting Teal's name.

"Teal! There you are!"

Cyan ran forward, arms out for a hug, but Teal took a step back.

"Hi Cyan."

"Babe! I've been looking for you everywhere! This building is massive."

"What are you doing here?"

"You told me you were here, so I came. It was super complicated to get across town—half t' public transport is down. It's war out there!"

"Okay," said Teal, still confused. "Cyan, this is Aq and Moss."

Cyan shook their hands and threw Aq a look when he said his name. "Glad to see you've got your clothes on now."

"Excuse me?" said Aq.

"Forget it," said Cyan. "Teal, what happened to you? Who are these people?"

Suddenly there was a loud crash, and everyone stood. Moss nearly lost his towels. Teal knocked over her chair. Aq squealed. There was the faintest smell of smoke.

Cyan looked terrified. "Fuck. I guess t' protests reached Union already."

Teal stood forward. "I think it's time we were leaving."

"To t' villa?" asked Aq.

"I guess so."

"What villa?" demanded Cyan.

"If we're going to t' park I probably need some clothes," said Moss. "And Aq here seems to have stolen my shirt. Be right back."

"What villa?"

"Cyan, honey," said Teal patiently. "This isn't your story. By all means, come along, but stop demanding things from me. I don't have time to catch you up and I don't have time to look after you."

"I never asked you t—"

Teal turned to Aq.

"Do you have a car?"

"I have a chauffeur."

"Right, of course you do."

"I call him. And I grab Moss. Let's meet at reception?"

They heard more shouting somewhere in the building. "Second thoughts, let's go together."

He pulled his phone out of his pocket, dialled and headed for the door, Teal ran after him and Cyan, spouting, followed closely behind.

All of the reception windows were smashed but one when the group reached it, and there was a small fire behind Moss' desk. As they ran, Moss pulled on a sweater he had found outside the sauna. He had both arms in the same hole.

"Uff, Aq help me!"

"Meet you on t' steps!" shouted Teal, and she and Cyan ran through what used to be the door out into the night.

Aq stopped to adjust Moss' sweater and liberate him. Aq adjusted his hair for him and pushed his fringe out of his eyes.

"Do I look ready for t' revolution?" asked Moss, his eyes glowing with excitement.

"You're beautiful, mate."

Moss didn't respond. There was nothing to say.

They kissed. Aq felt himself pulling away beyond reflex. He was fading. Journeying. He was almost halfway to another place. But his best friend's tongue was in his mouth and his hand was cupping the back of his neck. He tasted like sugar and cream. He couldn't leave now. He wouldn't. They were alone in the world and Aq had never been more present in his life.

A bottle exploded through the remaining window and fire was suddenly everywhere on the floor. Moss squealed. Aq grabbed his hand and they ran together out into the street.

Chapter seventy-two

A hundred people, a thousand. Protests and banners and molotovs and a burning police car. Still holding hands, Aq and Moss found Teal and Cyan and they moved as a group down the Union stairs away from the fire. They ran down across the courtyard, which was strewn with uprooted organic vegetables, and reached the road.

"Over there!" shouted Aq, pointing at the car, which was parked well away from the riots. Beige stood nervously, his hand in his pocket as if he held a gun.

Probably a banana, thought Aq. *But who even know anymore?*

"Let's go!"

The four of them ran together, heads down, towards the car. They were barely a hundred metres away, when a massive unmarked Espera vehicle pulled up and blocked their way. The side door opened, and four armed men jumped out and grabbed Moss.

"What t'—?"

"Mr. Moss," said one of the men. "We are here for your comfort and protection."

"But I don't—"

The man pushed Moss towards the open door.

"You are an Esperan asset now, we protect you."

Moss resisted, but he was no match for four soldiers. They pushed him in to the van and slammed the door behind him.

Aq and the others stood frozen. Through the tinted glass, Aq could just see make out his friend's face pushed up against the window as the van drove away at top speed.

Chapter seventy-three

"No no no!"

"I'm so sorry, Aq." Teal touched his arm lightly. "But we need to get out of here."

She looked over her shoulder as another room in the Union Building burst into flames.

"What was that about him being an asset?" asked Cyan.

"He... Moss killed someone," said Aq, not quite sure why he was telling them. His voice was choked with smoke, or tears, he couldn't tell which.

"He killed someone?"

"A woman, from t' resistance. Espera have made him into a hero for it. For protecting t' park or something."

"A woman from t' resistance," repeated Teal slowly. "When was this?"

Aq looked blank and tried to think.

"God, time make no sense anymore. Was it yesterday? It couldn't have been yesterday. It feel like a month ago."

"It was yesterday," said Teal firmly, suddenly understanding.

"Okay..."

"We deal with this later. We need to get t' fuck out of here."

"Come," said Aq, leading them to where Beige still stood waiting for them.

The drive to the villa took just under an hour. Security was sparse at the park entrance—the guards detailed there had been called back to crack down on the rioters—and once they got away from the city, there was no traffic at all. The lights of the villa flickered on as Aq unlocked the gate and Beige pulled the car into the driveway.

Teal and Cyan got out and stood together, open-mouthed.

"Wow, Aq," said Teal. "That's quite a house."

"It's a long story. But look, we still got power here," he said. "That's something."

They stood for a moment taking in the sheer enormity, the columns, wind turbines and palm trees. Even Cyan looked impressed. Teal had the strangest sense of déjà vu.

"Here," said Aq and gave her the keys to the house. "You gonna be okay here for a while? I gotta go find Moss."

"Erm, sure," she said, uncertain.

"I know," said Aq. "We're supposed to be here together, but right now I got bigger things to think about. My friend is in trouble."

Teal nodded.

"Go, we're fine. How you gonna find him?"

"Didn't you hear on t' radio? A big press conference has been called in Dignity Square. That's him for sure."

"Okay. Good luck, Aq."

Aq smiled. "Enjoy t' hot tub."

Teal saw him speak briefly to Beige, then they both got back in the car and drove away. She turned to Cyan, who still stood staring at the house, hands on their hips.

"This is a weird fucking day," they said. "What are we doing here again?"

"Hold on," said Teal. "Just gonna lock t' gate and I explain everything, okay?"

"About time you did."

Time, Teal thought as she walked back to the heavy gates, swung them closed and turned the key in the lock. *It's all about time.*

She remembered the feeling of her journey. Watching herself running down this same gravel path with Aq and throwing open the gates to let the resistance in. Helicopters. The screaming of the injured. She looked around her.

And this same dark forest.

She could see the blackberry bush where she and Azure had crouched together. She could remember Azure's smell. Lavender and rose. She felt pain in her chest at the memory, her breathing slowing, almost stopping.

"I miss you," she whispered. "You showed me everything. You connected me."

Teal heard a high-pitched peep-peep-peep of something flying past her at great speed.

A kingfisher. But in t' forest? At night? Impossible...

Ahh, she realised, calmly. *I'm already leaving.*

Chapter seventy-four

Finally, it was happening. It felt like she had been waiting for a lifetime for this moment and at last she was here. Teal stood on a riverbank. It was a bright spring day. She could smell pollen and hear ducks calling from upriver. A buzzard flew above, high in a clear sky.

A wave of nausea passed through her, but Teal was already getting used to this, already integrating this new part of her life. The kingfisher flew past her again. Electric blue in the sunlight.

A hundred metres up the river she saw a boat. She knew exactly where she was and more or less when. She walked towards the boat, in a dream, her heart pounding with anticipation.

"Hello," she called. "Anyone here?"

There was silence.

"Hello?" she tried again.

Then the door squeaked open and an old woman with a dignified posture stepped out onto the deck of the boat. Teal's heart skipped and she thought she would burst into tears, right there on the river bank.

"Ash..."

6. Beginnings

Prelude

A sonic boom echoed across the land. Another cloud of dust filled the sky. Workers, arriving for their shifts in droves, poured out of their biofuel-powered buses with tools in hand. But already the explosions had begun. The ground shook as its very insides were blown apart, extracted and taken away to the refinery. For the many beings who lived here, this looked like an epic disaster; the end of everything. For the economists in the city, it was just a rising line on a graph.

Chapter seventy-five

"Who the fuck are you?" asked Ash, her hands on her hips.

She didn't like unexpected visits.

"I—I'm super sorry to disturb you. Are you...Ash?"

"I'm Ash." She crossed the plank onto the riverbank to get a better look at her visitor. "Wait, you're not really here are you?"

Teal paused for a second to catch her meaning.

"Right!" she said. "I'm—" She realised this might be the strangest thing she would ever say to a perfect stranger "—from t' future."

"So you are," said Ash thoughtfully. "When?"

"2118."

Ash made an impressed sound through her teeth.

"You're in 2036 now," she said. "I knew I couldn't be the only one."

"You're not!" said Teal excitedly. "There's another person as well. Well there *was* I guess, I mean...well, something terrible happened, but in fact she's t' granddaughter of someone you know! Kit! And Danny!"

Ash looked blank and rubbed her eyes. She was quite interested in going back to bed.

"Who are they when they're at home?"

Teal found it hard to understand everything that Ash said. The odd pronunciations—that 'th' in 'they'—and strange word order were confusing her.

"Kit! Danny! Oh wait, 2036! You didn't meet them until *2040*! Oh no, but what if this is like a paradox or something? Now that I told you, something's gonna change…"

"Sweetie, I doubt very much if I'll even remember *your* name tomorrow, so I shouldn't worry. What is it by the way? Your name."

"Teal," said Teal.

"A beautiful duck."

"Oh, it is? I'm named after t' colour! I can't believe this is happening!"

Ash seemed unimpressed.

"You're very excited, young Teal," she said, looking longingly over at her boathouse. "Why don't you come in for cup of tea and relax a bit?"

"Oh my god, yes!"

Twenty minutes later they were sat together on the deck of Ash's boathouse watching a group of ducklings swim by on the river and sipping lemon balm tea.

"You've been here quite a while," said Ash between sips.

"Oh," said Teal, "I should leave? I'm so sorry…."

"Gosh, no. I'm not *that* rude. I just mean that my journeys never last long in general. But then, I almost never go to the future. It's always the fucking past and always the worst parts." She looked distant for a moment and stared at the water. "How long have you been journeying?"

"This is my third time, or fourth." Teal flashed back to the night she slept at the beach. The tear gas in the park. This same woman before her running towards the hotel. "Maybe fifth I guess? I'm not sure really."

"Yep, that's how it goes."

"Ash, I have so much to ask you, so many things I want to know."

"Drink your tea dear, all in good time."

A noisy flock of ducks flew overhead, and Ash watched them in admiration.

"So, tell me about this other person who can journey, who are they?"

"Her name was Azure. She... well, she died, or she's gonna die or something. She was shot."

Ash nodded. "The State?"

"What? No! Some guy in Esperan security—in fact, I might even know who. At t' park, like just a few kilos from here. Oh wait, no never mind. No park yet. Well, anyway, Azure was amazing and she told me that you told her... or you're *gonna* tell her, I guess, that this would happen, that we—you know—*would* meet, or something. How amazing is that?"

Ash stared at her for a long minute.

"My dear, I barely understand a word of what you're saying, and your accent is very difficult."

"Sorry."

"But I understood that this Azure was important to you."

"Yes, she was resistance."

Ash nodded.

"Right, good. And you?"

Teal felt a little pride rising in her chest.

"Yes," she said. "And there's more. She showed me how when two people like us, people who journey—"

"Temporally divergent, Pin calls it."

"Right... so people like us, when we come together, it change t' journey. Like we can direct it, decide what we want to see. With Azure she showed me a future I had glimpsed already. At a villa in t' park. And there was this guy. He's with me now in t' future but—"

"You've lost me again. So what happens?"

"We can control t' journey."

A look of recognition flashed across Ash's wrinkled face.

"Then I know what comes next!"

"You do?"

"Absolutely. Come with me, Mallard." Ash stood up suddenly.

"Mallard?"

"Teal, sorry. Teal yes, *that's* your name. God, names... sorry. Come sit on the riverbank with me. We'll need the soil beneath us for this."

Teal followed her, and they sat together in the grass. She couldn't remember a time when she had been happier. She had dreamed of this time since she was a little girl—Ash and Pinar, the resistance, the Exodus—these were her bed-time stories. Without a doubt, this was the best moment of her life.

"How does it happen?" asked Ash, scratching her stubble absently.

"I'm sorry?"

"The shared journey. I don't know how this works."

"We hold hands."

"That's it?"

"That's it."

"I had no idea it would be so simple. Well then, are you ready?"

Teal had never been as ready for anything in her life.

"But wait, two out of three!"

Ash stared at her.

"Azure told me, that you told her—gosh this is confusing. We're gonna journey three times, but you can only come t' first two."

"Why?"

"That's what you told her to... um... tell you?"

"Well, I'm sure I had a good reason," said Ash finally. She put out her hand. Teal could feel the warmth of her. The dry softness of her wrinkled palm. The world shifted ever so slightly, and they were gone.

Chapter seventy-six

Teal and Ash stood together in a street, surrounded on all sides by people in wheelchairs, people signing, people walking with crutches. A float went past, pumping loud music out into the street. Light rain was falling, but nothing could dampen the smiles. There were at least ten thousand people.

"No more cuts, no more austerity!" a person with a white stick shouted into a megaphone. The crowd echoed them. "Disabled pride!"

"Wow," said Teal, finally finding her voice.

People were still flowing past them on all sides. Teal was careful about guessing such things, but she saw so many people around her that looked queer, trans, homeless. They looked nothing like the trans politicians she had met in the Union or the business people she saw talking on TV. This was a different class of queer, a different intersection of poverty.

An intersection that isn't taking any more shit.

"This is amazing."

Ash smiled. "It is, isn't it? Any idea where we are?"

"You don't know?"

"No clue."

"I thought you would know!"

Ash shrugged.

"I had no idea there were others like me out there. I mean I guessed I wasn't alone, but you're the first I've met."

"Azure was t' first I met."

"Was she trans?"

"I... erm..." *Well, this is Ash after all.* "Yes, and me too."

"That makes sense I guess."

"It's only trans women that can journey?"

Ash shrugged.

"Who knows?"

"Oh wait, and Aq."

"Aq?"

"Yes. He definitely journeyed. And he's a guy. Or like, looks like a guy. I mean that's how I've read him until now. I hadn't thought about it. But then... I guess I was also mistaken for a guy at some point."

"That happens."

"Gosh, I wonder if—"

A loud bang at the front of the crowd, then another. Ash turned to Teal.

"Have you tasted tear gas before, my dear?"

Teal gasped.

"Yes! God, is that what that is?"

Ash nodded. "Whatever state we're in, I imagine they'd prefer disabled people stay quietly in the shadows barely surviving, not coming out and blocking roads. I think we need to go."

"We should stay! We should do something."

"That's not how this works, dear."

The crowd disappeared suddenly into a cloud of white just as Teal heard the first sounds of horses' hooves coming down onto wheelchairs. Instinctively she grabbed Ash's hand.

And it was all gone.

* * *

They stood on a forested hill, overlooking a river. It was night with no moon. Teal fell to her knees with a groan.

"Fuck, that was awful. Why couldn't we do anything?"

"It doesn't work. Trust me, I've tried. We can only change things in our own time. At most we can pass on messages."

Teal wrapped her arms around herself and shook.

"I know dear, it's hard. And fucked up."

"I could never get used to that."

"I know—wait, look over there!"

On the other side of the river a building was catching fire. Ash looked confused.

"Any idea?"

Teal looked up and stared for a moment, taking in the details. The rainforest, the slow-moving river. She heard shouting from the building and recognised Guatemalan Spanish.

"Wow, I think I know," she said, standing up. "I mean, maybe. I researched this place when I was looking at a job in park planning. If I'm right, that's t' San Pedro research station. A national park was built here, Laguna del Tigre, if I remember right, but it's been largely destroyed by petrol extraction. I think we're in Guatemala."

"Okay, Guatemala," said Ash, unfazed. "Wasn't there also a civil war here?"

"Right. From 1960 to 1996." Teal had always been a thorough student. "Indigenous-led leftist groups fighting against t' national government."

"Did it gain power through a US-backed coup d'état by any chance?" asked Ash.

Teal nodded.

"Like so many of them. With support by Apartheid South Africa, Israel and Argentina. A genocide against Mayan people."

Teal paused to watch. The flames were growing higher, illuminating the river banks and the edge of the forest.

"God... I can't believe we're here."

"It takes time to get used to it. Tell me more about this park. Why is the station burning?"

"Well, because of t' war, this land was full of squatters for a while. T' park was supposedly built to protect this forest but was also full of officially-sanctioned petrol extraction. They evicted t' squatters and left them homeless."

"Sounds like a familiar story," said Ash with an edge.

"And in 1997—today, I guess—about sixty squatters came back and burned down t' research station. I learned it as an example of Big Conservation ignoring national politics and being doomed to failure. In this case, t' park clearly prioritised petrol before people. And t' people pushed back."

Ash nodded. "Resistance takes many forms."

"Yes. I work on a research camp in a protected area. Maybe I needed to see this to put things into perspective."

"Maybe. Back to the boat?"

Ash offered her hand. Teal took a final look at the burning station and they left. The sky was empty and blue once more. With just the remains of a memory of smoke.

Teal tried to catch her breath. She was afraid she might throw up in front of her heroine.

"Shall we have some more tea?" said Ash. Her voice was calm.

"I want to, but I guess I have one more journey to make."

"Right."

"Am I gonna come back here after that? Am I gonna see you again?"

"My dear, you seem to think I have all this planned out. I thought my day would involve taking a nap, checking my carrots and maybe paying Pin a visit. Then you appeared out of nowhere to take me on a whistle-stop journey of oppression and resistance."

"Sorry..."

"Nonsense, it's been a pleasure."

Ash and Teal hugged. Teal could feel the muscles of Ash's back through the heavy sweater she wore. She smelt like cinnamon.

"This has been amazing, thank you."

There was a pause, a flock of birds passed by and they sat back down on the warm river bank.

"Ash, how do I do it?

"Journey?"

"Yes."

Ash shrugged.

"I'm sorry my dear. I'm clueless. I've never been able to control it."

They sat for a moment. Nothing. Teal tried to imagine herself somewhere else, but her mind was blank. She tried to listen to the sound of the wind as Azure had taught her, but the air was unmoving and silent.

"Still here?" Ash asked after five minutes.

"I guess so."

"Let's get some tea," she said and stood offering her hand.

Teal took it and stood up too quickly. Her head spun. The river was where the sky should be and suddenly, beyond her control, she was journeying again.

***

"Ash! Ash!"

Teal reached out, but she was already gone.

She stood on the deck of a boat, a much bigger boat, moving fast upstream. There was an incredible wind blowing, lightning tearing up the sky.

"Yes?"

It was Ash, appearing from inside the boat.

"Wait, who the fuck are you?"

Teal couldn't help but laugh. *What a greeting.*

"Wait, Pochard! It's you, isn't it?"

"Teal..."

"Teal! Yes, yes. Ah so this is where you came to!"

"I guess so, I'm so confused. When are we?"

"2040, or it might be '41 by now, I'm not honestly sure."

"T' Exodus!"

"Is that what they'll call it?"

"You escaped t' City!"

"For now. They've been chasing us for weeks—our fuel is nearly done."

Teal looked up and saw the other boats spread out behind them moving fast through the rough water.

"Are Kit and Danny here?"

"Back there," said Ash, smiling. "I guess they become famous?"

"You all did. And Pinar—Pin?"

Ash pointed inside the boat.

"Sleeping. She was up all night fixing a leak that half-flooded our little boat. I thought it was the end there for a while."

"It's not—t' end I mean. You're gonna be okay."

Behind them, someone cried out. And another and another. Looking up, Teal and Ash saw people pointing ahead, they turned and, sure enough, where the river met the horizon there were shadows coming towards them.

Boats, Teal realised. *Hundreds of boats.*

"Fuck," cried Ash. "Pin, wake up! The State got the drop on us somehow. Pinar get up here now!"

"No, Ash," said Teal as calmly as she could. "It's Espera. This is how it happened. This is how t' State was liberated."

"Espera? What the hell is that?"

"You knew it by another name, but it doesn't matter. You've already left t' State now. This is Espera, things are gonna change."

"For the better?"

"Kind of."

Ash's face looked concerned. "Teal, my dear. You look sick."

"I don't feel right."

"Come here." Ash held her strong. "It's going to be okay. I've got you."

The door opened and Pinar appeared onto the deck.

"Ash? What are you doing, hon?"

Ash put her empty arms down, her heart heavy.

"Nothing."

Pinar looked up.

"God, what the hell's that?"

"Boats."

"State?"

"Espera, apparently."

"Never heard of it."

"A little bird told me. It's gonna be fine."

Pinar gave her a curious smile. "You and your little birds. Shall I put the kettle on for our new guests?"

"Good idea."

Pinar stepped towards the door but turned back.

"Ash. Is this it? Are we finally safe? Are we home?"

Ash smiled and softly touched the hand of her best friend in the world.

"My love, I've been home since the day we met."

Chapter seventy-seven

Teal? Teal?

"Cyan, I...oh my god. You saw?"

"I saw. Are you okay?"

"I'm back now."

"You were...this is it, isn't it? T' changes you told me about."

"Part of it. I was in t' past."

Cyan tried to speak but couldn't.

"It's a lot to take in, I know," Teal said.

"No, that's just it. I knew you were telling t' truth. I just didn't know what to do with it. I was scared, I guess. I was scared of Azure and t' village and t' whole thing."

"Imagine what it's like for me."

"I'm sorry, Teal. I haven't supported you." Cyan bowed their head just a little. "I've been so crappy."

Teal took their hand.

"I know. And I forgive you like I always forgive you."

Cyan was crying.

"You're too kind to me. But I feel terrible. I should have done more for you. I should have—"

"Do you want to feel guilty, cry a lot and have me take care of you? Or do you want to do something useful and help me get ready?"

Cyan lifted their head. "For what?"

"T' resistance is coming."

***

"Let me go! Let me out of here!"

Moss was shouting at the top of his voice. He wasn't restrained, but the three men next to him in the van made it clear they would get violent if they needed to.

"Sit down and shut up," shouted the driver looking at him in the rear view mirror. "You're not a prisoner. You are our very *special guest*, Mr. Moss. We're gonna protect you whether you like it or not. T' state protect its assets."

"T' state...?" said Moss slowly.

"*Espera*. T' Esperan state. You know what I mean. There's a clean shirt in t' bag—" one of the guards in the back passed Moss a bag "—you have a TV interview in five minutes."

"I...shit," said Moss and, turning his back to the guards, he changed his shirt.

"Here's your mic. You're on stage in two minutes. Half of Espera is out there to see you."

Moss stood silent as the microphone and sauvite power pack were attached to his very expensive shirt.

"And remember," whispered the assistant. "You denounce *everything*. T' strike. T' protests. And t' rioters because they are enemies of conservation. They are enemies of Espera. Espera is t' resistance, blablabla... have you got that?"

Moss was still silent.

"Yes?"

"Yes."

He couldn't think. He was still trying to process what had happened at the hotel, the kiss, the new arrivals. He had no idea what it all meant—Aq's connection with Teal and all this talk of Ash and time travel. The riots. Jail. Azure. He was part of something here and he felt like he had no control.

Aq seemed to know, seemed to understand something of all of this. So it would be okay. He would follow Aq to the ends of the earth if he asked him to.

The assistant gave him a strong push and Moss walked out into the bright lights and onto the stage overlooking the city square. There was applause. He could barely see a thing. Lights and cameras were pointed at him from all directions. From the voices in the square he guessed there must be hundreds of people in front of him.

"Hello?" he said into his mic. There was a squeak of feedback. "My name's Moss."

More applause.

"I...as you know, yesterday, I was sent to protect t' park. T' great Espera conservation park."

A final burst of applause and the audience and film crews fell silent ready for the big speech.

"I was sent out to t' perimeter in a uniform with a gun that I barely knew how to use..." He could feel the assistant to his side shifting nervously. Moss pushed on. "I was given a gun and sent out to protect t' park."

A pause while he tried to calm his racing heart. "But from what? This has been t' worst day in my life. I woke up this morning in an Esperan jail. I've been thrown into vehicles against my will."

Out of the corner of his eye, he could see more security guards were gathering at the side of the stage.

"Because yesterday I killed an old woman who was just protecting her family. I shot her dead and I'm never gonna forgive myself for that."

He reached into his pocket, pulled out his phone and held it up. "*This* is what she was protecting her family from. Sauvite mining, Esperan work camps. We think we're t' greatest nation on earth, we think we brought t' State to some great new future. But who is it great *for*? Who get to enjoy this future and who don't? What are we conserving here?"

He swallowed and continued. "We're so fucking proud and sustainable, but what are we sustaining? Shit work. Exploitation. Shops full of over-priced crap and t' poverty of Oak Grove." Moss caught his breath. He felt invincible. "*Development*, in other words. That's what we're sustaining. Enough is enough."

Moss knew his time was up. More guards were gathering, and they looked ready to run onto the stage to grab him. But then the silence of the crowd and the film crews was broken.

"Long live t' resistance!" someone shouted. There was a crash. Moss heard something breaking beyond the lights.

"An end to *all* oppression!"

"Fuck t' state! And fuck Espera!"

Suddenly the guards disappeared from the stage. As the lights turned away from him, Moss saw them reappear down below him. They rushed at the crowd, batons raised, and the crowd pushed back. A camera exploded. The lights went out. Something dark and heavy flew towards the stage.

Moss ran. He pushed past the assistant who stood frozen behind the curtain. He ran away from the stage, away from the crowds and the burning square. He ran and ran but had no idea where to go.

"Moss! Stop!"

He stopped and turned on his heels, and suddenly Aq was there, holding his hand and pulling him towards the car where Beige stood, holding open the back door. Moss climbed in and Aq climbed in behind him.

"Back to t' villa!" shouted Aq. Beige got behind the wheel and drove full speed towards the park.

"Mate! How did you—?"

"You didn't think I'd leave you behind?"

"T' others?"

"At t' villa already."

"Fuck. Aq. Thank you."

Aq pulled Moss towards him in a hug. Not the bear hugs they had always shared. Something softer. Something different. He could hear that Moss was crying and pulled him even closer.

"I've got you mate. I've got you."

Chapter seventy-eight

As they drove through the grand park entrance, Aq and Moss could see that the lights were off. The power grid was down. There wasn't a single guard to be seen anywhere.

"This is t' part where t' dinosaurs escape..." joked Aq.

But Moss, his head on his friend's lap, was fast asleep. Aq ran his hand through Moss' hair.

He's exhausted, poor thing.

"To t' villa, sir?" Beige asked in the rear-view.

"Yes, please mate. And Beige?"

"Yes, sir?"

"I don't care what your contract says, please call me Aq." The driver nodded. "And if you don't want to keep driving us around, you don't got to, okay? Carl is long gone and I guess he isn't coming back. So you should do whatever you want."

Beige smiled and swerved around a branch in the road. "I'm good where I am, thank you, si— I mean, Aq. Honestly, I'm kind of enjoying all this adventure."

"Okay, but t' city is falling apart. If you need to be with your family..."

"No family," said Beige softly.

"Oh. I guess I never asked. I'm sorry."

I should call my family too, thought Aq.

"No problem." Beige was driving more slowly now as he turned onto the gravel lane that lead to the villa. "Is your friend okay?"

Moss sniffled a little in his sleep and tried to curl up smaller on Aq's lap.

"He's gonna be okay. It's just been a hell of a day."

* * *

"Here, help me move t' sofa over here. That's right, next to t' door."

"But Teal, won't that stop people getting in?"

"That's t' point."

"To stop t' resistance?"

Teal paused and stared at them for a moment. For all their degrees and educational privilege, Teal realised that Cyan wasn't always so good at keeping up.

"To stop t' state."

Cyan stared back and then continued to push their end of the sofa. It was massive and heavy, but together they managed to move it far enough to barricade the back door of the kitchen. Cyan looked tired, but Teal had never been more energised. She moved around the villa as if she lived there, rearranging furniture and giving Cyan instructions.

"We need to check food supplies as well. There's a lot of people coming. Most of t' villages as far as I know. We might be here for a while."

"Right," said Cyan, remembering. "Azure said something about visiting a cemetery? That t' village comes back to t' park every year?"

"Exactly. A little help...?"

Together they moved a heavy dresser to cover the French windows. It scraped a long welt into the wooden floor and some plates fell out and smashed. Teal seemed not to notice.

"Teal, I want you to know that I'm really sorry about Azure. I know you became close."

"We did." Teal grunted, pushing the dresser and stood back to check its position. "She was important."

Cyan nodded.

"Is that where you were, during your...*journey*, at t' gate? You were with Azure?"

"Ash."

"Ash? God. There's so much I don't understand."

"I know, love."

Teal lightly touched Cyan's shoulder and said seriously. "What's coming isn't going to be easy. With t' demos in town and t' invasion of t' park, we're going to have t' full force of Esperan security down on us. This villa will be our stand-off."

"How do you know it's here? How do you—"

"I saw it. With Aq."

"Aq? Random security guard, Aq?"

"Yes. That's why we're in his house."

"Okay."

"He's... like me, I think."

"Okay."

"Do you trust me?"

"I respect you and love you, Teal, you know that."

Maybe I know that.

"Cyan, do you trust me?"

"Kind of?"

Teal laughed despite herself. "Well, that's gotta be enough for today."

There was a loud honking sound and Cyan visibly jumped.

"It's okay, babe. It's just Aq back with t' car and Moss." Teal looked through the window. "Look, there they are. T' moon doesn't rise for another few hours and that's when t' villagers gonna get here—about three in t' morning I think."

Cyan stared at Teal in amazement and followed her outside to the gate.

"Welcome back," said Teal, as Beige, Aq and a very sleepy Moss got out of the car. "Welcome to my luxury barricaded villa."

Aq smiled.

"I like you," he said. "You seem so calm about all this."

Teal was surprised. One thing she had never been described as was calm. But the journeys with Ash had reassured her. They were part of something bigger. A chain, a history of resistance as old as time. She knew it now as surely as she knew anything.

"Well, it hasn't really started yet," said Teal. "We have a few hours to prepare."

"It's coming tonight, isn't it?"

"Yes."

"Two seconds." Aq's phone was beeping in his pocket. He turned away and scrolled through his messages.

18.00 Aq Hass: Hey mom, dad. Are you guys okay? I'm staying with a friend out of town but wanted to check on you.

18.15 Mom: Thanks love. We're fine—your dad has barricaded t' front door and made a mess of t' walls. And your brothers won't stop climbing on t' furniture. But Oak Grove is quiet tonight. I think everyone's gone into town to do their rioting. Glad to hear you're safe. I love you.

Aq typed 'Love you too' and turned back to Teal.

"Sorry about that."

"No problem.

Teal pointed at the villa.

"We... kind of turned your fancy mansion into a fortress. Hope that's okay."

Aq smiled. "Well, that's what it's for, right? That's why I got t' damn thing."

"I think so."

Aq smiled and took Teal's hand.

There was a buzz. An electric spark between them. But they didn't journey. They were needed here, now, and they were stronger together.

"To t' barricades?"

Teal rolled her eyes.

"Sure thing."

Chapter seventy-nine

"Teal..." Moss stood awkwardly in front of her, his hands in his pocket. "I filled t' baths with water in case they cut us off. Aq and Cyan are making space in t' basement in case we have to go down there. What else need doing?"

"We should talk."

"Talk?"

Moss swallowed loudly.

"Yes. T' woman you killed, at t' perimeter. She was my friend."

Moss looked at the carpet.

"I thought so. I wasn't sure if I shou—"

Teal cut him off.

"Her name was Azure."

"Yes."

"And she was important to our story." Moss kept staring at the carpet. "But I don't hate you, I want you to know that."

He looked up, surprised.

"They had no right to send you there and you had no business being in uniform. You're just a kid."

Moss nodded just a little.

"This is bigger than you and me. It's about war and occupation and industry. But yes, it is also about you. You *did* go there, to t' fence. You followed orders and you killed my friend. There were other options, but you went there, picked up a gun and shot her. So this is also about you, Moss."

Moss' eyes were wet.

"That's it. That's what I wanted to say. Maybe we can talk more after this is all over."

Teal walked to the centre of the grand living room.

"Here, help me lift this box over to t' window. More people gonna come in t' morning. T' city resistance is on its way and folks from beyond Espera. We just need to be able to hold back t' army until they arrive."

"Got it."

The thundering of the helicopter was the first clue. The second was the moon. Teal, Aq, Cyan, Beige and Moss stood out on the balcony watching it rise over the treetops, casting the world in a silver light. There was absolutely no wind and the forest was silent in that way that could only mean trouble.

"Is it...?" asked Aq.

"Yes."

They left the others to barricade the bedroom windows and they went down the grand staircase together. As they reached the foyer, Aq looked down for the first time in hours and noticed he was still wearing Moss' security uniform.

"I guess I had to wear this, no?"

"I would never have found you otherwise."

"Right."

"You love him, don't you?"

"Moss is awes—" Aq stopped himself. *Why do I do that?* "Yes, I love him. I think I always have." They stepped out of the door onto the steps. The helicopter was closer now.

"When this is over, you gonna be great together."

"Do we survive, Teal? Have you seen it?

Teal shook her head.

"You?"

"No idea. It was just that one time."

"Well, it's nice to be surprised sometimes. Ready?"

Aq smiled and took her hand.

They ran then, down the stairs and the gravel driveway. To the gates.

Teal glanced over to the blackberry bush.
There I am. God, I had no idea what was coming.

Aq saw himself too. And there was Azure, silently taking in every detail. They heard the shouts and the sirens of security vehicles coming towards them through the *cerezo* trees. Helicopter lights flooded the driveway. Teal turned the key and together they pulled the gates open.

Chapter eighty

The kitchen table was a hospital bed, the bathroom floor full of bloody bandages. People that Teal vaguely knew from the village talked in panicked Polari as they made plans, took in the space and lined people up on the balconies with boxes of bricks.

Teal didn't know what to do with herself. Cyan was lost somewhere in the crowd, giving people water. Aq was showing someone the basement. She stood in the busy living room, overwhelmed by the voices, the smell of panic, the endless thundering of the helicopter pounding through her stomach. Someone came running through the crowd, grinning.

"Indi!" She hugged Teal tight. "Oh my god, what t' hell are you doing here?"

Indi was grinning. "You real don't know?"

"I can't begin to imagine. I figured you were in town somewhere."

"Teal, I've *always* been resistance. Why did you think I had so many meetings all t' time?"

Teal stared at her colleague. Indi laughed.

"You really didn't pay attention, did you? You and your Cyan drama!"

The crowd cleared a bit and a person rolled their wheelchair over to join them. An elegant ball-gown, green satin, with a long slit. Silver heels that refracted a thousand colours. Teal knew that pretty face anywhere.

"Verde?"

"Of course," they said, grabbing Indi's hand. "You know, we've been planning this for months." They looked around the grand salon. "Well, not so much t' barricading ourselves in a forest villa part but, well, that's how these things go sometimes."

"And Jade?"

Indi shrugged.

*　*　*

Jade was running and grinning. He had no idea how much fun rioting could be until he smashed his first window. It was a family-owned grocery store and the owners were nowhere to be seen.

Unlike some of the young guys from Oak Grove who he'd seen filling carts with food, Jade decided not to take anything this first time. He figured there would be too much risk getting in and out and besides, he wasn't in it for the stuff.

Jade quickly learned that property destruction aroused him like nothing else ever had. The release as the brick shattered glass. The scream of the alarm and the flash of the approaching police cars as he dived behind a dumpster or disappeared into an alleyway. The dizzying power of breaking the rules.

No-one to stop me this time.

He was addicted. A small group of young women ran up to him. They wore political badges on their hoodies.

"We're targeting Rak Industries!" announced one of them excitedly. "Want to join us?"

Jade ignored them and continued on his way. He wasn't rioting for the politics either. His next target was a wellbeing store. He filled his pockets with bottles of vitamins for no good reason except that he could. Then a traffic stop sign—he was amazed at how easily it came down. Then he set fire to a dumpster.

What a fucking rush.

He stood on the other side of the road to watch the flames. His clothes were filthy and his hands reeked of gas. He had never been so euphoric. A homeless person who had been sleeping near the dumpster pushed their cart quickly away, throwing a look at Jade.

"Fuck you, old man," Jade shouted. "You can't tell me what to do!"

He felt powerful. He knew this night was special. Once the riots had passed—as he knew they would—he would return to his job in the forest.

Hopefully write a paper on t' Red Shadow-Tail. Hopefully get some of t' success I deserve. Get a nice apartment in Dignity Park one day—write some books.

Life in Espera would resume, he knew. But for that night, Jade was free and had no-one to control him.

Not mom. Not Cyan or those other fucking women.

He would see the city burn.

***

No clue what happened to him," said Indi with an edge. "Last I heard, he was arrested but released again after five minutes."

"Yes, I mean it was only domestic violence after all," Teal sighed. "Nothing compared to all those very dangerous refugees who were born on t' wrong part of t' planet and needed to flee for their lives."

"He's a privileged little shit," declared Indi.

Teal smiled. "For all we know, he's out there right now shooting at us."

"Fuck that guy."

"Yep." Teal looked down at the mud on the wheels of Verde's wheelchair. "By t' way... how did you two get here? Did you come through t' fence?" she asked carefully.

"Of course not," said Verde with a smile. "Me and Indi shut down t' power and let t' resistance through."

"You did?"

Indi laughed. "You didn't even notice all t' wire cutters and ropes I've been collecting in t' base tent for t' last three years?"

Teal laughed too.

Then a window in the kitchen exploded.

Chapter eighty-one

Passing the abandoned park gate and speeding up along the gravel lane through the park, Carl was so excited that he could hardly breathe. He could see the moon above the trees. The dashboard and his pale hands on the steering wheel were illuminated.

He was driving too fast, but the park was quiet. Once he had got past the police blockades with a flash of his Guest Speaker badge and a wad of notes in the right palm, he hadn't seen another soul. He had thought of letting his Boss know he was coming, but he decided not to send a message. He wanted it to be a surprise.

He knew that Aq had kept the villa. When the paperwork hadn't gone through, Carl had checked with the water company. As Aq still seemed to be taking a lot of baths Carl had signed the papers for him and sent them on. Forging Aq's signature was one of the first things he had learned to do in their week together.

"I'm gonna be t' best for him," Carl muttered to himself as he swerved around a pothole in the road. "I'm gonna be t' perfect servant this time, I'm gonna..."

He stopped talking and slammed on the brakes.

There was the villa, the gates. But everything was wrong. A helicopter was hovering above it, beaming a bright light onto the back patio and the pool. There were people inside the house; Carl could just make out faces pushed up against the upstairs windows.

That's Aq's room.

Security vehicles were everywhere, flashing red and blue onto the surrounding trees. Lines of men were scaling the massive gates. Men with guns. Soldiers, attacking.

No. Impossible.

Carl was far enough away that the soldiers didn't notice him. He turned the car around slowly, steadily, holding his breath as he went. He glanced back at the villa and saw that someone had stepped out onto the balcony.

He slammed into gear, and as fast as he could, Carl Kingson escaped.

Chapter eighty-two

Teal could hear a hail of bricks falling from the master bedroom onto the patio. Gunshots fired from outside. Another window exploded. She wanted to help but knew she should stay with Indi and Verde. This was the time to be together. Cyan arrived with blood over their shirt. Aq and Moss, holding hands, joined them.

Then for a moment the sirens stopped and the crowd inside the house fell silent. Teal felt herself fading.

Shit. Not now.

She stayed in the moment, but she also began to see her body from above. She was disassociating, she knew.

But it's more than that.

From up in the chandeliers, Teal looked down.

She saw the crowd, the resistance from the villages and from the city. And others. People whose clothes looked wrong for this time and place. Someone in a firefighter's uniform. Someone in what might have been a brightly-coloured Andean dress. Someone in a Victorian suit. People all over the gender map.

She noticed someone over by the window standing tall and proud. Someone who looked a lot like Azure.

A balcony was burning. The pool was unlit. Teal was outside the building now, high above the villa and the trees. And she could see the others. A flock of starlings creating a night cloud so dense that the moon had disappeared. An animal on a branch with a red tail and eyes full of flames.

Teal heard the sound of hooves and feet approaching from beyond the villa in such numbers that the ground shook. She saw faces in windows and knew they had a chance and no choice.

She lifted her head high and smiled.

If you enjoyed this novel, please consider helping the author to write more transfeminist speculative fiction by supporting her through Patreon, spreading the word on social media or leaving reviews online.

www.patreon.com/otterlieffe

About the author:

Otter is a working class, femme trans woman. She has been involved in grassroots activism for nearly two decades, in Latin America, the Middle East, Europe and North America, and has at various times found herself involved in queer community organising, land reclamation and language teaching in migrant communities.

She adores hearing from readers and fans and always has a full schedule of readings and events, so follow her website to stay in touch.

www.otterlieffe.com

Since Otter's first novel, Margins and Murmurations, was published, she has been proud to work with LGBT Books to Prisoners getting copies of the book to trans folk incarcerated in the USA and is currently founding a UK group to do similar work.

www.lgbtbookstoprisoners.org

Action for Trans Health hosted two speaking tours for Margins and Murmurations in 2017 and is an essential organisation for trans communities in the UK.

www.actionfortranshealth.org.uk

Printed in Poland
by Amazon Fulfillment
Poland Sp. z o.o., Wrocław